A **FLORENCE GRAY** MYSTERY

NOT A THROUGH STREET

JUDITH DECHESERE-BOYLE

For Rick

"*Life takes its own turns, makes its own demands,
writes its own story, and along the way, we start to
realize we are not the author.*"

Barack Obama

ACKNOWLEDGMENT

With the final words of this work finally written, I would like to acknowledge two important people. First, my son, Justin, whose insightful dedication and tenacity in the field of law enforcement for many years has been stunning and inspiring to me. He makes me proud. Secondly, I would like to acknowledge Rich Carnahan, creative coordinator at Publish Pros whose support, talent, and expertise have been invaluable and deeply appreciated.

CHAPTER ONE

SUSAN

It's been a long road. How did I arrive at this place, I wonder? Susan Wallis, not quite fifty, sat quietly in a wicker chair just outside the front door of her home. From her perch on the veranda she could see across a wide swath of valley terrain to the Sierra foothills far in the distance. The morning was brilliant. The sun had crept over the horizon only an hour before, setting the landscape ablaze in dazzling light. It was spring and deciduous trees had leafed into stunning, chartreuse marvels. In contrast, prickly leaves that had held on stubbornly to the limbs of countless gnarled and ancient oaks all winter were a dusty, dark, olive green. They looked tired. Yet sounds abounded around them; they were alive with new life. Finches, sparrows, hummingbirds, and jays flitted in and about the branches. A flock of turkeys strutted and gobbled in a field nearby. From not far away an owl could be heard calling its farewell to the night. The sound, both haunting and soothing, spoke to Susan of change, and created before her the image of her beautiful mother, dead now, but so lovingly remembered. *Oh, Mother, how did I arrive at this place?*

Of course there was no answer, but Susan recalled her mother's words of wisdom. Years before her death, the old woman who proudly held claim to her Yokut ancestry, had told Susan emphatically, "You are my daughter, Susan, and like I do, you hold within you the spirit of the owl. It's a gift."

Ah, my mother . . . what wisdom and insight she possessed. It was as though she knew what would happen before anyone else. How was it that she seemed to foresee every occurrence? The thought of her mother issued a trace of palpable pain in Susan's chest, but she countered it with a wistful smile. *Oh, how I loved her.* In her heart, Susan knew her mother had been correct about the animal spirit she had been granted. Intuition had been Susan's mindful partner and a guide all of her life. And when transitions had arrived on her doorstep unexpectedly, she had been undaunted by them. It simply had been her way. Susan listened to the soulful call of the owl once more and, despite her awe for the animal, hoped that it would sleep now, silencing its song of death and change for one more day.

⌘ ⌘ ⌘

The cup of hot tea Susan held was cooling. She stood to go inside and freshen it just as her own daughter, Jenny, appeared at the door.

"Hey, Mom."

"Good morning. You're up early."

"I am. Here, let me take that. I'll make another cup." Jenny slipped away quickly to the kitchen, hoping that her mother had not detected her exhaustion. With any luck Susan had been sleeping soundly when Jenny's friends had dropped her off not three hours earlier that Friday morning. The fact was that Jenny had not slept at all.

"Thanks, honey. Make one for yourself too and then come out and chat with me. It's such a gorgeous morning."

Jenny returned in several minutes with two steaming mugs of creamy tea.

"Ah, just as I like it," Susan said. "Thanks."

"You're welcome. How long have you been out here, Mom, and what are you doing? Thinking. I know." Jenny answered her own question and smirked, diverting attention from herself.

"Yes, of course. You know me well, always churning thoughts around up here." Susan tilted back her head and her eyes rolled upward as if she really could see into the workings of her brain. She grinned. "I was actually thinking about my mother. Sure do miss her sometimes," she admitted.

Thank God. She's in her own little world. Jenny was off the hook. Her mother had no clue that she had slipped into the house like a thief only hours before, having spent almost an entire night dealing with her friend, Courtney. Courtney. She could be her own worst enemy.

"Wish I had known Nana better," Jenny offered. Actually she had only a dim recollection of being in the presence of her grandmother at all. Jenny had been four when Nana passed away on a cold, rainy night in January. Her grandmother, clutching a dram of whiskey, had been rocking in her favorite chair in front of a roaring fire when it happened. Sputtering about the unrelenting rains, she simply had stopped speaking mid-sentence, "Rains are awful this year. Mudslides, floods, don't know how poor folks . . ."

And that was it. Her head had dipped to her chest, her hands had fallen open on her lap spilling the nip of alcohol, and she had let out one last sigh. A malty, phenolic smell filled the air. Jenny remembered looking up at the slumped figure in the rocking chair. At that inauspicious moment, to the little girl's eye and mind, her nana somehow had transformed from a diminutive but formidable, old woman into a grand, contented giant. Her grandmother, whose daunting demeanor had made some folks wary, had softened in one, startling instant. Jenny never had forgotten; the imposing image of her grandmother that night was captured forever in her mind's eye. A clear visual of Nana on the night of her passing hauntingly had surfaced at odd times all of Jenny's life.

"She was simply too tired to carry on," Susan had determined. "She probably knew all along that it was time. She is at peace. That's all that matters."

Jenny had been shuffled off to bed, a coroner had been called to examine the body, and Nana had been carried away from the house forever. Her spirit remained, however, in tales and stories. Susan made sure Jenny knew the woman almost as well as if she were still alive. In some ways, Jenny supposed she was, for her mother's ability to remember, and her inherited gifts of intuition and imagination had granted Nana an awesome immortality.

As she thought of that time so many years before, Jenny's face drew serious. It was anxiety perhaps, or trepidation. She had plans to reveal and she was not certain how her mother would react. Suddenly she blurted, "Are you happy, Mom?"

"Now that's a interesting question, and a serious one, actually. Why do you ask?"

"Just wondering." Jenny scooted her chair a bit farther away from her mom. "Are you?"

"When the day's done and I crawl into bed, I'm satisfied. I may not be overcome with happiness, but I'm not sad, and any real depression, fortunately has escaped me. I don't think living somewhere else, or having had some other occupation would make my life better, or for that matter different. In fact, if I lived on the other side of the world, I likely would be doing the same things I do now. In so many ways I have been fortunate."

Jenny stared at her mother in surprise. "How can you say that? Don't you want to shake up things in your life a little bit, Mom? What the hell! Aren't you tired of living in this dreary, old town? Nothing happens here. It's an event if a dog shits on the sidewalk."

"Jenny Wallis!"

Susan responded to her daughter's comment with mock shock. She sneered at her as she pulled the mug of tea to her lips. That was Jenny, a slight, and delicate girl with the vocabulary of a thug. Though Susan had tried her best to curb her daughter's bad habit of cursing incessantly, it had been to no avail. Furthermore, the acid approach to life that Jenny possessed concerned Susan more than she wanted to admit. *How will she manage to get by if everything becomes an argument or an indictment? It makes me worry and feel weary. Why, look how quickly Jenny has turned my morning of contemplation and sweet memories into a mild confrontation. I wonder what's next?*

"Well, really, Mom, don't you ever want to protest something, or make a flippin' scene? Don't you want to be noticed for doing something good, or bad for that matter?

Aren't you bored here, and how can you say you're satisfied and that you're fortunate. Don't you miss Dad?"

Jenny's long, silky hair, the color of dark copper, shimmered in the morning sun that filtered through the twisted canopy of the wide oak beside the house. She was eighteen and restless. She had lived alone with only her mother for seven years. Her father had made his exit the day after her eleventh birthday. Gone. No one was certain why, although Susan had speculated.

"He had an edge to him. Impatient. Angry. He wanted more, more than I could offer, more than he could accomplish here in this tiny, valley town. So he went away. I understand. It took awhile, but it's all right. I'm not mad," she had explained to Jenny, and this day, she answered her daughter's question with a blunt, "No," before adding, "I don't miss him. Not any more. I don't miss him at all, but I understand that you would. You're so much like him."

Susan Wallis gazed at her daughter's face, so pretty now. Jenny clearly was eager, as her father before her had been, to move on. Susan knew it was inevitable, and though the thought of her daughter's departure made her heart quiver noticeably, she would not protest. *A revelation is coming.* And it did.

"I'm moving out, Mom," Jenny announced, "with Courtney. We've decided."

The news, not surprising, settled in a moment of silence before Susan spoke. "I knew you would be leaving some day. I think you should." She smiled a tiny grin that she hoped would conceal a sudden, alien sadness. She would miss this girl.

"Will you be okay without me around?"

"Of course I will. I have my job, my students, books, the garden, my long walks, and a few friends here and there. I'll be fine," Susan told her.

"I'll come back to visit. You know I will," Jenny stammered, the tone of her voice revealing uncertainty.

"Of course you will."

Jenny's eyes looked away from her mother. She scanned the horizon, searching. "I love you, Mom, but I have to get out of here. I hate this shitty town."

"I know. Go when it's time. Find yourself. And when you come home again, if you come home, I'll be here. I'll be waiting."

⌘   ⌘   ⌘

Susan Wallis was a smart woman. She read constantly, anything in print: newspapers, magazines, textbooks, and novels, the latter of which she savored one after the other like rich morsels. Books took her away, to places she never could have visited, and into the worlds of people she did not know. Fantasies toyed with her, her imagination ramped, and she began herself to write, journal after journal until there were dozens that she locked in an old trunk at the foot of her bed. Putting words to paper had been her therapy when her husband went away.

It was understandable that Susan felt a bit stricken when unexpectedly, and callously, in Susan's mind, her husband left her. Zach had disappeared one morning immediately after she had driven away to a job she adored, teaching first graders at Mountain View Elementary School in town. She had been unaware of his leaving, of course, until she had arrived home. She remembered the autumn afternoon vividly, an unusually warm day with a sun that had cast an eerie, white, all-encompassing light on the landscape. Everything had looked tired. Dry, crisp, multi-colored leaves had been dropping for days, one by one, from myriad trees that surrounded the house. A blanket of the fallen ones had crackled and crunched beneath Susan's feet as she had stepped from her old, black Buick and walked toward the back porch. When she had entered the rear of the house, plunged by then in ghostly shadows, it had been strangely silent. Zach would not have been there anyway, for his job at a local grain mill kept him occupied from midday until early evening. That day something had been different though. It was as though the rhythm of the old house had been thrown off balance, as though the very breath of life had been sucked out of it.

"Of course," Susan had mumbled, not comprehending, really why she suddenly knew.

She had noticed first, the absence of his leather jacket that had hung like a primordial hide on a hook beside the back door for years, and his boots, his beloved hikers. He had worn them on countless trails throughout the Sierra.

"Best pair of shoes I ever owned," he had said over and over.

Two shotguns that had hung over the mantle were missing too . . . and the binoculars and some books. When Susan had observed the gaping spaces in the bookcase that lined one wall of the living room, her breath had caught and she had gasped audibly. She had dropped her hands to her sides and had looked around, turning in a complete circle before she had re-entered the hallway and had climbed the stairs to the bedroom she had shared with Zach for fifteen years. When she had reached the closet she had peered in cautiously, knowing instinctively what she would find. Not one item of Zach's clothing remained there. A strange emptiness had overwhelmed her but she had been unable to do anything but stare. Any definitive emotions immediately had eluded her. She had backed numbly from the closet and had sat gingerly on the edge of the bed. *I'm going to have to tell Jenny. How am I going to do that? I have no idea what to say.*

Susan wasn't clear why Zach had chosen to leave on the heels of his daughter, Jenny's birthday, or why he had gone away without a word, though strangely, in recent months, prior to it actually happening, Susan had considered the possibility. As a result, when his departure finally occurred, she was not staggered, only mildly shocked. In fact, she surprisingly felt a certain sense of relief knowing that the waiting was over. And how odd was that? Zach had grown edgy and aloof in recent months. He had become impatient with Jenny and snippy with Susan. He was so antsy at times that it seemed as though he wanted to crawl out of his own body. And so it had happened. Just like that, he was gone and reading and writing became a salve to the aching heart that plagued Susan for a time, for a long time really, until she told herself, "Enough." *He's never coming back. Buck up, for Jenny, for yourself, Susan Wallis. Guess he wasn't worth the effort after all. But fifteen years. I spent fifteen years of my life with him.* The sudden realization of spent time, over and done with so abruptly, is what had blindsided her.

Seven years had passed and Susan was about to endure another loss, that of her daughter, Jenny. Yet this was different. It had been expected since the moment Jenny was born and Susan soothed her misgivings by assuring herself that it was a natural parting. *This is what children do when they come of age. They move away. They want their independence. Be excited for her.*

CHAPTER TWO

COURTNEY

Courtney sat up reluctantly in bed when she heard pounding on her bedroom door. It was loud. Demanding.

"Courtney? Open Up." It was her father, Bennett Taylor, of two last names fame. He carried them both with a fabricated sense of importance.

Still wearing the black tights and bright, orange sweatshirt she had worn when she fell asleep eight hours earlier, she sauntered to the door, glancing as she did at the digital clock - eleven on the dot. *God I was out of it.*

She opened the door slowly, knowing already what to expect. Her father, his dark hair slicked back from a perfectly-put-together, handsome face, stood before her attired, as only he could, in one of his many, color-coordinated, golfing outfits. Dominating this day was a brilliant shade of blue – broad blue and white stripes on his shirt and pants the color of cobalt. *He's such a dork.*

"What time did you roll in last night?" he asked, not really wanting an answer though his deep-set, brown eyes intimidatingly bore down on Courtney. His was simply a cursory, obligatory question that he assumed qualified him as fatherly and interested, however remotely. He had all but given up on Courtney by the time she was a sophomore in high school. She was as headstrong as he. The two had clashed more times than he could count and for an inconceivable reason, at this very moment, he suddenly remembered the particular rant that had changed everything. *You look like a fucking whore dressed in that get-up. You're an embarrassment to the family. Now get upstairs and change. Wash your face.* He had said the words in anger, and in fear as well, because he was a man, a father. He was convinced that he understood at an innate, gut level what any male whose gaze fell upon his daughter would assume he had coming. *She's too naïve and young to get it.*

In reality, though Courtney's evening garb that night, years before, may had been considered somewhat provocative, there was no question it was to Bennett's eye; his assessment solidified his conviction that his trepidation was not unfounded. *I'm right.* However, nothing was same after those words were spoken, heaved into the space between them, an acid vitriol that could not be retracted. Silence had set in then and father and daughter had maintained a hostile distance thereafter. Now he waited for his daughter's response.

"Not late, around one," Courtney lied as she set her lips in a practiced pout and stared coldly. She flipped her long, straight, blond hair with one hand as if to brush away her father's very presence. *Get out of my face. You'll never know the truth.* The fact was that Jimmy Nelson had dropped her off just after three a. m. She had been sloshed. *Thank God for Jimmy. Saved my ass again last night.*

"We didn't hear you come in," her father acknowledged, speaking both for himself and his wife, Jill. "Usually do."

Courtney looked at him, her face emotionless, masking the loathing she harbored for the man. *What the fuck does he want anyway? I'm sure his question is not one of concern for my wellbeing. No way. More likely he's here to tell me I'm a slut for having a fucking life or that he's off to the club for another round of golf.*

"Clean yourself up, Courtney. You reek of pot, and God knows whatever else."

She stared at him unspeaking. *Whatever!*

"Your mother and I are going to the club. There's a golf tournament. We'll be home after it's over for a bit before we head up to Bear Valley for the weekend. We'll be home Monday night. Late."

"Have fun," Courtney managed as she watched her father abruptly turn away. Her eyes narrowed and her right fist clenched. *Jackass.*

Since she had turned fifteen, Courtney had spent countless weekends alone in her parents' sprawling, country home. Their property lay adjacent to that of the Nelsons, Jimmy's folks. The two families had, in all likelihood, more money than the entire populace of Hollow Vista, or perhaps the county, combined and touted it with enormous, garish houses, luxury cars, lavish parties for a privileged few, staffs on hand to cater to their requests, and arrogance that settled into the lines of their faces. These facts had set Courtney and Jimmy apart from many others for a lifetime, and most notably when they became students at Hollow Vista High School. They were rich. Untouchable. Enviable. Marked.

The two, Jimmy and Courtney, had been forced together at family gatherings since they were toddlers; they had grown up, spoiled, lacking for not one tangible desire, and the result was that each possessed a laundry list of hateful traits, not least of which were bossiness, selfishness, and, in Jimmy's case, an irrepressible bent for bullying. To make matters worse, each was their parents' only child. With no competition they were obscenely overindulged and quickly grew into self-centered, ungrateful brats, unmistakably miniature replicas of the couples that had spawned them.

In time, the Nelsons and the Taylors hired nannies, one after the other, to look after the children whose behaviors made them weary. It was not uncommon for the twosomes to leave the little terrors for days at a time so that they could cavort on the ski slopes of the Sierra or fly away to Baja or Oahu for a breath of fresh air. Though Courtney and Jimmy were incorrigible children, they were not unfeeling. Coping with what they perceived as their parents' periodic abandonment, both children often lapsed into fits of unabashed anger and frustration. The combination took its toll. Sulking, temper tantrums, and malicious pranks became the norm as the years progressed, but what else might one expect? And with their little lives reflections of each other, it was only natural that they gravitated together, becoming fast friends. Courtney had more memories of her escapades with Jimmy than she could count, and as she settled back into her bed after the departure of her father, the files filtered though.

"Watch what happens," Jimmy had whispered after pouring olive oil onto the entryway tile. "Go outside. Ring the front door bell. I'm going to hide." Fueled by mischievous curiosity, Courtney had obeyed although in reality she hated Jimmy's much too frequent demands. While Jimmy had peered from his hiding place inside a hall closet, his Nanny, Miss Ada, upon hearing the door buzzer, had rushed to the entrance, had slid through the oily mess, and had landed feet first against the front door. Her wide bottom had hit the floor with a thump, her head had slammed backwards on the tile, and she had been rendered unconscious for over an hour. Miss Ada unceremoniously had resigned that very day.

And there were the firecrackers. How many times had those come in handy? Courtney and Jimmy had thrown them from the balcony into a knot of their parents' friends at more than one extravagant event; they had burned a foot-wide swath into the deep pile of the imported, Asian carpet beneath Jill Taylor's grand, dining room table; and on one unforgettable summer night, a handful of lighted, illegal rockets had been tossed with precise accuracy just inside the Nelson's stable, stampeding the horses that almost crushed one of the handlers in their attempt to escape. Courtney actually smiled as she remembered. Jimmy had gloated with that success for days.

A litany of pranks filtered through her thoughts: red food coloring in the pool and Tide detergent in the spa, trip lines that had flipped a stable worker and a newly-hired, Russian cook, both within minutes of each other; flower gardens stripped bare of every blossom in a nighttime raid; ripe tomatoes tossed against crystal-clear windows, and Elmer's glue poured into Jill Taylor's bottle of conditioner. "This is so much fun," Courtney had tittered to Jimmy when she heard her mother's shriek of dismay.

As the two grew older and had access to cars, their shenanigans intensified. *Ah, the horse shit. Unforgettable.* They had hopped the fence of the corral, had filled paper bags with every ounce of excrement they could find, and before the night was over, had placed burning containers of the foul-smelling dung on various porches around town, that of the Hollow Vista High School's principal being the highlight. Lanky, old Cunningham had rushed outside at the sight of the flames, stomping and stomping to extinguish the blaze. Concealed by a hedge of boxwood, holly, and laurel, Jimmy and Courtney had held hands and had covered their mouths to hide the sounds of their snickering. "Mr. Cunningham's a dick. Did you see that jackass? He was knee deep in shit," Jimmy had laughed later.

The best fun though had been driving as far into the vineyards as possible late at night. Several small houses were situated on the periphery, one of which, Jimmy discovered belonged to Flo Gray, the tiny, female custodian who had been cleaning hallways, bathrooms, and student messes forever at Hollow Vista High and who gave Courtney a royal pain in the ass. Though Flo never smiled and seldom said a word, she always was watching, her eyes narrowing as she observed the goings-on with eagle eyes.

"She gives me the creeps," Courtney had whispered more than once, "staring at me from behind her stupid cart like she's going to turn me in for something. Bitch!"

"Don't get paranoid," Jimmy had told her. "She gawks at everyone, not just you, princess."

"Fuck you, Jimmy," Courtney had snarled.

"Love it when you talk dirty," Jimmy had retorted, licking his lips vulgarly. It was all he needed though. Courtney's distaste for Flo was enough to spur his twisted pleasure for intimidation, and she was an easy target.

It became routine for Jimmy to speed by Flo Gray's bungalow well after midnight with his horn blaring, and yelling, "Wake up, Mousey," for no reason other than to harass the woman and to make Courtney giggle.

Even more amusing had been maneuvering farther out of town toward the Flack house. Rumors had it that Bertha Flack was a witch, pure and simple, and her son, Chester, a backward, dimwit, who barely graduated from their own high school, Hollow Vista, way back when. Jimmy, Courtney and a few other believers, their bravery bolstered by bottles of beer or Red Ripple, had made it a monthly habit of piling into Jimmy's pickup, driving at a crawl with lights out toward the old, stucco structure that was the Flack house, and then pelting it with rocks, empty beer bottles, cow paddies, or dog poop stashed in plastic bags. Without fail, Chester Flack would appear on the front steps and yell, "Get out of here, you brats! Get out! You've got no right to trespass. This here's a dead end."

It made no difference. Taunting Chester and old Bertha Flack was a reward in itself because Chester lashed out, and because Jimmy, Courtney, and a few wayward friends got away with their stalking, belligerent behavior time after time. They puffed up with their clout. Throwing his truck into drive, Jimmy would slam on the gas, and in an extemporized shriek like a hillbilly, scream, "Yee ha," into the night.

Courtney could hear his voice even now. She cocked her head to the side, wondering how Jimmy had managed never to be caught, even when his aggressive behavior had gone way over the line as it had only months before with poor Willard Dunn, a relatively new kid at school. Jimmy's bellicose tendencies had peaked when he made a fool of poor Willard. He had knocked him out cold, stolen ever stitch of clothing save his underwear, and kicked him while he was down. "No mercy. Move on, turtle boy. Stay on your knees," Jimmy had bellowed, and Courtney, with a host of other adolescents had looked on, urging Jimmy with their snickers. Courtney had chortled the loudest. "What a kick!" *Who will be next?*

She was deep in delicious memories when her phone rang. She looked at the name on the tiny screen: Jimmy Nelson.

"Hey," she mumbled.

"Hey," he said. "You okay? Just checking. Did your old man hear you come in this morning? You were pretty fucked up."

Courtney sighed. "No, I lucked out. You saved my butt again, Jimmy."

"Getting to be a habit," he admitted. "Not a bad job. Be better if you'd give me some payback though."

Courtney sighed again, understanding the innuendo. "Don't be a sicko," she said. "You're like my brother."

"I'm not your fucking brother though, Courtney, and you know what I want."

Courtney did know. She always had managed to keep Jimmy in his place but in recent months his inferences had taken on the tone of intimidation.

"You don't always get what you want," she giggled, though her stomach pitched uncomfortably. She understood the emptiness of her words. Jimmy had everything he wanted, always had, and with each additional possession, tangible or otherwise, he appeared ever more eager for more, at any cost. Ironically, though equally indulged, the glut of Courtney's possessions had the converse effect. They weighed upon her, leaving her anxious and often depressed. She had learned through the years that a fabricated attempt at humor, booze, and sexual favors gave her the attention she lacked on the home front. Jimmy was well aware. He had been by her side, picking up the pieces more than once. *I do owe him, don't I?* She was afraid to answer her own question. Instead she listened.

"The more you resist, the more I persist," he stated. "Simple as that."

Courtney fell silent. She knew what she was up against. She and Jimmy had slept side by side more times than she could remember, as pals when they were little, in tents, on blankets outside on a summer night, side by side, arms touching, beside the Nelson's pool, or on an overstuffed couch in her living room. Later, in high school, after being left alone by their folks again, Jimmy would find Courtney, or Courtney would locate Jimmy almost out of habit. Lying at each end of the huge, leather couch in Jimmy's family room their toes would touch, their hands reaching out. Courtney's bed was more threatening, for they would fall back together to watch television, often falling asleep only to wake up curled together like lovers. They never had been though, for reasons neither could have articulated.

"Jimmy, enough of that talk," she said, finding her voice again.

"For now," he replied abruptly. "You know I'll be seeing you later though."

It was true. Jimmy would show up after her parents' SUV had pulled away from her house. He'd be watching.

⌘   ⌘   ⌘

She thought about the night before. It was a carbon copy of so many others.

Courtney had made plans with her friend, Jenny Wallis. "Let's get the hell out of Hollow Vista," Courtney had said, "just for the day. Let's drive over to Turlock. We can get there by mid afternoon, cruise around, walk around the university, and see what we can get into."

"Fuck yes, I'm with you," Jenny had agreed. "Nothing is ever happening in this hell hole."

"Check this out," Courtney had said as she had slid into the front seat of her tiny BMW. She had held up a paper bag. "Vodka and a few beers to get us adjusted."

"Sweet."

The day had played out as they had planned, up to a point. After a late lunch at a small café near the university, the girls had wandered the campus until it had grown dark and had emptied of students. They had known no one there anyway, and as high school seniors had been a bit out of their element, though neither would have admitted that simple detail. Alone and tipsy after consuming their stash of alcohol, they had drifted back to Courtney's car.

"You okay to drive?" Jenny had questioned. "Cause I'm not."

"Sure, I'll make it home, just like I've done a million times." And one more time, holding fast to her faith that she was invincible, she had, driving straight into Jimmy Nelson's circular driveway as though magnetically drawn there. It appeared that every single light in the lower story of the house was on; in contrast the second floor was eerily dark.

"Must be party time," Courtney slurred as she exited her car. It was in the nick of time for at precisely that moment she dropped to her knees beside a manicured row of low boxwoods and vomited until her stomach emptied. Jenny rushed to Courtney's side in time to grab a handful of her straight, blond hair and keep it from falling into the mess. She waited there, holding her breath against the dreadful stench of bile and puke until Courtney could move; when she could, she scooted backwards and leaned wearily against the front tire of her car. Her head lolled to one side while she dabbed at her mouth with her cashmere scarf. "Shit."

"Holy crap, Courtney, how in the hell did you drive when you were that fucked up?"

"Don't know. Just drove. Felt like I was in a tunnel wearing blinders and going downhill. Was holding on for dear life."

Courtney gazed through glassy eyes and smirked.

"What the hell?" Overcome with a jumble of emotions Jenny stared down a Courtney. *We could have fucking died. Courtney's too careless for her own good.* Jenny closed her eyes, her own head swimming. *And I'm not much better.* As she touched the car to balance, she envisioned her dead nana, hands on hips, disapproving. *God, Nana. Not doing that again.* In Jenny's mind, Nana shook her head from side to side, not believing.

When Courtney could stand, Jenny followed her to a narrow sidewalk that led to the back of the house, all the while thinking that fate, if one could call it that, clearly had been on their sides. She shivered in the face of that realization.

Jimmy and a few of his friends were visible through a bank of wide windows. A cluster of stocky athletes sat at a poker table in the family room while others milled around, beers in hand.

"Crashing the festivities," Courtney announced as she pushed her way into the kitchen where she perched, in seemingly perfect control, on a bar stool and surveyed the room. It was filled with friends from school, all in varying degrees of intoxication, some laughing hysterically, one girl sobbing, a few couples locked together in corners, and two, notable bodies passed out on a carpet in front of a roaring fire. Jenny moved in their direction. "I'm fucking freezing," she said, "Going to hang out by the corpses and warm my ass up."

By midnight the crowd began to thin, couples leaving arm in arm for their vehicles and home. Jenny had remained planted by the fire. Cole Jackson, a well-built wrestler, who was known also as a math genius, not unpredictably had joined her. He had been circling Jenny like a vulture for months.

"Looks like Cole has captured his prey," Jimmy chuckled as he handed Courtney another IPA.

Courtney stared at Jenny and Cole for a long time before slipping off the stool and walking slowly toward Jenny. *Have to get her away from him. He's a creep.* "Hey, Jenny, let's go. We can crash at my house," she offered, swaying toward Jimmy who had kept pace with her. Jenny looked up gratefully, though her body did not respond. *She's had way too many, just like I have.*

Jimmy took notice as well. "You two can't go anywhere just yet," he said. "You need to sober up."

"You just gave me another beer," Courtney complained as thought it was his fault. She took another sip.

"Last one. I'll get you both home safe before your folks think you've completely skipped out of the country. God, Courtney, here you are again, different night, same scenario."

"And for you too," she grinned wryly. She gazed for several unsettling seconds at her friend, Jimmy. He was handsome, muscular, self-assured, and as misguided at times as she often was, but they were a pair. They had been allies, first out of necessity, and best buddies by choice, for a lifetime.

She swayed slightly once more and then as if pulled backwards by a specter, plopped onto Jimmy's parents' oh-so-familiar, leather couch. Leaning her head back, she closed her eyes. *What is it about Jimmy Nelson? He can be such a jackass with so many people, but he takes care of me like a brother . . . or else a would-be lover?* The question had a valid place in her thinking. *Don't think I'm ready for that yet though. It would probably be like incest.* Courtney was unable to ponder her predicament further though, for within seconds, she had fallen asleep, waking two hours later with her head leaning on Jimmy Nelson's shoulder. He had wrapped a soft blanket around her and had watched her sleep until he knew it was time.

"Let's go, Courtney," he said, his voice husky. "It's late, really late. I'll drive you and Jenny home."

CHAPTER THREE

CHESTER

Chester Flack detested three things: mornings, small talk, and people, probably in reverse order. His character was developed by the time he was a toddler, it seemed. His mother, Bertha, certainly maintained that it was. While most young children were up early, badgering their parents for breakfast, bathroom, or play, Chester had been satisfied to lie in his bed, eyes closed, sleeping or perhaps feigning it, until late morning. When he finally did crawl from bed, he transformed, as though seized by an alien, into a terror, racing around the house, urinating on the floor, throwing toys, badgering the cat, kicking the walls and furniture, and making Bertha's life a holy nightmare. He spoke very little, but instead resorted to screams, grunts, and shrieks that annoyed the hell out of his mother. She was powerless though. The boy simply would not listen.

"Chester, you stop that yelling now. Just stop it," she would demand.

"No!" he would shout. "No, no, no!" And he would lunge at her, stomping on her toes or scratching her arms.

He was in constant motion from noon until dinnertime when he stopped dead at the sound of his father's heavy footsteps on the back porch. Chester then retreated to his room and silence.

"What's wrong with that kid?" Herbert Flack asked Bertha over and over.

Or to Chester, he'd blurt, "Cat got your tongue, boy? What the devil's gotten into you?"

The days played out in similar fashion for years with Bertha being unable to control or justify Chester's bizarre outbursts and inexplicable behavior. Herbert never would have believed her anyway. He was convinced the boy never made a sound at all.

When he was six, Chester was forced to begin school. It was the beginning of a new battle for Bertha who literally had to drag her son from bed and dress him as best she could. He offered no help, refusing to stand up straight, instead going limp while she tugged and pulled clothes over his skinny frame. She offered food that he seldom accepted and then shoved him out the door to catch the school bus that rumbled along, stopping at the end of nearly every lane on the rural highway that led into Hollow Vista.

If Bertha had thought she had troubles before, she was about to enter into a whole new realm of unrest. From day one, Chester made his presence known at school as *that kid*, the one who could not sit still, did not listen, instigated fights, and spent the majority of his playground time standing on the long, red line where disciplined students were separated from other children. It didn't take long until Chester became a target himself, as others pointed at and taunted the boy they found odd and a bit frightening. The goading only made things worse because Chester retaliated against any child who made the mistake of mocking him in any way.

"Chester tripped Bethany, yesterday," his first grade teacher, Ms. Butcher, informed Bertha by phone three months into the school year, "and today he bit Billy Barnes, right on the shoulder. Drew blood. We can't have that. Do you know how nasty a human bite can be, Mrs. Flack?"

Bertha was speechless when she heard Ms. Butcher's report, but in all honesty, not surprised. She had been enduring Chester's outbursts for years. When she finally was able to respond, she murmured, "I'll come get him. Maybe his father can straighten him out."

Herbert's answer was the belt. He yanked the wide, leather strap from the loops of his trousers, grabbed the buckle, wound the belt around his thick hand, and had at Chester with seven quick whacks. Though the boy winced, he voiced not one word. Nor did he cry. Bertha stood back, horrified by her husband's choice of punishment, but like her son, was unable to utter a sound in protest. *Bastard. Last time I'm telling Herbert a thing.*

Bertha kept her promise to herself. Though all the way through elementary school Chester continued to pester his classmates unmercifully, to irritate his teachers and administrators, and to infuriate more than a few parents whose children became the brunt of his outbursts, she did not mention reports of Chester's wild and unruly behavior to Herbert ever again. Instead, she bore the burden of her son's atrocious behavior in silence, and her anger at having no outlet for her frustration gnawed at her unceasingly. *This is not the life I was looking to have.*

Ignorant of the goings on at school, Herbert seldom reacted to Chester's presence at all until the day the boy

turned fourteen. "Get dressed, Chester," Herbert called
one Saturday morning. "It's time you become a man. Get
on out here. I'm taking you to the range. I'm going to teach
you how to shoot. Then, we're going to hunt."

⌘ ⌘ ⌘

The lessons at the range created a precarious bond between
Chester and his father but, moreover, they had an impact
on Chester's behavior. Oh, at his high school, he still continued to annoy the hell out of his classmates and teachers
with pranks, harassment, profanity, and provocations that
assured hours spent in a straight-backed chair opposite the
principal's office.

"Don't you move from that chair," he was instructed.
He reluctantly obeyed time and again for he had no other
choice. He was guarded like a criminal. When the final bell
rang on the days he was stationed there though, he would
leap from the spot as though sprung from a trap. Ignoring
everyone, he would launch to the front of the school, slam
open the double doors as hard as he could, and run home.

"I'm out of here," he'd yell. *Assholes.* His rage accompanied him home, but he knew not to say a word.

While Bertha suffered knowledge of her son's infractions in silence, Herbert Flack remained clueless. He mis-
takenly believed Chester had learned his lesson. Had he not
made it clear early on that he would not tolerate reports of
misbehavior? It was a fact. Neither he nor Chester had forgotten the beating. As a result, at home the two eyed each
other cautiously as if squaring off for a fight, and although
a verbal confrontation, much less a physical one, never occurred again, an underlying current of loathing lay hiding

like a silent specter between them, and both keenly were aware. Oddly enough, however, despite the unspoken animosity that existed between them, on more weekends than not, the father and son would don their khaki, camouflage pants and jackets, pack up a lunch, grab their rifles, and head for the foothills to kill whatever animal they could catch in their sights.

With a firearm in his hands, Chester was a changed adolescent. He could focus. Perhaps the reason was because hunting put distance between himself and people – the teachers, administrators, and students whose simple presence in his world exacerbated the anxiety that always had plagued him and provoked his aggressiveness. In Chester's mind, it was the whole of humanity that set him off. He acted out in defense against them. He had no way of understanding his fear of people or why his interactions with them drained him of his energy. Years of rowdy, inappropriate conduct had solved nothing though and Chester was lost. His behavior had kept others at a distance, and yet paradoxically as an integral part of his life. He never clearly had understood the complexity of that conundrum, so, in frustration, he had lashed out. *They're a bunch of fucking jerks.*

Though his angst continued, he embraced his newfound means of coping. Hunting ultimately became the means to an end for Chester. The ability to center himself for the first time ever, combined with the emotional, gripping charge of power and excitement that accompanied a kill, exhilarated him. When hunting, his anger dissipated and calm set in, a deep river of contentment. The two sensations, so unfamiliar three short years before, secretly bolstered him. Not for one second, would he have admitted his feelings to his father though. His emotions were too delicious to share.

On the outings Chester spoke very little unless Herbert engaged him and that was not often. If he did, it generally was to rebuff his son for moving too quickly, for making too much noise stomping through underbrush, or for mishandling the Ruger he had provided him. Despite the awkwardness of their togetherness, Herbert did teach Chester how to shoot, and moreover, how to hunt. By the time he was seventeen Chester was an excellent shot, bettered only by Herbert who lauded his expertise over his son. It was important to him to keep the boy humble and in his place. He was a master at doing so. His critical eye caught Chester's every misstep and his acerbic judgments were the only comments that passed between the two.

"Chester, you dimwit, lower that weapon until you're set to shoot. You're going to nail another hunter."

"Goddamn it, Chester, quit moving in the brush. Every goddamn rabbit within a mile can hear you. You scare away my kill and you're in for it, boy."

One autumn day when Chester missed his shot at a large, four-point buck not thirty yards away, Herbert became unhinged. "I let you take that shot, you little punk. I gave it to you, jackass. Could have been mine. Mine! God help me, but more often than not, I wish your sorry ass had never been born."

Though Chester appeared to brush off the abuse like dust, deep inside, his father's comments settled, and they festered.

⌘ ⌘ ⌘

It was an accident, wasn't it?

"It was an accident," Chester shrieked to his mother from only steps inside the rickety gate of the front yard. The cold, January air burned his lungs, as he panted for air. He had run a mile home.

"Come with me. Come now," he ordered, clawing at his mother's arm as she ran from the warmth of the house to meet him.

"What? What's wrong?" Bertha's breath caught as she stared at her son. His lips were quivering, his eyes were wide, and the rifle was shaking awkwardly in his hand. "Just come. An accident."

Bertha, clad only in a pair of her husband's corduroy trousers, a thick cable-knit sweater, and rubber boots, began to trot after Chester who had turned the moment after he had spoken to retrace his steps. She trailed behind her son, the gap between them growing. Though her heart was racing, she followed on, able to keep up only because she had a strong will and because she was experienced. She had tracked prey herself as a young girl and though, in minutes, she lost sight of Chester's bobbing figure, somehow, she instinctively knew where she should go.

She jogged for half a mile before she finally stopped, her side aching from the exertion. She stood perfectly still, panting to catch her breath, and gazing around at the thick, brown brush, tangles of it, choking beneath a canopy of California Black Oaks, gnarly, rusty Madrones, and towering, Ponderosa Pines that dotted the hills. For a split second she scanned the bushes in front of her and she recalled her father's blustering advice. *"Three plants to avoid like the plague: poison oak, stinging nettle, and Mountain Misery. All three will tie you up in knots."* He had lectured to her many times.

When she could breathe again, she irately pushed away any thoughts of her father, thankfully dead now, and moved forward, more slowly than before, but determined. The path had narrowed and branches, like low, camouflaged daggers, ripped at her pants legs and tore at her boots. She lowered her head against a cold breeze that bore down the hillside. *It's going to storm. I can feel it.* She pulled her hands up into the sleeves of her sweater, drew her arms to her chest, and marched on with gritty tenacity, unsure of what she would find ahead of her, but fearing the worse. And then she was there, at a scene that never, never would she be able to erase from her memory.

A few feet off the trail, Chester was squatting beside her husband. The young man's hands were still gripping the Ruger with such force that his knuckles had blanched white. Beside him lay Herbert, dead, a plume of blood oozing from a gaping wound and saturating his jacket. He had been shot, dead on, in the heart, and again in the groin; his trousers splayed open exposing bare and bloody flesh.

Bertha gasped first, and then she sighed, a long, mournful sound issuing from her lips. "It's finally over," she said, and was filled with a strange, unsettling sense of relief.

"It was an accident," Chester muttered, his head bowed as if in prayer and resignation.

Bertha did not believe. "Look at me, Chester."

Chester tilted his head upward toward his mother. Their eyes locked.

"Was it?" she asked point blank. "Was it an accident?"

"I shot the bastard," he admitted. "It was no accident."

Chester addressed his mother calmly for the first time in his life.

"It was an accident," Bertha said flatly, refuting his claim and affirming exactly what she wanted to believe, what she would have others believe. "Let's drag his ass out of here." They managed to pull the body to the edge of the trail before Bertha hiked back home and called the police. Chester stayed behind ready to take out any animal that made a move on the corpse.

Bertha led a troop of paramedics, armed with a stretcher, blanket, a shroud, medical supplies, and flashlights, up the trail to the spot where Chester kneeled, silent and pale, beside his father's body. A pair of police officers, weapons at the ready, accompanied them. When the officers were convinced that Herbert Flack was, indeed, dead, they photographed the scene as best they could in the waning light and made the call. "We've seen all we need to see. Let's head down to your house, Mrs. Flack, where we'll need to ask you and Chester a few questions." The medics packed up the body and trudged downhill to the road where an ambulance was stationed ready to take Herbert for his last ride, to the morgue.

It had taken little to convince authorities that indeed Herbert Flack's death was simply a gross mishap. "Herbert and Chester were pals," Bertha had lied. "They've been hunting the foothills for years. They lived for their outings together."

Aside from asserting that the shooting had been accidental, Chester said nothing to the police. His face bore no discernable expression although inside he churned with shock, satisfaction, and bravado, a disparate mix that made his heart race. He was unable to find his voice however, even though, for once, he felt in control having finished off, once and for all, the man, who when not ridiculing him, had regarded him as a useless, human speck.

Instead, Bertha explained details of the accident. "It's just horrible," she said, dramatically, alleging that she was heartbroken and that Chester was too upset to regurgitate details of the event one more time. "It was hard enough the first time," she declared. She sniffed into a tissue and began her tale.

"After a couple of hours wandering up the trail, Herbert apparently wrangled his way into the thick brush leaving Chester behind," she told police. "He said to Chester something like, 'I'm going on up that slope yonder. You stay here and get ready to shoot if you hear anything. You can tell by the scuffed marks on a few trees around here that some big, old bucks are vying for territory. If you hear rustling, shoot the fucker.' That's the way Herbert talked most times. Used profanity in practically every sentence. Well, Herbert was gone for an hour, Chester told me. Everything was real quiet . . . until it wasn't."

She continued. "Chester waited a long time and then lowered his body to the ground and sat with his back leaning on the trunk of one of those ancient oaks up there. Says his rifle was on his knees, and he stared into the foliage until his eyes stung. He closed them for a minute and must have dozed off when, all of a sudden, he heard a loud crack. Chester said he jumped to his feet, leveled the rifle, and fired, twice in quick succession, at what he assumed would become his prize buck. Instead of the bellow of a buck or the grunt of a doe though, Chester heard a man's cry. It was a shriek of pain, my boy told me, and then he heard Herbert's voice. 'You goddamn motherfucker.' And then all was quiet."

"Chester came after me right away," she told officials. "He was sobbing and shaking like a leaf. Devastated. I followed him as fast as I could to the place up there, just off the main trail to see for myself. It was an accident, plain and simple, officers, and Chester's likely never to get over what

he's done by pure chance. Why, he can hardly say a word."
Bertha embellished the lie to save her boy.

It's what any mother would do, isn't it?

⌘   ⌘   ⌘

In the aftermath of the shooting, Chester's relationship
with his mother changed. He owed her. No longer did he
lash out at Bertha as he had for his whole life. Instead, he
drew quiet, even at school, and perhaps that was best. Not
everyone believed Herbert Flack's death had been accidental, but if anyone had voiced an opposing opinion, there
might have been hell to pay. They knew. Chester knew. As a
consequence others kept their distance and he completed
his last few months of high school in somewhat of a daze . .
. up until the last day when he made a decision. *These jack-
asses can go fuck themselves.*

The moment he had crossed the stage at graduation,
diploma in hand, he ran from the ceremony to the front of
the school and launched six cherry bombs through a window into the principal's office where they exploded, one
after the other, before lighting the carpet on fire. The interior of the office was gutted. And Chester never was caught.

CHAPTER FOUR

FLO

A pall of sadness tugged at Florence Gray's sensibility. Flo was astutely aware why. The chaos at her workplace only the day before had left her wrestling with an annoying melancholy that, like an evil despot, so wanted her in its clutches.

It was Saturday. She had slept late and fitfully. Her mind had not rested; instead it replayed, over and over, the terror that had unfolded in the halls of Hollow Vista High School where Flo had been a custodian for years. She closed her eyes. Images of frightened adolescents, panicked teachers, and worried parents played before her like a picture show, face after face, all displaying differing emotions: fear, anger, sadness, shock, and at last relief. Surely every one of them had been traumatized, just as Flo had been. A distinguished and respected, female teacher had done the unthinkable. With one clandestine murder, that of a well-known real estate agent behind her, she had launched into a near-lethal rampage that had left the high school's principal, his secretary, and a fledgling teacher injured, the latter two critically. No one had foreseen such madness, but in an instant the school had become a war zone. The school secretary surely was crippled for life, and the young teacher left maimed beyond belief.

Flo, and a few others who had lingered at the scene, had learned the details of the women's injuries immediately, and most others in the small town almost as quickly. Folks chattered, whispered, gossiped, and speculated, all searching for a logical reason why a seemingly normal individual could had fallen into such an abyss of hate that she saw no way out of her angst other than through violence. Flo, as many others were, was baffled. *It's hard to fathom that a crime like this could happen in little Hollow Vista, but it did, like a lighting strike. Well, it's behind us now. That murderous witch will be in prison for a good, long, time, forever, I suspect . . . and the others? Who knows? Life will go on though. It always does, until, of course, for some reason or another, it doesn't. Makes me wonder what's around the next corner.*

⌘ ⌘ ⌘

Flo lay in bed much longer than usual as though trapped there by her overactive mind. She had felt overwhelming despair before, the ominous feeling threatening to drag her downward into a mire of depression. She never had surrendered to the maddening sensation though; nor would she now. The possibility was unarguably present, but it was not in Flo's nature to acquiesce to the negative. She could not stop herself from pondering her own past losses though.

First had been her father, a man both as soft as fine leather and as strong as steel, whose horrific death still haunted folks at the cannery in town. A callous, careless truck driver had sped backwards into a loading dock, spilling his load and crushing three workers into a pulpy mass all at once, Flo's father among them. Flo's heart had ached with grief, but she had been unable to dwell, for her mother's need seemed greater. It took only three months for her mother to die as well, she from a broken heart. Flo was sure of it. And much later, it was Randall.

Randall Gray had been Flo's lover, antagonist, and friend, a soul mate who at the prime of his life was snared by cancer, the evil monster Flo so abhorred. In only months, her poor husband had withered to a skeleton before her eyes, his leathery, yellow skin stretched over an emaciated frame. The couple had suffered together in silence, until Randall finally gave up the fight and died. Armed with the wherewithal not to renounce her own existence as her mother before her had, Flo embraced her life. It was hers, and hers alone, as paltry as it might have appeared to others.

Though her husband was gone now, he was with her still, the memories of the man vivid and alive. In fact, she needed only to peer out her bedroom window at the mature vineyard beside her house to feel his presence, for he was most certainly there. She had scattered his ashes on a cool, autumn night, four weeks after his death, the swirling fog being her only companion. Overwhelmed by sorrow and loneliness, she had sobbed well into the night, but was done with the outward display of grief by morning. It seemed a waste of energy. *Have to go on.* Though tears had threatened a time or two, Flo had learned to stifle them. She had not cried openly again until she had reached home only the night before. Though she had tried to suppress the tears, weeping had won out and actually had served her well, washing away a tangle of emotions and calming her.

The horror that had occurred at the high school was behind her, she believed, and with her senses deadened somewhat, it would be easier to face another new day.

Flo believed that her own tenacity was her greatest strength. *Too many folks are bogged down by emotions. And what do they do? They react or behave in ways that wreck their lives. I want no part of that kind of behavior. No. Not me.* Flo knew her strengths, and stolidly maintained strict control of her demeanor. It was safer that way.

⌘ ⌘ ⌘

At midday, Flo finally slid her legs from under the blankets and sat on the side of her bed, tightly clutching her pillow for several minutes before letting go. She looked down at her toes, not quite reaching the floor. They dangled in repose, unmoving. *I'm going to plant my feet on solid ground now.* And she did, vowing to herself, with any luck, to leave the previous day's horror hidden away.

Slipping to the floor, Flo wandered into the bathroom and stared at her face in the mirror. Her hand went immediately to the large, black mole lodged high on her cheek below her eye and she fingered the thing hatefully.

"I'm a sight," she mumbled. "I'd have the damned thing hacked off, but, hell, I wouldn't recognize myself without it."

It was a truth. Although all of her life Flo had been self-conscious about the hideous growth, its presence, in an odd way, had given her existence stability. She was not beautiful, but she was balanced. Seldom did she seize up in anger or regret; nor was she giddy with happiness. Instead she moved through each day with her head down, sights set, and her integrity in place. She was nobody's enemy, no one's real friend, and that was all right. Her position as a custodian at the high school fit her like a glove. She quietly finished her duties, interacted politely with teachers, administrators, and students when need be, and when the job was done, went home to Freddy, her cat, and the silence that she treasured.

⌘ ⌘ ⌘

As she had every morning of her life, Flo left the house that day for a walk. It was her daily constitution . . . two or three miles, rain or shine. The exercise gave Flo time to think, with few thoughts latching on for long. Instead, ideas, impressions, considerations, memories, and even the odd judgment surfaced and then retreated, never settling. Her thinking mirrored her life, a tidy ebb and flow that pushed her into each new day, and then dragged her back to the solitary comfort of her home at night. She didn't mind. No one bothered her there.

Flo had pulled her long, brown, grey-streaked hair into a tight bun at the nape of her neck, donned a tattered sweat suit, her trusty tennis shoes, and a baseball cap. She was ready. She stepped from the wooden porch onto a narrow pathway that led to the road. She looked up at the sky, cloudless, an endless blue, on this spring day. The sun already had risen high and Flo realized she was starting her walk later than usual. *Going to be a warm one.*

She was looking upward at the very moment her toes reached the black- topped roadway and was startled by the loud roar of an engine. She instantly reeled backwards to avoid being struck as a rusty, red, Ford, pick-up truck tore past her, the driver, Chester Flack, hell bent, Flo assumed, on meeting his maker. The man drove the same way, like a bat out of hell, day after day. *"Pedal to the metal," Papa would have said. Chester Flack. Now, that's a character.*

Chester Flack had lived for years with his mother in a small, stucco house identical in size and construction to Flo's, on a cul-de-sac that jutted from the main road a quarter of a mile west. Bertha Flack was as old as the hills and never left the place except on Sundays when Chester drove her to the nondenominational, community church in town. He would strap her into the front seat of his pickup truck and speed like a madman with no consideration at all it seemed to Flo, of the poor woman's well-being. *She has to be ninety, if she's a day. Don't have a clue why she puts up with Chester the way she does. Always has though. He was the same way when he was a kid.* Of this, Flo was certain. Chester Flack had graduated from Hollow Vista High the year after she entered. He had left his reputation behind.

CHAPTER FIVE

GEORGE

"No. Leave her alone." Through clinched teeth, George hissed a growl of fear and loathing into his stuffy, darkened bedroom. Unaware, he was drenched in perspiration. He watched the event unfold before him, seeing every movement all so clearly. Momentarily he was paralyzed, his body betraying him.

From his bedroom window, beyond his reach and much too far away, he could see that his daughter, Angie, was being jerked into an old, dented van of some kind. Her slender arm was held fast by the huge mitt of a faceless monster, while her free hand flailed, searching for anything to grab onto, but to no avail. Someone had her. Panic, like quicksand, threatened to pull George under. He couldn't breathe.

"No," he gasped as he reached for his service weapon, his hand, like his daughter's thrashing wildly but finding nothing. "Damn! Where in the hell is it?"

He sprang forward, launching himself down the stairs, onto the front porch, and onward toward the street, but before he could reach her, before he could stop the madness, the door of the vehicle slammed shut with a haunting screech. The dilapidated van swerved sideways for a moment before racing ahead down the street. He charged after it, barefoot, and nearly naked. "Stop, Goddamn it!" He yelled the command over and over until the van's taillights at last were but miniature specks.

In a nanosecond of time the van vanished from sight as if it never had been there at all; he could see absolutely nothing. Sharp stones and shards of glass had torn into his feet as he ran, faster and faster. He stopped still finally, feeling crippled. Instantly he was submerged in such darkness and despair that he understood surely that this disaster would destroy him. He was too late. He had failed again. He called out one last time, "No! Stop. Angie!" His bellowing cry, a deafening scream all unto itself, dissolved instantly into an eerie silence.

And he was awake. "Shit."

⌘   ⌘   ⌘

George sat absolutely still for several minutes listening to the echo of his heartbeat pound in his ears and then, eventually to the familiar sounds of the house as it settled in the night. Had Angie heard him cry out? No. It was not quite midnight. She was with Willard and George was alone.

Perhaps it was, *no, certainly it is*, the newness of Angie and Willard's relationship that had those two unwilling to be apart. *Is it really love this time?* After observing three years of Angie's unhealthy alliance to Brad Browning, George cautiously hoped it was. Strangely, the thought of such irrepressible emotion buoyed his mood and memories fell open like the unfurling petals of a rose. George remembered with absolute clarity the initial juncture in time when he and his wife, Linda, had been new, unable to learn about each other fast enough, intimately enough, thoroughly enough.

Linda's beautiful face, golden hair, and unsettling smile had captured him, and he pictured her perfectly in his mind's eye. Nearly eighteen years had slipped by since her passing and he mourned her as much now as he had the moment he had seen the doctor's stricken expression that fateful night. "I'm so sorry," the man had murmured, "The bleeding could not be stopped."

Until the day he died, George would not forget; nor would he let go. His memories of the love of his life, combined with the intensity of his devotion to his daughter, Angie, had allowed him to move forward. He had managed so well, until recently, when frightening dreams, night after night, had begun. And what had precipitated them? He knew. A murder too close to home, his exhausting investigation into the crime, and a mass shooting at the local high school, Angie's school, all within a matter of weeks had left him beyond fatigued and on edge. It was out of character for George, a respected police detective, to lose his composure, but he had, at least at home when the reality of life's more sordid side closed in on him like an a vise, the pressure unrelenting. *No one else can know.*

Having awakened again from another alarming nightmare, he felt more alone than he had in many years. That realization was new and disconcerting. When his wife, Linda, had died giving birth to Angie, George had felt he would never recover . . . ever . . . but that notion had changed incrementally beginning with the moment his baby girl had been placed in his arms for the first time. Burdened with grief, George did survive, but he became driven, his protective instincts dominating him. He would not fail Angie, as he irrationally believed he had failed his wife. His little daughter became his reason to live and he had dedicated himself to her for a lifetime . . . until now.

What had changed? Why was he feeling so anxious, so unsure? Angie would be beginning her studies at the university in Turlock soon, not far away, really, but removed, and when she did come home, Willard Dunn surely would dominate her time. And where did that leave him? George took inventory. Had he made a mistake? Had he lived his life, after the death of Linda, wearing blinders? Should he have remarried? Was it too late? Being alone was not what he had bargained for, but the veracity of that fact becoming a reality weighed on him. He stood suddenly, walked into his bathroom, stared at his reflection, and evaluated. He was not young, certainly, at fifty, but he was fit: tall, muscular, his looks passable. He had a strong jaw line and high cheekbones, perhaps an inherited trait from his mother who believed her father to have been a descendant of the Miwoks or Yokuts. George's hair might attest to that for it was full and dark with only a smattering of grey at his temples. A few lines had settled onto his forehead, the result surely of worry, of concentration, of his commitment to his profession as a detective and, of course, to Angie as well. Tiny wrinkles had formed at the corners of his deep, green-brown eyes; they deepened when he smiled. Should he smile more or less? He shook his head then, embarrassed by his self-assessment. *What the hell's with you, George?*

He wandered down the stairs to the living room, turned on a small lamp, picked up a tattered paperback, and thumbed through it blindly. *What is this anyway?* He turned the book over and read the title, *On The Road* by

Jack Kerouac. *Geez, read this years ago. Wonder what it's doing here. Guess Angie's reading it for school.*

He thought then about what he remembered of the story – two young men traveling the country in search of, what was it? Excitement. Experience. Knowledge. Enlightenment. George had not been able to relate for his path had taken him in another direction. He had played it safe. No travels for him. He had had little choice, really.

"Get a job, George," his father, Ervin, had told him. "Get some education, no matter how hard it is, and get yourself a real job. Otherwise, you'll be lined up alongside of your mother and me down on cannery row. You won't like it."

George took his father's advice to heart. He had watched his parents stumble home exhausted day after day from jobs that offered no stimulation, no future, and little money. Both, like so many others in the community, had secured employment at one of the local canneries right after high school. Quite a number of students, bored with their studies, quit school altogether, looking at income, no matter how insignificant, as an incentive to move on.

For years, George's father had boxed cans and jars of vegetables and fruits to be shipped throughout the United States and beyond. As a result his arms were ripped with muscle but his shoulders were bent slightly and permanently forward having borne the burden of repetitive, back-breaking maneuvers that changed his entire body shape in time. George's mother, Sylvia, had been a bit more fortunate. She was smart, pretty, and laced her conversation with jokes and innuendo that won her many admirers, and an office job, sorting through invoices and packing slips. Her tasks were redundant as well, but kept her off an assembly line and for that she was grateful. Sylvia's quick wit captivated Ervin before he knew what hit him and she fell in love immediately with his hearty, good looks, broad smile, and tenderness. By the time George graduated from high school, his parents had been married for twenty-five years, and though Sylvia and Ervin worked from sunrise until sunset, they were happy, and their home filled with laughter and love. George had been lucky. He knew it. His parents had taught him well the basics that enabled him to find success: determination, commitment, perseverance, acceptance, and kindness.

Though many parents in their circumstances might have insisted that their son go to work immediately, his folks had not. Instead, George commuted to a small college near his home and in two years was accepted into a police academy in nearby San Jose. Never were two parents more proud than when George was offered a position with a local police department in the central valley. He would be set.

George thought with affection of his parents, now retired and living together in a mobile home park in Santa Cruz. They were as content and devoted to each other as they ever had been. George worried though. They were aging and he had overheard his father tell Sylvia, in no uncertain terms, to watch her pennies because, "Sylvia, honey, we don't have a pot to piss in." Directly to George, however, Ervin assured his son that he and Sylvia were getting along just fine. "Got a roof over our heads, food to eat, and after all these years, Sylvia is still damn good company."

George had to appreciate his father's desire for autonomy for as long as Ervin and Sylvia's luck and decent health held. He seldom saw them, but they spoke weekly by phone and always made it a point to be together for the holidays. Angie adored her grandparents, calling them Erv and Syl when she was a tiny toddler. Their full names had been a mouthful for Angie so the first syllable of each name had come to suffice. The idea of eventually resorting to the more common *Grandma* or *Grandpa* was out of the question for Angie and in her little brain were alien names for her grandparents Erv and Syl. Ervin and Sylvia found their nicknames charming, buying in to their little granddaughter's creativity without batting an eye.

As the years passed, the physical distance between George, Angie, and Ervin and Sylvia meant nothing at all. George knew it to be a fact. Love in this tiny family definitely was intact, and for George, something of a relief.

⌘   ⌘   ⌘

A rustling of footsteps on the front porch drew George from his reverie. Angie was home. Still holding the copy of *On the Road* in his hand, George stood silently waiting for the door to open. It was late. Several minutes passed before it did. *Can't get enough of each other.*

"Dad? You're still up?" Angie asked, "You're usually asleep by now."

"Yeah. Couldn't get to sleep for some reason," he fibbed. "Did you and Willard have fun?"

"Yeah, we did. He's really sweet," she answered. Her face softened with a wistful expression as she spoke.

"You like this young man a lot, don't you?" It was a statement more than a question, because George knew it to be true.

"I do, Dad. He's different from most of the guys I've known, and a hundred and eighty degrees from Brad. Thank God that jackass is out of my life."

"Well, I do believe you've moved up in the world. Willard is a definite improvement, not that Brad is a terrible person,

I guess. But I do have to say that I cringed a few times when Brad displayed his attitude around you. You didn't deserve it. Willard, well, this kid seems to have character and manners. Old school. I like that."

"Me too." Angie grinned and then changed the subject. "Were you reading?"

"No. Saw the book here, though. Recognized it. Read it years ago."

"Yeah, I just finished it, last book of the year. Guess it was an appropriate choice since everyone who's graduating will be, in essence, on the road to somewhere. Hard to believe."

"It is, "George replied, his throat tightening unexpectedly. "Where have the years gone? Yesterday you were five."

Angie smiled. "I can almost remember being five," she said.

"You were the cutest, little girl in the world, well, in my world anyway. Nice memories." George bit his lip and stared away from Angie. His eyes stung with tears. "Bittersweet," he managed.

Angie moved toward him, grabbed his arm, and rested her head on his shoulder. "Love you, Dad."

It took a minute, but George found his voice. "Love you, too, honey. I have conflicting emotions, you know. I want to keep you right here, a little girl forever, but I want you to go too. My real hope is that you'll fly, really fly, and in time, you'll find your perfect place in the world, but I have to be honest. I'm going to miss the hell out of you."

"I won't be far, and I'll be back. You know that."

"I do, but your leaving at all is a reality check."

CHAPTER SIX

SUSAN

Armed with little else but resolve to accept the inevitable, after Jenny's abrupt pronouncement, Susan moved through the rest of the weekend as though nothing had changed. She had no choice. She was not a complainer, never had been, and had learned to lock her emotions safely inside to be shared with no one, barring perhaps Jenny, on rare occasions. It was her way.

She puttered in her garden that Saturday, pulling stubborn weeds until her nails were black with dirt. Although she knew she should wear gardening gloves, she detested them. They were uncomfortably confining. *Aw. Doesn't matter. Dirt washes off. Who's going to see me anyway?* She stared at her hands for a moment. They were prematurely aging, with wide veins protruding and radiating like tiny tunnels beneath the skin from her wrists to her knuckles. Dark spots were clearly visible too. Freckles? *Hardly. These are age spots. That's what Mother used to call them. She hated them*. Susan remembered Jenny as a small child holding her grandmother's hand firmly and running her fingers over and over them, pushing down on the purple bulges hidden beneath the skin. "Nana," she'd say. "What are these things?"

"They're veins, Jenny."

"Make them go away. They're ugly."

"They are ugly all right, but I'm lucky to have them. They keep Nana's blood flowing. Wouldn't be a nana without them."

Susan had been a bit embarrassed by Jenny's disrespect, but her mother, Rachel, had taken the innocent abuse in stride, instinctively understanding that her granddaughter, simply a curious child, would never believe that her nana's hands once had been as soft and smooth as little Jenny's were. Life's hardships had hewn them though into a worker's hands – thick, puffy, calloused, and unsightly.

Susan recalled watching her mother draw her hands away from Jenny, clasp them together, and touch them to her lips. She had grown silent then, her eyes downcast, shoulders hunched forward, pulling away into her own world. Susan had observed this exact response, an instant retreat, time and again, but could only watch. At moments such as this, her mother truly mystified her.

In truth, Rachel never could have revealed that, in fact, much too often, myriad worries, gnawing inside, oddly and quite unpredictably pulled her to another place. *Susan and Jenny are oblivious to what lies ahead*. Rachel's battered and aging hands had prompted her musing. She had been tugged again, rather unwittingly, into another of her reveries because they reminded her of a truth. *The passage of time appears an ally early on, but in the end, it is an enemy, and I know in my heart that my time is near*. The old woman grasped that notion at the deepest level for she had lived for over eight decades. She looked soulfully at her daughter and grand-daughter knowing that their lives would play out as well with victories, failures, joys, and sorrows, a diverse and con-tradictory mix that was life itself. Rachel could do nothing but stand by and let it happen.

Susan's memory dissolved almost as quickly as it had surfaced. "I have my mother's hands," Susan said aloud, a catch of astonishment and sadness betraying her and tear-ing at her heart.

She looked longer, turning her hands first palm down and then up. Deep lines there, like haphazard etchings, held predictions and quite likely could have revealed sto-ries, too many to count. Susan knew that to be so. *Ah, what answers lie here? I never expected at this juncture in my life to be here, in this place, and I believe I'm a little bit afraid. I have no clue what the future holds for me, for Jenny.* She clinched her hands together as if in pain. Dirt had lodged in the crev-ices of each finger. One nail had split; another was cut to the quick. She stared until her eyes grew blurry. One fat tear rolled down her cheek and plopped onto her arm. *Oh, Mother, how did I arrive at this place?*

⌘ ⌘ ⌘

Shadows began to fall across the garden that had been planted in an array of now decaying containers built long ago by Zach after Susan's pleading.

"Please, Zach, would you make boxes for the vegetables? The gophers are making my life a misery. Half the things I plant in the ground disappear by morning. The little bas-tards must have their burrows packed full."

He had chuckled at her. "Sure, honey, I can do that. Easy project."

Though their personalities were the antithesis of each other, Susan and Zach had been in love then, early on. Life had seemed so simple. Of course, with the passage of time, events began to complicate their lives: an unexpected pregnancy; Jenny's birth, a difficult one; their adjustment to parenthood; Rachel's sudden death followed by Susan's prolonged, untenable grief; Zach's dissatisfaction with his job at the mill that spilled over into black moodiness at home; and finally, his departure, sudden, yet not unsurprising. In the days after Susan had been left, she had plunged into a sadness that strangely was tinged with relief. It was as though she had known he would go, long before he actually did, and with the waiting over she oddly breathed more easily. And now, it was Jenny's time. Though accepting, and even, to some degree approving, Susan could not escape an alien, aching feeling, as if her very body abruptly had been gutted. *I feel hollow.*

She stood slowly, feeling a twinge in her lower back. Perspiration had dried on her face and arms. It felt gritty to the touch, like fine sandpaper. Her arms tingled a bit from her exertion, but she ignored the sensation and moved toward the house. *A bath. That's what I need.*

A long, soapy soak in the claw-foot tub upstairs relieved her tight muscles. When the water began to cool, she stepped out onto the bathroom mat and rubbed herself dry. She was refreshed and clean, even those pesky fingernails.

After sighing deeply, she whispered aloud, "I'm hungry. Don't think I've eaten all day."

She dressed quickly, pulled leggings over her slender legs, and slipped braless into an ancient, soft sweatshirt. *Aw! Comfort.* In moments she was in the kitchen preparing a meal, just for her. She was alone, but oddly not lonely. *A new normal, I guess. Get used to it, Susan.*

Susan sipped creamy, tomato bisque from an earthenware bowl that had been Rachel's favorite, bit into triangles of buttered toast, and sat quietly, anticipating reading the morning newspaper that had been tossed aside earlier when Jenny had announced that she was moving out with Courtney. Susan's normal, Saturday morning routine had been disrupted; reading had become out of the question, and she knew: *Get busy. Do some mindless work.* It was not that she would not think. Indeed she would. Routine chores, however – mopping, gardening, folding clothes – gave Susan permission to process her thoughts, in her own way, at her own pace. Such randomness worked for her.

She reached for the folded newspaper, flipped to the front page and gasped.

"Another mass shooting . . . oh God, no," she said, speaking directly at the newspaper as if it were an animate object. "This happened last night. What the hell? Why do these horrific events keep happening?"

She absorbed details as she read: twenty-three dead, sixteen others injured, assault rifle and handguns found, gunman killed by police, cell phone video discovered, carnage everywhere, motive unclear. The column left little to the imagination. *Fear – Anger – Disbelief* - were the words boldly printed beneath a photograph of a group of survivors huddled together. Anguish clouded every face. *Makes me sick.* Susan realized immediately that her body had tensed.

She moved to the living room, turned on the television, and instantly was absorbed in a prolonged rehashing of the mass shooting that had taken place in a small, shopping mall somewhere in southern Mississippi. The gunman had not yet been identified . . . nor had the dead and injured.

Susan watched, drawn to the coverage of the manic scene while at the same time admonishing herself for her anxious curiosity in the wake of such tragedy.

She watched as a sober, male reporter looked directly into the camera. His eyes were wide and his lips moved just slightly out of sync with a line of dialogue that was being streamed across the television screen beneath the taped footage. "It will take some time, I've been told, before details can be released. Authorities are conducting a thorough investigation as we speak but are very tight-lipped about this seemingly random act of violence that has shocked the residents of this quiet, rural town."

Behind him, a bevy of police officers, investigators, and first responders were entrenched in their duties, oblivious to the news media that had been cordoned off, away from the bustle of activity. Countless eager and stressed news correspondents, straining to see more, bobbled and swayed like an angry ocean. The lights of ambulances and police vehicles flashed red and yellow in the distance displaying a disordered array that illuminated the scene in a haphazard rhythm that bore absolutely no sense of order. Chaos reigned.

Though the footage was hours old, Susan had not yet seen it, so she watched in stunned silence until, without realizing, over two hours had passed. She felt suddenly tired. *Time to turn this off and get some sleep. Tomorrow's another day. Wonder what in the hell it will bring.*

A sudden banging on the back door startled her, but she relaxed a bit after she had walked into the kitchen and recognized her daughter, Jenny, looking at her through the glass. *Forgot her keys, I bet.*

Susan's momentary sense of calm disappeared instantly when she pulled open the door. Jenny was barefoot, her hair a disheveled mess, and her mascara streaked beneath her eyes. Her blouse was ripped at the shoulder revealing a large, purple abrasion and a long, fresh, puffy scratch flared red on her neck. She looked at her mother soberly, although it took only seconds for Susan to assess that Jenny was more than a little inebriated.

"Oh Jenny. What in the world happened?"

Jenny said not a word. Instead, she stepped solemnly into the kitchen, sat down on a wooden chair, and began to sob.

CHAPTER SEVEN

COURTNEY

Courtney heard her cell phone ringing . . . or did she? She heard something, a remote clanging close by. What was it? She tried to open her eyes but could not. They were stuck together. Wait. Was she blindfolded? She attempted to move her hands to pull at a smelly rag that had been tied too tightly around her eyes and forehead, but found she could not move them. She was bound, both her hands and feet. She lay still for several minutes, her mind searching for answers. How did she get here, to this place that smelled of animal feces, hay, and mold? And what was that clanking sound? Twisting slightly, she felt the prickle of a stick, perhaps straw, piercing her cheek. *What the hell happened last night? Where am I? God, my head!* She drifted back into a light sleep, but was awakened again by persistent clanging, by the whinny of a horse, and by the shuffle of footsteps, slow, heavy, deep thumps that grew louder as they came closer and closer, until they stopped still.

She felt a presence. Was she imagining? No. Someone was there. A man? He cleared his throat noisily and spewed a wad of saliva and mucus onto Courtney's upper leg, her bare leg. Though she could not have know for sure that she had been spat upon, she was well aware of the sound and of the moist sting, both hot and cold, that had struck her thigh. *Shit. What the hell's happening?* She felt a kick then. Perhaps it was more of a firm nudge, low on her abdomen. It hurt and she recoiled slightly. She wanted to speak, but her voice betrayed her. Only a sad groan issued from her throat, but that was enough. He knew she was conscious.

"Well, well, missy. Guess I have you where I want you," he chuckled. It was a deep voice, strange, and yet the cadence of it oddly familiar.

"Who are you?" she managed in a whisper. "And where am I?"

"Why, you're in my palace, bitch, my stable, with all the other animals that serve my needs. You'll fit in just fine, missy."

⌘　⌘　⌘

Only the day before, mid-afternoon, on the last Saturday before the end of the school year, Courtney and Jenny Wallis had sat in Courtney's bedroom, flipping through fashion magazines and drinking weak, wine coolers from fragile, crystal tumblers Courtney had pulled from her mother, Jill's, prized, china cabinet. Her cunningness gave her satisfaction and allowed her surreptitiously to abuse her mother who would have had a fit had she known her daughter had been rummaging through her fine porcelain and crystal. Courtney could imagine her yelling – *"How dare, you,*

Courtney! Those are mine and they're expensive." – the last word drawn out for emphasis. *It serves her right. She cares more about her stupid crystal and china than anything.* Courtney rubbed her finger along the rim of the glass and smiled in approval at the sound, a sharp screech that filled the air. *Yeah, the real shit.* She grinned at her friend when Jenny's shoulders inched up with irritation.

"Stop it, Courtney," she begged. "That's fucking annoying."

Courtney quickly broached a new subject. She smirked, "So your mom didn't know what time you came home this morning?"

"Fuck, no," Jenny replied. "I had sneaked in only a couple of hours before I heard her up. Don't know how she does it. She's up by five every day."

"Old people do that shit. My dad's like that too. Up at dawn and off to the club, or the gym, or driving around the ranch from one end to the other. Don't know how they do it. It kills me to get up by 7:00 on school days, but thank God that shit is about over. Do you realize we graduate on Friday? Can't fucking wait."

"Me either, and then, off to a new life. I told my mom I was moving out, that we're getting a place together."

"What'd she say?"

"Not much. I mean what could she say? I'm doing it." Jenny watched Courtney gather a thrown pillow from a pile behind her. She clutched it tightly to her stomach as though protecting herself from something and stared blankly for a moment before she spoke. *What's she thinking?*

"Yeah, well I haven't talked to my parents yet. They're never around long enough to have even a half-ass conversation with me. The only thing my mom has been talking about is my graduation party, or I should say *her* party, next weekend, as if anyone there will give a shit about me. It's just another excuse for old Jill and Bennett to get sloshed with their friends. Maybe I won't even show up."

"You have to be there Courtney, for the presents, if nothing else."

"Yeah, I guess that's something. Should score a shitload of cash," she grinned. "Hey, what do you want to get into tonight?"

"I don't know. Maybe we should just drive around and let the night happen to us. Be spontaneous," Jenny suggested.

"Yeah, sounds good to me. I'm sure Jimmy's house will be open for partying again, but think I'll stay away tonight. All of a sudden he's being pretty demanding."

"For sex? But you guys are best friends," Jenny replied somewhat incredulous to the idea of Courtney and Jimmy as a couple.

"That's what I keep telling him. Don't get me wrong. I like Jimmy. I actually love the guy, but not the way he wants. Can't really imagine actually having sex with him. He's like my brother."

"True, but he's fun and he's handsome, not to mention, rich," Jenny grinned.

Courtney's retort was swift and a bit caustic. "Well, my family's rich too. Rich doesn't mean shit."

⌘ ⌘ ⌘

By eight o'clock, Courtney Taylor and Jenny Wallis were ready. The wine coolers had them feeling properly adjusted with a light buzz. Both were dressed in tight jeans and skimpy camisoles, over which they wore loose, gauzy blouses. Courtney tugged on hers, pulling it off one shoulder.

She turned to Jenny, pursed her lips, and then licked them. "Too bad Jimmy can't have a piece of this," she smirked.

Jenny studied her friend, Courtney. She looked like a model – tall, thin, blond, and beautiful, a classic nightmare to other girls who could, in no way, match the standard she set. No wonder Jimmy Nelson was smitten. Half the guys in high school had been, but Courtney had given not one of them a chance to claim her, not that she hadn't slept with more than a few. How she had managed to maintain her reputation was a mystery to Jenny. Any other girl would have been labeled a slut, or worse. Quite likely it was simply status that kept Courtney at arm's length away from any would-be slurs, or perhaps, nearer to the truth, it was Courtney's own sense of self, her own reckless independence, that set her apart. She appeared to pride herself on answering to no one. *The world revolves around her. It's trite but true.* Jenny secretly wondered how she, of all people, had managed to break through the invisible barrier that Courtney had created around her. Their lives were different in so many ways, yet they had glommed on to each other in sixth grade, shortly after Jenny's father had disappeared, and they had been best friends ever since. Besides Jimmy Nelson, only Jenny, it seemed, had been allowed into Courtney's world.

"Let's get the hell out of here, see what the night has to offer, " Courtney suddenly blurted, grabbing the keys to her BMW, her cell phone, and a tiny bag that held her driver's license and a few credit cards. "We'll stop by the bar on the way out. Old Bennett had it stocked yesterday, ready for *my* party. There's so much booze stashed in there he won't miss a bottle or two. And there's beer in the fridge. I'll grab a six pack."

⌘ ⌘ ⌘

With a few lights strategically left on, and with the house securely locked, the girls set out for a night that unraveled in ways they never could have imagined. First, after driving for only a few miles into town, Courtney's car suddenly jolted to the left, and the steering wheel began vibrating awkwardly within her grasp.

"Shit. I've got a flat,"

"Great. Can you make it to that old, gas station at the edge of town?"

"Hope so. Yeah. It's only two blocks down. Shit. Hope this doesn't screw up my wheel."

Courtney was quick to charm a middle-aged, station attendant who sidled up to her car the moment she drove into the lot. He looked down at the right, front tire and grinned, revealing crooked, tobacco-stained teeth.

"Got yourself a flat, I see. Hope you haven't been driving on it long."

"No, only two blocks. Had to get it here," she cooed. "Sure hope you can help us out, Lou." She had honed in immediately on the attendant's nametag and was quick to feign familiarity.

His smile widened. Although the man's principle job was collecting cash and selling chips and sodas, for a price, he was capable of making minor, vehicle repairs in the grimy, disorganized garage adjacent to the office.

"Reckon, I can fix it," he said. "Not many people passing through here evenings, so I got the time. Don't regularly do repairs for folks, but hell, looks like you could use a hand. Do you know how to change a tire?" Lou asked.

He was short, heavy-set, and had a thick, greying beard, shades lighter than his hair. He tugged at his trousers that were cinched beneath a fat, beer belly and stared at Courtney and Jenny as though they were from another world.

"Honest-to-goodness damsels in distress don't show up around her too often," he smirked, "and I got nothing better to do. Pop the trunk. We'll jack this puppy up."

Courtney looked at him blankly, her bottom lip in a pout. She was playing this for all it was worth. Jenny watched, amazed at her audacity. When she said nothing, Lou began to chatter again.

"Okay, now, move aside. You don't want those hands of yours getting all greasy and dirty. Reckon you need to watch what I'm doing though. Your daddy never gave you lessons in changing a tire?"

Courtney visibly cringed at the mention of her *daddy* and muttered hatefully, "My dad probably has no clue how to change a tire himself and I can promise you, he'd never get his hands dirty doing it."

Lou glanced up at Courtney and sneered. "Guess the old man isn't in your good graces," he said. "What'd you do, have a falling out?"

"We don't see eye to eye," Courtney replied smugly. She wanted to say more, like, "It's none of your damned business," but refrained. She needed the help.

"Well, he's sure set you up in a nice, fancy car. Dude can't be all bad."

Courtney said nothing, but Jenny watched her eyes pull into a deep squint. *She's fuming.*

Fortunately in less than forty-five minutes, Courtney's tire had been patched and remounted. Lou stood up, wiped his hands on a filthy towel, and spoke once more. "What are you willing to pay?"

Having no idea what such a repair might cost, Courtney pawed through her bag and indifferently handed Lou a one hundred dollar bill. He snatched it from her without offering change, and Courtney proffered not one word of thanks. Within seconds the girls had plopped into the front seat, Courtney started the engine, and she pulled back onto the highway, her tires squealing. Neither she nor Jenny looked back at the gas station or at the lone attendant, Lou, who stood gawking at the little sports car as it sped out of sight.

"What a fucking weirdo," Jenny uttered.

"No shit, but had to play my cards. Needed my tire fixed. Not a great way to start the night. Hope it's not an omen or some shit. What the hell's next?" Courtney's question clearly was directed at no one but she had voiced it and it hung there like a dark shadow.

She planted her foot on the gas pedal and sped down the narrow highway without any clear plan as to where she was headed.

CHAPTER EIGHT

CHESTER

Chester tripped clumsily across the threshold of his mother's small, stucco bungalow and onto the front porch to listen to the familiar, night sounds that gave him some semblance of satisfaction in a life that had been wrought with countless disappointments. It was the only time he was truly alone and he could think.

Mornings aggravated him and had for thirty years. Each day, from the moment he opened his eyes, angry thoughts pervaded his mind. First and foremost were memories of his father, the hateful jackass Chester had shot dead. Not one day had passed since that fatal day in the woods years ago, that Herbert Flack's ashen face or bloodied trousers were not the first, vivid visions Chester saw upon waking. It was as if the old man was still taunting him with a persistent, ghostly presence. Chester often squeezed his eyes shut tight to make his father disappear, but Herbert's image held fast. And Chester could hear him, a voice from the dead, criticizing relentlessly, mocking every failure, goading Chester to pay attention, *"For Christ's sake,"* and fueling his son's silent rage.

Anyone who knew Chester Flack maintained a distance, even his mother, Bertha, whose worthless life, as Chester perceived it, had pushed her well into her nineties. He had had about enough of her, but was tied to her because of a lie. He knew it; she knew it. So he tolerated her and silently wished she would fall asleep some day and never awaken. Perhaps then he would be free.

Bertha, however, had no intent of simply giving up the ghost. She had a job to do, to take care of her Chester, just as she always had done. She watched her son with both cautious reverence and profound anxiety, her tired, bespectacled eyes, red-rimmed and weepy and her hands often caught in a grip so tight that it whitened her knuckles. Wary though she was, she continued her vigilance. The baby she had borne had been a terror as a child and as an adult could alarm with little or no forewarning. He was that unpredictable. He could sit for hours out in the back yard cleaning his guns on the rickety, picnic table that was so dilapidated it was a wonder it held Chester's weight or he might lean over the front fender of his rusty, red, pickup truck tinkering with coils and wires until his hands were black with grease. Other times he could not sit still at all. He often raced down the country lane clear to Flo Gray's cottage, a carbon copy of their own. He hiked for hours through vineyards that separated several, small houses, all the same ilk, or he headed for the dark woods where he could hunt and hide safely in the shadows. And, of course, there was his pacing. Usually that occurred in the middle of the night. Bertha would lie awake in her tiny bedroom that was adjacent to Chester's and listen, staring out into the blackness and clutching a blanket to her chin, ever mindful of her son's erratic behavior. A cold, adobe wall was all that separated them; both of their bedroom doors opened to a narrow, t-shaped hallway that led to a kitchen on the right, a bathroom on the left, and a living room at the front. When Chester's bedroom door squeaked open, Bertha knew she would be awake until morning. More often than not, on the days following Chester's nighttime marches and his departure for work at the local Bending Vine Winery, Bertha would doze in her rocking chair all afternoon in order to gain enough strength for the next round. For over thirty years the routine for mother and son had altered not one iota.

⌘   ⌘   ⌘

Night sounds, eerie though some could be, had a soothing effect on Chester who otherwise was wound tight as a tick. He had moved stealthily to the edge of the wooden porch as though he were being observed and stood in the darkness, as still as a sentry, listening. A cacophony of sound filled his ears. The humming and clicking of insects - crickets, cicadas and grasshoppers - created a simmering foundation of noise over which larger creatures made their presence known. An owl or two hooted in the distance causing Chester to wonder. *Is someone dying? Is someone going to die?* Never did he hear the owl's call without pondering the possibility for hadn't he heard that owls were the messengers? Rustling amid a thicket of live oak, buckeyes, and western junipers nearby alerted Chester that he was not alone. His eyes followed the sound and he stared until he could make out the dim outline of a large buck, its stately rack, now completely still. *He knows I'm here.* Chester stepped backwards, his back touching the wall. He sank down until he was sitting, his legs drawn up and his arms encircling them. In moments crackling among the trees resumed, this time louder. *There's more than one, and they're agitated. I wonder why?* And then Chester knew. The huge buck, two does, and three fawns trotted rapidly in tandem directly past the porch to the road beyond. Behind them, a mountain lion pounced forward, its sights surely set on one of the fawns. It was denied however, for one of the female deer turned, ran toward the cougar and reared. Its front, cloven hoofs caught the side of the cat's head. The stunned animal flopped to one side momentarily and then it was up, skittering away in the direction it had come. The buck lowered its head, the massive antlers aimed for attack should the mountain lion return. When it did not, the small herd of deer hurriedly trotted off down the country lane, an odd, indistinct odor of sheer panic permeating the night air.

Chester stood once more, peering into the darkness. Many times he had positioned himself there on the wide porch but not always had he stood somewhat peacefully as he did now. No. Much too often he and his mother had become the victims of vicious individuals, teenagers probably, who had waited until late at night to back their trucks up the dead-end driveway so that they faced forward, toward the road, for a quick get-away before beginning a barrage of abhorrent heckling. Over and over again, the intruders would begin their orchestrated abuse for no rhyme or reason other than to be cruel. Like clockwork, they had yelled obscenities, had called out crude names, and had thrown beer cans, feces, and other garbage onto the barren, front lawn. Without fail, alarmed, and in an effort to retaliate, Chester had charged through the front doorway, rifle in hand to confront faces he could not see in the dark, while Bertha had huddled inside, the old woman shaking and mumbling incoherently.

"Witch! Where's the witch?" voices had hollered time and again.

Even in the aftermath of the taunting intrusions, Chester could hear the cat calls both high and low, female and male, screams from thoughtless kids who could have cared less that an old woman was stunned and terrified by their contemptible behavior. His blood boiled, remembering. He had had no recourse, however, except to stand his ground, searching his front yard blindly, only to be assaulted with more abuse.

"And you, old man. You're fucking crazy. You're loony tunes. You're nothing but white trash, you and that hideous witch. It's extermination time, wacko."

"Get the hell out of here," Chester had yelled each time the tiny home had been assaulted, and he had cocked his shotgun menacingly. "Get off my property."

He had screamed, and screamed louder, as he had faced the perpetrators whose faces, without fail, had been obscured in the darkness. The same scenario had repeated itself so often that Chester had begun to expect it, though each time it occurred, adrenaline had churned angrily through his body and his hatred of humanity had intensified. His rancor was rock solid.

He sighed deeply as he recalled the threats that always had left him furious and had frightened his poor mother half to death. They had endured the cruelty together though for years, and because of it had bonded even more closely despite Chester's abhorrence to the fact.

In the relative quiet of this night, Chester began to perspire, droplets of sweat sliding down his cheeks and into his scraggly beard. With a dirty handkerchief, he wiped his neck and moved his feet, a silent shuffling on the redwood planks beneath them. *Feeling unsettled.* The fact that he could identify the sensation was remarkable in itself but that did not calm his unease. *Something is out there. I can feel it.* He stared for minutes, subconsciously holding his breath as if exhaling might summon his demise. He knew the buck and deer had moved on, that the mountain lion had scampered away in the opposite direction, and that no vehicles had backed up to his front fence. So what was it?

Not seconds later, it happened. He heard the screeching of brakes on the country lane not one hundred yards from where he was standing. And then he heard a crash, followed by one, terrified scream, and then nothing. As if in competition with the noise of the collision, the chorus of insects suddenly seemed to grow so loud to Chester that he covered his ears and stifled the urge to shriek a mighty cry of trepidation into the night. Dread as to what he might discover on the rural road beyond overcame him. He had no idea what to do. He began to saunter slowly down the long driveway toward the road, but stopped sharply when a truck barreled toward the scene of the accident. He slithered behind the wide trunk of a Valley Oak and held steady for minutes until he heard two doors slam shut. The truck then drove away, its tires crunching first on soft gravel and then squealing ominously as they found traction on the blacktop.

Chester had two choices and either likely would alter his life, if only a fraction. *I can go on back to the house and pretend I didn't hear a thing, or I can wander on down to the roadway and check out what's happened. Guess that's what I'll do. Looks like something down there's steaming. Don't want a fire, dry as it is.* His eyes had adjusted to the dark well enough to make out the boundaries of the driveway. He need walk only fifty more yards. He made his way forward but stopped short when he saw the car, a small, sports car, wedged in a ditch, its doors swung wide open, one smashed against the branches of a stand of Manzanita trees and the other lodged awkwardly into the edge of the pavement. A steady stream of vapor from a cracked radiator spewed eerily into the air. Not one soul was within shouting distance. *What the hell?* He reached the car and peered inside. In the dark, he could make out the front seats, the steering wheel, and a bundle of some kind lying on the floor. The smells, however, were what alarmed him. The sweet, overpowering aroma of a woman's perfume, mixed with the sour smell of brandy and beer were smothered by another odor: a heavy, pervading, foul stink of perspiration. The combination was so powerful that it made Chester gag and he backed away from the vehicle as if he had been scalded. He held his breath for as long as he could before he turned and ran toward the house. When he reached the front gate, he paused, listening again to sounds around him. All was quiet except for the persistent drone of industrious insects and several, deep, soft, hooting sounds from a duet of owls hidden from sight. *Had someone died?* Chester shivered slightly, clearly understanding the decision he must make. Despite his lifelong, inherent aversion for interactions, planned or otherwise, with any other individuals, he made his way inside the house and made a phone call. Within half an hour, on his very own front porch, he stood face to face with two, stony-faced police officers.

CHAPTER NINE

FLO

Flo had spent Saturday and Sunday forgetting, or trying to, and although hours had passed, she knew she was doomed. *God damn it, Randall, will you give me a little peace? I miss you like the devil, but you need to stop pestering me.* The manifestation of Randall's presence was as stubborn in death as it had been in life, and it tormented Flo at times when she was alone, as she had been for two days. Randall's random, although persistent, ghostly appearances always put her on edge.

Friday's horrific rampage at Hollow Vista High School had done it - brought Randall back so vividly. Since daylight an avalanche of memories had ensued, beginning with the day that Flo, a newly hired custodian at Hollow Vista High, had met Randall Gray. He was a pitifully introverted painter who, *God only knows why,* had shed his inhibitions that day and had fallen headlong in love with Flo, the plain, diminutive janitor he had encountered for the first time in his life. Why he had chosen Flo, she never could have explained – *I'm sure not much of a catch* – but he had, and by virtue of his simply wanting her, she reciprocated. They endured moments of fiery passion interspersed with long hours of mutual solitude until fate took Randall away forever. So, yes, though the dreadful shootings at Hollow Vista High School had precipitated Flo's unease, it was Randall's eerie intrusion that had thrown her off balance for two, solid days. She didn't like it.

Aside from a couple of short, two mile walks along the dusty shoulder of the roadway, Flo had done little all weekend – nothing except think, and she was sick and tired of it. On her second outing she spied her neighbor, Susan Wallis, who Flo knew was an elementary teacher in town. The two had never spoken at length, but as distant neighbors and as employees of the same school district, were remotely aware of each other.

Susan had been strolling by herself in the middle of the narrow driveway that led to her house, set back a bit from the beaten track, just as Flo strode by. Susan visibly started when she noticed Flo.

"Oh," she said, her voice cracking, on the word, "You startled me. I didn't expect to see anyone out and about this afternoon."

Susan's voice, strained and edgy, made Flo flinch as well. *Does she think she's caught me trespassing?* Flo wasn't, of course. Her feet were planted squarely on the shoulder of the county road. Nonetheless, she found herself stumbling over words to explain why she was there. "Well, uh, sorry. I didn't mean to scare you. Was walking like I always do. Every day, well almost every day, I walk. Needed to get out of the house for a bit; you know, wanted to shake the stink off." Flo tittered nervously after uttering the idiomatic phrase, that to her made absolutely no sense. The words were engrained though; Flo's mother had used the same phrase time and again throughout her youth.

Flo uncharacteristically chattered on. "Ever since Friday I've been pent up at home rehashing what happened down at the high school where I work. Guess you heard about the shootings there. I've been nothing but a tangle of nerves. Walking seems to clear my mind, so here I am. Can't get over what happened at the high school Friday though," she repeated.

"Oh my, wasn't that awful? My daughter, Jenny, was there too, hiding under a desk in one of her classes. Believe it was English, but I'm not sure. Came home full of the gossip, but she didn't seem worse for wear. Went right out that afternoon with her friend, Courtney; drove off like they didn't have a worry in the world. They're seniors, set to graduate, and raring to take on anything that comes their way. Pretty much full of themselves." Susan paused. "Oh goodness. I'm rambling."

"Well, I'm glad she's okay," Flo muttered. She looked down and away from Susan Wallis then. She had run out of words and suddenly was aware of her appearance. She blushed uncomfortably and placed her hand on her cheek, covering the black mole before she looked up once more.

"Well," she started again, "better get on home before dusk. Folks can't see so good that time of day driving. Apt to run you over in a heartbeat."

"I know what you mean," Susan said. "People can . . ." She stopped talking and gazed down the narrow, county highway in the direction of town, her eyes searching. Her arms had dropped to her sides and her mouth had turned slack. In an instant her voice had grown dull, almost lifeless. Flo could not stop staring. Susan's sudden change in demeanor was unnerving and Flo shifted her feet uncomfortably. *What's wrong with her? Looks like she's slipped off into another dimension. It's making my skin crawl.* Her attention shifted to Susan's eyes, red-rimmed and glassy. *Has she been crying? I wonder.* Flo knew that Susan's husband had disappeared some years before, but doubted she still was mourning that loss. *Maybe it's the girl, Jenny. Is Susan looking for her? Maybe she's causing problems. Maybe she's leaving Susan too. She'll probably be off to college or to work somewhere soon. Susan's sure to miss her.* Flo was needlessly speculating, of course, but her focus had shifted. For a few moments, while speaking with Susan, she realized that she finally had lost sight of Randall Gray, who before those few moments had remained steadfast in her mind for two, complete days.

"Are you all right?" Flo asked. She was unsure what to do.

"What? Oh, sorry. What did you say?

"I asked if you were all right. You, well, you seemed to go off. Your voice changed."

"Yeah, yes, I think I am. Think the mention of Jenny threw me off. I worry, you know. Mothers do."

"Well, I don't have my own children, but sure am around a lot of kids down at the high school. From what I've seen a good many of them must worry their folks silly," Flo spouted. "Oh, but I'm not saying that about Jenny."

"She's a good kid, but she is a kid. She has a lot of growing up to do." Susan stared at the little woman in front of her as never before. Flo's hair was beginning to escape from a bun that had been tied back at the nape of her neck and her dark eyes searched the air above Susan's face. She clearly was avoiding eye contact. Susan watched Flo's body sway slightly from side to side as if she wanted to flee and in all honesty, Susan wanted nothing more than to escape this awkward conversation as well.

"Well, I better get on home," Flo muttered for the second time. She turned then, threw up her hand in a hasty wave and ambled away in the direction she had come.

Susan watched Flo momentarily before turning away. As she trudged up the driveway she was overcome with an uncanny sense of dread. She was confused as to what had precipitated such an intense feeling of trepidation, but it had set in, a tedious and unrelenting response to an unknown.

"Something awful is going to happen, isn't it, Mother?" she moaned. "It is. I know it."

⌘ ⌘ ⌘

Flo arrived at her front door just as the sun was sinking behind a bank of Ponderosa pines that lined a stretch of low hills to the West. The brisk walk home alone, away from Susan Wallis, had not revived her spirit, for the interaction with the woman, however brief, had zapped her energy, not only because of their seemingly inane conversation, but also because of Susan's unusual manner that spoke of trouble. *She's sure wound up, that woman.* Flo's reaction was accurate, but she admonished herself for her concern. *Let it go Flo. She's only a neighbor, not your ward.* Flo knew, in all honesty, that she could put the awkward exchange behind her. She had a capacity for staying out of others' business. She stayed to herself, and always had. It was safer that way. The only person, after the death of her parents, whom she had allowed into her life, was Randall Gray, and look where that had taken her. So, yes, she was done with Susan Wallis. Fate is fickle, however, and though little Flo Gray believed she had control of whom she let into her simple, adequate existence she was mistaken. She was, in fact, blindsided by what lay ahead.

⌘ ⌘ ⌘

After a light dinner, Flo poured herself a glass of Merlot and settled on her couch to read. Freddy, her cat, was her only companion. As was common for Flo, the red wine, the toasty room, and reading made her sleepy. Rather than going to bed, though, she gathered a warm afghan around her shoulders, placed her head on a small pillow, and with Freddy nuzzled in her arms, fell asleep. She dreamed she was running, running away. *A burning sun bore down on her as she ran faster than she ever had run before, although she was barefoot and dressed only in a thin nightgown. The late afternoon winds whipped at her, tearing at her hair until, at last, the bun at the base of her neck came undone and her dark, grey streaked hair fell free. She passed through a parched field of grass and brambles that scratched her legs until they bled, but she could not stop. She forced herself forward until she reached a deep canyon, the walls of which were covered, every inch of them, with a massive colony of black bats, their leather-like wings seeming to pulsate in a choreographed display that made Flo shiver in fear. How had she gotten here? In her effort to escape the place, she tripped clumsily, landing hard on her stomach and whacking her forehead as she did on a huge boulder. She was stunned for a moment, recovering her senses at the exact moment a snake slithered away into a crevice not three feet away. Terrified, she scrambled forward for several yards more, falling at last into a dry creek bed lined with sharp rocks that cut into her feet. She screamed in pain.*

It was her own voice that awoke her. Freddy no longer was in her arms, her book lay splayed out on the floor, its spine upward with pages bent beneath, and her wine, what had been left, was overturned, the glass shattered on the floor. Flo bore in on those details in seconds, but it took longer to realize that her little home surely had had an intruder. *While I was sleeping?* She knew she had been exhausted, but had she been sleeping like the dead? Had someone entered her house and disappeared without her knowing? She had heard nothing. How could that be?

With difficulty, Flo gained her wits. She pulled the afghan tightly around her and sat up, gazing around the room as if seeing it for the first time. The front door was open wide. She glowered at it apprehensively. Finally, she stood, shivering in the cold air that had shifted inside and inched her way toward the opening. As she pushed the door shut, from far outside, she heard a desperate squeal, followed by a high-pitched shriek, and the loud rumble of what must have been a truck. She listened to the sound of the vehicle grow fainter and fainter until it was gone. Someone, perhaps more than one person, had been in her home, wandering through it while she slept. *How could this have happened?*

Flo locked the door firmly and then turned her back on it, staring toward the darkened, central hallway. Though her heart pounded, and her body coursed with adrenaline from her sudden waking, she was not afraid. She wandered from the living room and peered first into the kitchen to her left and then into the bathroom to her right, flicking on lights as she did. At the back of the house were two bedrooms, one her own, and the other a place for storing Randall's paintings, hundreds of them, that virtually had lain undisturbed since his death. That was until now. Randall's major works, though seemingly untouched otherwise, had been vandalized, splattered with foul smelling whiskey and red wine, the remainder of her own bottle that now lay in the middle of the floor like an empty torpedo casing. Flo spun around, glaring in every direction, and surveying the mess. Several of Randall's precious drawings and watercolors had been ripped in pieces and tossed into a soggy pile in a corner. Flo gasped, and wailed at the sight that pulled the essence of her repressed grief to the surface of her very being. She could ignore her sorrow no more. Who could have done this, and why? Neither she nor Randall had hurt anyone in their lives, save perhaps, on occasion, each other. Neither had an enemy in the world. *So why?*

Flo backed to the doorway, strangling on her own saliva and mourning the sight before her. She had never felt so violated. A singular, astonishing fury consumed her. At last, with every ounce of her strength, she slammed the door shut and paused trembling. When, at last, she could stand without wavering with anger and sadness, she phoned the police. "My house has been invaded and vandalized," she stated flatly. "My name is Florence Gray."

CHAPTER TEN

GEORGE

George entered the police station at five o'clock on Monday morning, having had no sleep at all. It had been one hell of a night. He nodded at the clerk on duty who looked as exhausted as he felt. Her name was Jan, Janice Cochran, and she had been planted at the same desk for years, even before George had arrived there as a young, police officer. She had to be pushing seventy-five, but plugged along at the job she seemed to love more than anything and in actuality, it likely was everything to her. She had never married and had lived alone for years.

"Not about to go anywhere," she had announced over and over if anyone posed the question of retirement. "What the hell! If I have to leave this office, you might as well hammer together a goddamned coffin. What do you think I'd do with myself, twiddle my damned thumbs or go fishing? To hell with that! Besides, this place would turn into a shit hole without me around."

Jan wasn't beautiful, even in her youth, but she had a genuine smile and the kindest heart of anyone George had ever met. She countered that, however, with a saucy attitude and a foul mouth.

"You cocksucker, George, it you don't ask out that pretty, little Linda I'll kick your ass all the way round the block."

George had remembered her playful, though profane, threat ever since. And he had taken it to heart. Jan quite likely was as happy as George had been when Linda said *yes*. Jan became like an adopted, doting mother to the two: thrilled when they married, ecstatic when Linda became pregnant, and devastated when she died in childbirth. Even now, Jan's eyes swam with tears if Linda's name was mentioned. Quite conceivably Linda was, in Jan's world, the daughter she never had. With Linda's passing, it became clear to anyone who knew Jan, that her heart had been broken into a million pieces.

⌘   ⌘   ⌘

Poor Jan probably had been up half the night just as George had. Hollow Vista's police department was a tiny operation with only ten officers, the chief, Jan, and George, the detective, on the workforce. All worked in tandem with the Coroner's Office if a need arose. Staffing had seemed sufficient until lately when criminal activity appeared to be seeping from under the woodwork. In the past month everyone at the department had been working double time.

"Morning, George," Jan managed. "What the hell's going on in this damned town?"

"I'd like an answer to that myself," he replied, glancing as he did at a newly hired, young officer engaged in conversation with a middle-aged woman. It was Florence Gray. George recognized her from the high school where she worked as a custodian; he understood from an earlier police call that Flo's home had been broken into two nights before. He had not taken the call because, unfortunately, he had had more pressing issues with which to deal: a car accident first, followed by the disappearance, or more likely the abduction of a teenage girl, the daughter of the one and only Bennett Taylor, one of the richest men in county. Saying that dealing with the man had been unpleasant was putting it mildly. Bennett Taylor had the manners of a jackass and the sensitivity of a scorpion. Though Bennett and Jill Taylor, without warning, had been wrenched into a crisis that had them both reeling, and though any parent would sympathize, George never had been so happy to leave the two alone after his initial encounter with them. He was weary to the core.

⌘ ⌘ ⌘

George gratefully accepted a hot cup of coffee from Jan, smirked in appreciation, and then moved to his private office to think. *Jesus, what's next?*

The evening had begun so normally, well, perhaps not. He had been at home ready to enjoy a much-needed respite from work. In the aftermath of his investigation into the shocking murder of a real estate agent in town, combined with the sudden and chaotic shootings at the high school, he was exhausted and hungry for sleep. Instead of welcome slumber though, his nights had been bombarded by nightmares full of strange, irrational visions that had him tossing and turning incessantly. Why, just the night before, he finally had edged from bed, dead on his feet, and had stumbled down the stairs to the living room. He had dozed finally in the old, overstuffed chair that was his alone, but subconscious thoughts had sabotaged his effort to rest there as well. Memories, from those deep-rooted, to recent, had made sleep impossible. So he had read until Angie had come home, ready to chatter and lovingly share as she always had.

How lucky he was that any lack of communication with his daughter seldom had been an issue. He and Angie had loved each other since the moment he carried her home alone, a motherless infant swaddled and capped in cotton candy pink and dependent on him, on George, alone. As the years had passed, their mutual respect had grown as well and was an integral component of the father-daughter relationship. And that's the way it had been until now. Quite suddenly, someone new, in the person of Willard Dunn, remarkably had stolen Angie's heart, in effect, leaving George's a bit empty, despite the fact that the love he and his daughter shared was secure. He had known the time would come. Of course, it would, and more importantly, should. Angie had had other boyfriends throughout the years, but this was different. George instinctively had known from the first time he saw the two together. It was in the tilt of her head, in the way he leaned in, in his goofy grin and her shy smile; and it had been in her eyes, a sparkle he never had seen present before. Angie. His little girl, his focus for a lifetime, and now a young woman, was ready to make her way into the next chapter of her life. The reality of that fact had left him feeling slightly and uncomfortably desperate.

After Angie had kissed him on the forehead, whispered *I love you* and gone to bed, George had closed his eyes and had concentrated on an alien heaviness in the pit of his stomach. His heartbeat had revved up and he had swallowed hard. For the first time in many years, he had wanted to cry. He had been deep in thought when his cell phone had rung, jarring him into a new reality.

"George get on down to the station. We have a situation," he heard. The chief's voice had been strained, his plea urgent.

"On my way," George had stammered. He recalled swaying a bit as he stood up from his chair, and he remembered glancing backward at the book he had held. *On The Road* had fallen onto the carpet, its pages spread out and bent shamefully. It would lie there until he returned home late the next day.

⌘ ⌘ ⌘

The *situation* as the Chief had referred to it, took George to the driveway of Chester Flack whose reputation as an eccentric apparently had followed him since he was a teen. George had heard countless stories of the man's escapades, but didn't dwell on the gossip. He had met Chester up close and personal though, first when George was a young officer. Completely oblivious either to the speed limit or to the danger, Chester had been driving his red pickup truck over eighty miles an hour on the crooked, country road into town. George had been driving a squad car in the opposite direction and had been nearly blown off the road when Chester had passed him. It had taken only minutes for George to begin his pursuit, and though his lights had been flashing and the siren blaring, Chester had appeared not to notice a thing. Three miles had passed before Chester pulled over on the shoulder, spinning out in a cloud of dust.

"Why the devil did I get stopped?" he had asked immediately when George had stepped cautiously to the window.

"License and insurance, please," George had demanded.

"Sure. Sure. I got them," Chester had muttered before asking again. "Why'd you stop me?"

George had ticketed Chester no fewer than ten times over the years, always for the same infraction: driving like a crazy man and endangering the public. He was the crustiest of characters, a man who, in all the years George had known him, never had been able to slow down. George had been convinced, very early on, that Chester did not possess a lick of sense.

⌘ ⌘ ⌘

When he had stepped up on Chester's front porch two nights before, however, George had been taken aback by the change in the man's appearance. Chester was wearing camouflage pants and jacket and wore a filthy, white baseball cap with, of all things, the initials of the local, high school, HVHS, emblazoned on the front in red and gold. *Why, that hat is as old as the hills.* The man's face had shocked George the most though. He had not seen Chester close up for several years and was astonished to see how much he had aged. Deep furrows dominated the man's forehead and cheeks and his eyes seemed half-closed because of an abundance of fleshy, sagging skin around them. He appeared to have no eyelashes at all making his black eyes look like deep holes. In contrast, his eyebrows were thick and bushy and he sported an outgrowth of whiskers at least a week old. *I know this guy is close to my age but he looks eighty. Hard living, I'd guess.* Behind Chester, just inside the door stood a woman. She was a wisp. *Can't weigh more than ninety pounds.* George was aware that Chester had lived alone with his mother for years but never had seen her in person. Her silver hair was pulled back in a tight bun and she wore a dirty, blue, chenille robe that dragged on the floor. The hem was black with dirt. Like her son's, her face was etched with wrinkles and she smelled, the awful stench of someone old and whose hygiene was lacking in every way. George held his breath.

At last he spoke, "Need to talk with you, Mr. Flack, about what you heard and discovered this evening out there on the roadway."

"Yeah. I reckoned you'd be coming around. Didn't know Hollow Vista's police force was so big. Looks like every one of them, and their brother, have been roaming the road out there tonight." Chester stood with his legs spread and his hands on his hips; he stared into the darkness as if trying to conjure the details.

"I know you already have spoken to our officers but it seems there is more to this situation than a simple car crash. I need to ask just a few questions, if you don't mind." George was polite.

"Shoot."

"When, Mr. Flack, did you hear or notice something out of the ordinary?" George asked.

"It was probably on the edge of nine o'clock," Chester replied.

"And you heard a noise from inside the house?"

"No. No. I was outside here, on the porch. Needed some air," Chester said, casting a wary look at his mother who was eavesdropping on the conversation from the kitchen door.

"Was listening to all the critters out here, when I had me a feeling."

"A feeling?" George tilted his head, confused.

"Yeah, that something was out there in the dark. See, we get these kids, blasted teenagers, coming around sometimes, backing their cars or trucks up the driveway. Thought maybe we were in for another bout. Little bastards start yelling shit, calling us names – *witch, wacko, crazy* – been going on for years."

"Have you reported this?" George was somewhat alarmed to hear Chester's disclosure.

"No. Take care of them myself. Little chicken shits don't want to mess with a man with a rifle. Oh, don't worry. I don't shoot it, don't even have ammunition," Chester lied. "Just step outside, level that sucker, and that's all it takes. Brats hightail it faster than a freight train."

Chester was breathing heavily. This conversation was beginning to exhaust him. He hated chatter of any kind.

"So it wasn't anyone harassing you?" George's statement took the form of a question. At the same time, he made a note on a pad. *Check on what guns, permits Flack has.*

"No. I was standing here when I heard brakes squealing and then a crash. Loud. Didn't know whether to ignore it, or investigate. Was going to go back inside, but on second thought, figured someone might be hurt or worse. Heard owls screeching tonight, so reckoned I'd better check."

"Owls?" George did not understand the connection.

"Yeah, owls. Owls hooting means something's going to die." Certain of his assertion, Chester stared at the detective mildly astounded that the man was unaware of that plain and simple fact.

George, a bit startled by Chester's comment, bore in on the man but said nothing for a moment. "And then?"

"Well, I was walking down the driveway when I heard a truck, big engine, maybe a diesel. I hid cause I sure as hell didn't want get into the middle of some mess. Truck stopped, some doors slammed, and in two shakes, it took off again, dust flying everywhere until tires hit the pavement. Damn thing screeched out of here like a bat out of hell."

"Did you actually see the vehicle, the truck? Make? Model?" George asked.

"No, too dark."

"And then you continued on to the crash site?" George wanted as much information as he could get, but could sense that Chester was hesitant now, and tiring. He had to be careful.

"Yeah. It was a little car, BMW, I think. Funny how I could make out that blue and white emblem, a cross in a circle, cause the moonlight was glaring on it just right. Radiator was steaming, one side of the car had slammed into a tree, and a door was wedged in the dirt, side of the road."

"Did you notice anything else? Blood, items of any kind?"

"Nope. Couldn't see blood. Saw a package in the floorboard but wasn't about to touch it. Stunk though." Chester's face actually skewed up with the memory.

"Stunk? What was the smell?" George asked.

"Bunch of them, all mixed up. I smelled a lady's perfume, real sweet, and beer or whiskey, some kind of booze, but worst of all was sweat, real smelly man sweat. That stink did not come from a female. No sir. I'm damned sure about that."

"Did you touch anything?"

"No, sir. Wasn't about to touch a thing. Turned around instead and ran home fast as I could. Called the cops. Did my duty. Don't want to have another damned thing to do with it."

George was satisfied, although he wasn't sure he was finished with Chester Flack. "Thank you for your time and information, Mr. Flack. I understand this isn't easy. You're in the dark as much as any of us, but every detail is important. If you think of anything else, please give a call. Here's my card. "

Chester simply nodded. He was very much done with George Murphy and the Hollow Vista Police Department. George backed out of the front door and was gone, en route to his next stop, the home of two women he did not know, a mother and daughter named Susan and Jenny Wallis.

CHAPTER ELEVEN

SUSAN

Jenny Wallis stopped crying abruptly after several minutes, at the very moment she stood and began to weave from side to side in slow motion. She grabbed the edge of the table and looked up at her mother, two blurry mothers, one beside the other.

"Sick," she managed before hurling herself toward the kitchen sink where she vomited over and over until her stomach had emptied. She hung on to the faucet with both hands and continued to drool vile strings of rancid saliva into the sink.

Susan stood beside her daughter until the retching had eased and then reached around her in an attempt to steady her. Jenny flinched, drawing away, a look of horror shrouding her features.

"Jenny?" Susan's heart began to beat hard and she flushed with shock and a foreboding, intense uneasiness. *What in God's Earth has happened?*

"No. Don't touch. Don't touch me," Jenny begged, her voice pleading. "Go away. Please, leave me alone." She turned then and dashed into the living room, frantically turning in circles as if trying to decide which direction was the best to run. At last she careened sideways onto the couch, clutched a large, throw pillow to her chest, and stared wide-eyed at Susan as if she had no clue suddenly who her mother was.

Susan, clearly alarmed at Jenny's confused behavior, backed away and sat down on the edge of a large, winged-back chair. *Okay, Susan, one step at a time. Take your time.* After several minutes, she stood slowly, reached for the old, familiar afghan her mother had lovingly knitted years before, and walked toward Jenny. She gently placed the blanket around Jenny's shoulders and this time, Jenny did not resist. Instead, her head dropped to the wide arm of the couch, her eyes closed, and she fell asleep. Her arms were tight around the pillow though, a protective shield she did not release until much later.

Susan had not been able to assess Jenny's injuries closely, but now, as the girl slept, Susan peered cautiously at her face and neck. Jenny's cheeks were black with mascara, her nose had bled, and her lips, barren of any coloring, appeared chapped and dry. The abrasion on her neck had oozed blood, now dry and crusted. It looked as though black dirt had intermingled leaving a wide swath that ran from Jenny's ear to her collarbone. It smelled of feces. *That will need a thorough cleaning, if, oh my God, she will even let me near her when she wakes up. Maybe I should call someone. A doctor? No. No doctor is going to make a house call especially at this time of night. No. We'll wait, wait until tomorrow. No.* Susan was beginning to panic. She found herself mimicking Jenny's actions, turning in silent circles in the middle of the living room, assessing, fretting, and finally deciding. *I need to call the police. Now.* She walked quickly to the kitchen, rifled through her purse, and pulled out her cell phone. She did not bother trying to find the number of the police station; she simply touched the word - Emergency. And with that simple action, her life shifted in a direction she never could have imagined.

⌘   ⌘   ⌘

"My daughter, my daughter's been injured. She arrived home a short time ago, clothes torn, cut, and sobbing. She was frightened beyond belief. I think someone's hurt her," Susan blurted when a dispatcher took her call. Her hands were shaking and her voice betrayed her, cracking into a stifled snort. With Jenny asleep Susan's feigned composure had slipped away like an illusive shadow.

"All right," said the woman who had taken the call. "Try to be calm. It's going to be okay. Can you answer a few questions?"

"Yes. Yes, I can." Susan listened to her own voice that sounded now like the distant whine of a forlorn child. *Get it together, Susan.*

She supplied relevant information: names, address, ages, and more details as to Jenny's condition, including the fact that her daughter had come home drunk. It was not a painless task. How easy it would have been to omit that truth, but what would that have solved? Nothing.

The dispatcher assured Susan that an officer would be at her home within the hour to take a report. In the meantime she was to lock her doors, try to remain calm, and keep a close eye on her daughter. That would not be difficult. The poor girl was not simply asleep, but eviden-tially had passed out cold. She had not moved an inch and likely would be in the same position for hours.

Susan returned to the living room and stood beside the couch staring until her eyes blurred with hot tears. The day had taken her on a roller coaster that had not yet come to a full stop. She wanted off, but that was not likely to happen. First some cop, an unknown, would stop by to ask more questions. She had no ideal what to expect. *God only knows how that ordeal might fare, and then Jenny's going to be up, hung over, probably, and moody as the devil. She'll be embarrassed and defensive. Why, just this morning she said she was moving out and I virtually gave her my blessing. Christ, she's a long way away from being ready to leave if she's going to be so fucking irrespon-sible.* Susan flinched at her own rare use of profanity even though it had lodged in her rambling thoughts. Her fear had morphed into anger and suddenly she was livid about Jenny's obvious recklessness. Moreover, she was furious at herself for not being a better mother, for not looking close-ly enough. *Jesus, Susan, what else have you missed?*

A flash of light through the front window and a sharp knock at the entry door startled Susan from her musings. She imagined hearing her own heartbeat as she turned abruptly and shuffled like an old woman to the door. With anxious apprehension she opened it.

"Mrs. Wallis?"

Susan looked up at a tall man whose face was obscured in the shadows. He held a flashlight in one hand. *Is this a police officer? There's no uniform.* Though she wondered if she should slam the door shut, she made a hasty judgment not to do so. Her hand tightened on the doorknob.

"I'm Detective Murphy," the man said, presenting her with his police badge as identification. "I need to ask you a few questions about the incident with your daughter, Jenny, isn't it?"

Sighing with relief, Susan stepped back and invited the detective inside. "Come in," she whispered. "I will tell you what I know, which at this point isn't much, but I'm afraid you won't get much information from Jenny. She's out cold."

Susan pointed to the heap that was her daughter curled on the couch. The detective leaned over the young woman whose face was visible in the dim light. He made a quick assessment: the girl's face, chalk white, was smeared with mascara; her lips were parched and colorless; dried blood was obvious in one nostril; the long, dark, auburn hair was a mass of tangles; a fairly deep cut and an abraded swath surrounding it was noticeable, running from below the girl's ear the length of her neck; dirt was embedded in the wound and an acrid odor of feces and beer combined was evident. While the intake of alcohol likely had been a choice, Detective Murphy surmised, the injuries otherwise indicated foul play. *This night is becoming more and more bizarre as the hours pass.*

Susan motioned for the detective to follow her into the kitchen. "We can talk in here," she suggested. "Is that okay?"

"Certainly, although I doubt if we'd wake up Jenny even if we were right next to her. She's down for the count. Wouldn't expect her to rouse for quite a few more hours, but yes, let's move into the kitchen."

"Oh, sorry about the smell in here," Susan stammered, embarrassed by the stench of vomit that lingered. "Jenny threw up in here, in the sink." She shook her head sadly. "I have no idea what she had to drink, but it must have been a lot. Honestly, Detective Murphy, I've never in my life seen

Jenny drink. I know. She's a teenager. Kids drink, but I'm so aggravated with her, and scared too."

For the first time, Susan looked at George Murphy full in the face. *Handsome.* His eyes were greenish brown, with long, dark eyelashes as straight as an arrow. She felt suddenly self-conscious of her appearance, but quickly admonished herself. *Don't be silly, Susan. This man's a cop doing his job. You don't even know him.* Her cheeks grew warm.

"Could I make you a cup tea?" she asked, turning from him.

"Oh, no. No," he said hastily. "Thank you, though."

"Well, sit then."

The two sat across the table from each other, he in the exact spot where Jenny had been. If seemed odd to see him there. No man had been at this table since Zach disappeared seven years before. George took out a note pad, looked up at Susan, and actually smiled. It was a tiny smile, but it calmed her. He was not the enemy.

"Okay, so why don't you fill me in with as much detail as you can. I think that will be easier than me asking questions that might not get us anywhere."

Susan started with the morning: Jenny's announcement that she was leaving soon, Susan's acceptance, their mutual understanding that her moving from home had been inevitable, and Susan's mixed emotions. Jenny had gone to her friend, Courtney's house later in the day. "Courtney Taylor," she elaborated. "They've been best friends for years. Two peas in a pod, though I'm not sure why. On my teacher's salary, we live much differently from the way the Taylors do. They're very wealthy. Do you know them?"

"I know of them," George answered, harboring the fact that he was well aware of Bennett and Jill Taylor and was apt to learn much more as his investigation expanded.

The Taylors, having been informed that Courtney's BMW had been wrecked, that the vehicle had been abandoned, and that Courtney had not been located, were en route to Hollow Vista from their mountain retreat at that very moment. George would be meeting them at the station, his next stop in what appeared to be an endless night.

It did not take long for Susan to explain what had happened after Jenny's knock on the door. "I thought she had forgotten her keys," she said, but when I saw her, "Oh, what a state she was in!"

Susan gave George Murphy every detail she could recall: her daughter's physical condition, the sobbing, the vomiting, the confusion, and Jenny's passing out. "What shocked me most though was that she cringed when I tried to hug her, to hold her up, to help. She actually pulled away as though she was afraid of me. She was afraid, maybe not of me, but of something. Somebody hurt her. I just know it. She wouldn't talk though. Her only words were 'Go away. Don't touch me.' That's all." Susan's eyes brimmed with tears.

George did not take his eyes from the woman's face.

"And Courtney? What about her?" she continued." I don't think she brought Jenny home. I didn't hear her car, and would have heard a car. Courtney's little sports car is noisy. The exhaust rumbles really loud. I'm afraid she drives way too fast. I worry about that girl. She's on her own too much." Susan's digression was short-lived. "I don't know what to think any more. You know, I think Jenny must have walked home, but from where? And what about Courtney?"

Susan stopped talking then as if she simply had run out of words.

George had sat silent, absorbing Susan's chatter, but when she clearly was finished speaking, he leaned toward her reassuringly. "We'll get to the bottom of this, Mrs. Wallis."

"Susan, please," she responded.

"Okay. So, Susan, try to get some rest. I'll be in touch with you tomorrow. I need to speak with Jenny, you know."

"I know. I know."

"Take my card. I'll phone you tomorrow, mid-morning. Hopefully Jenny will be feeling better by then." George was depending on Jenny to fill in much needed information, but he could not reveal that to Susan Wallis. Not yet. The fact was, however, that Courtney Taylor somehow had vanished into the night, leaving her car, a shattered carcass, in a ditch on the side of a country road. It was George's job to find out why.

"Well, good night, Susan."

"Thank you, so much." Susan extended her hand and he took it. It was an electric touch.

CHAPTER TWELVE

COURTNEY

Courtney lay, bound and blindfolded, in a heap of straw for hours longer. She dozed a bit, necessarily so, because she was sick. Her head throbbed, she was nauseous, her body ached, and she was so thirsty she imagined she surely would die. It was thirst that had awakened her. Her mouth, opened wide, was parched, and her tongue, dry and swollen, lolled in her mouth like a salted slug. She had been gripped by a nightmare before waking, imagining herself crawling on her hands and knees through hot, abrasive sand toward water, a mirage, an illusion, a merciless trick, for each time she was within reach, the liquid shimmered away, mocking her. She squirmed to sit upright, managing finally to prop herself against what, in her blinded state, she thought might be a wooden post. She was able to shift her head from side to side until the blindfold loosened and slipped to her neck. The effort exacerbated her nausea, but at least she could see. In horror, Courtney surveyed her surroundings. She sat in an oblong cubicle, a small horse stall, she assumed, that was cast in shadows. Through an opening between boards in an outer wall, she could see outside, but not well. Daylight was waning and a chilly fog was settling. *Where, the fuck, am I and how long have I been here?* She shivered and swallowed hard trying not to take in the rancid smells, a mixture of animal dung and sweet, wet hay that was smothering. An odor of urine wafted up to her nose as well and she quickly realized it was her own smell. Clearly she unwittingly had urinated while she slept. *Oh God, where in the hell am I?* She looked down at herself. Her jeans were gone. *My best fucking jeans!* She wore only her panties and camisole. *Wait. Wait. Has a full day gone by?* Courtney struggled to remember, but could not focus. She was dizzy and oh, so thirsty. She smacked her lips and let her head flop backwards against the post again. *Shit!*

Think, Courtney, Think! Last night I was with Jenny. We were in my car, driving, drinking, drinking and driving. Shit. She remembered that much before she began sailing away and all went black.

⌘ ⌘ ⌘

When Courtney was conscious again, it was daylight, though the sun was obscured by fog, low Tule fog that swirled and eddied in the field outside. She could see that much from her vantage point inside her stall. *Wait. I can move my hands. Shit. Someone's been here.* Courtney was becoming more cognizant of her situation. Her hands and feet had been unbound and she had been covered with a dirty, scratchy horse blanket. *Oh my God, I have to get out of here.* She glanced up at the eight-foot gate of the stall. A heavy, chain had been looped through the latch and secured with a hefty pad lock. Escape from her creepy confines appeared risky, if not impossible. And who had put her here? In the dim light she began to crawl in a circle on her hands and knees looking into every corner, finally spying a bowl of water next to the wall. She scrambled to it, lapping at it like a starving dog before she lifted the container and took three huge gulps. The quick intake caused her to begin a coughing fit that was followed quickly by a choking sensation. The aspiration of the liquid made her dizzy and she sank back down onto the straw. She wanted to cry, but no tears formed. Instead she began to moan, a mournful whimper that she could not stop even when someone kicked at the wall of the stall repeatedly and shouted, "Shut up, missy. Shut the fuck up."

The sound of the deep voice caused Courtney to cower in fear. Pulling the dirty blanket more closely around her shoulders and up to her lips, she attempted to quash her cries. Then she scooted backwards as far away from the gate as she could toward the outer wall of the barn and leaned her cheek against the wood next to the gap that had been created obviously by years of decay and deterioration. The hole in the rotten board ran vertically for a full foot and was six inches wide at the widest point, tapering little by little to the top and bottom. Instantly this innocuous crack in the wall had become incredibly valuable - Courtney's only access to the world outside. *I could put my arm through it.* She peered through the space looking for something, anything that was familiar. The ground outside was barren of any vegetation save for a few tufts of stubborn weeds that had held on for dear life. Beyond was a wooden fence with open slats, and even farther beyond, another. Was this a racetrack? Courtney sighed heavily. Racetracks made her think of Jimmy and his parents' estate, where countless horses, mares and lucrative studs lived in luxury. *I wonder where Jimmy is right now. Where is he? He wasn't around to save me this time, not from this shit.*

Thinking of her friend, Jimmy, at this very moment, made Courtney's throat tighten and again, she felt like crying, but she could not. Not one tear. She stared through the opening in the wall at a sky that was now a cloudless, deep sapphire blue, the sun having quickly burned away the fog. She picked tentatively at the edges of the hole; rotting splinters came off in her fingers and she stared at them forlornly. She closed her eyes, trying to envision Jimmy's face, but she was denied. Instead a chaotic swirl of dark colors – umber, ochre, purple, and navy blue - frenetically swirled in and about each other until they faded, at last, to black. *Shit.*

With her eyes closed, Courtney began to listen to sounds, both near and in the distance. Concentrating on what she could hear distracted her from a sudden, angry, gut-gnawing hunger that had overridden her nausea. *I'm going to starve in this flippin' hellhole.* Leaning against the wall, directly behind her, she could make out a shuffling noise followed by muffled squeaks and chirrups. *Mice, or even worse, rats.* Holding perfectly still, Courtney perceived another sound, dull but rhythmic. Was it her heartbeat? Yes. A definite, irritating pulsing, seeming to grow louder with every beat, pounded in her ear. Her head began to throb again. The reality that she was alive and confined like an animal terrified her to the point that involuntary, unceasing shivers racked her body. As she pulled the blanket around her shoulders more tightly, she heard again the jangle of a harness. A horse whinnied. She heard a man's voice then, the same deep, raspy voice she remembered from earlier.

"Here you go, Satan. Some oats. Better eat them you mangy devil or there won't be any more." The man cleared his throat.

Though she could see nothing, Courtney imagined the man carelessly tossing a bucket of oats into the horse's stall and leaving immediately, for the gate had screeched open and was followed instantly by a heavy thud, metal against wood, she guessed. Once the gate had been slammed shut, she heard footsteps, slow and deliberate approaching her. She froze.

⌘　⌘　⌘

When, at last, she faced the man who was her captor, Courtney's entire body tensed, and she felt, for certain, that if he touched her with one finger she would shatter into a million, broken pieces.

He was tall, six feet at least, and as thin as a rake. He wore a fuzzy, grey, trapper's hat with the earflaps hanging straight down atop his head. Shoulder-length, filthy hair the color of mud stuck out below in brittle-looking clumps. Though he had an extraordinarily long, bushy beard that obscured the lower portion of his face, Courtney could see his gaunt cheeks and protruding cheekbones below dull, sunken eyes. He sneered at her, his mouth open and menacing. Most of his teeth were missing and the few he had were decayed and brown. He stood at the gate and began to remove his clothing. A dirty, camouflage, hunting jacket dropped to the floor of the barn first, followed by a faded blue, work shirt, and a white, sleeveless t-shirt. Courtney gawked at his hairless chest, sunken in to the point that every rib stuck out under pasty, white skin. Never in her life had she seen anyone so emaciated. And though it was quite cool now, with the disappearance of the sun, he was wet with perspiration. Rivulets of sweat ran from his neck downward, the beads dripping eventually in slow motion on the straw. She gawked at him unabashedly. *He's fucking hideous.*

Stepping farther into her stall, he angrily threw a sack into the corner and muttered, "There's some shit to eat. You're hungry, aren't you?"

Courtney could not speak. She simply stared at the man, her eyes pleading more for her freedom than food.

"Well, missy, seeing as how you aren't going to say a word, I'll say it for you. What you're going to do is you're going to give me what I want, a piece of that skanky, little ass of yours and then, maybe just then, I'll let you have some chow."

Courtney shook her head. "No!"

"Wrong word, missy."

Before she could stop him, he was upon her, stripping her of her blanket and pushing her hard against the ground. She fought back, kicking, punching, and squirming to move from under him. Though she struggled to free herself from her attacker, she was too small, too weak, and much too frightened to have a significant effect against him.

"Look, missy. You're not going anywhere. Stop thrashing, you fucking, little bitch," he spit, grabbing as he did a fistful of her hair, twisting and pulling it cruelly. The moment he hissed those awful words, a rancid odor from the man's breath permeated the air. He reeked of rotten teeth, a sour gut, and cigarettes. Courtney gagged and turned her head away, but he pressed down on her until at last she screamed, and at that moment, to silence her, with a tightly knuckled fist, he slugged her in the temple. She was unconscious the instant the blow hit her, and fortuitously so.

She would not consciously know that he had raped her three times that night, that he had fondled her from head to toe, lingering on her breasts, her soft neck, her hips, and her thighs. She was saved the agony of knowing that he had run his fingers through her hair, probed every orifice of her body, and at last urinated and defecated in the corner of the stall like an animal. She would not be cognizant of the abuse she had endured at the hands of a madman, a violent creature whose only love had become crystal meth – the drug he craved more than the air he breathed.

CHAPTER THIRTEEN

CHESTER

Chester took the long route to work, driving up the much too bumpy, country road past Flo Gray's driveway first, and then farther past that teacher's place. He didn't know the woman's name but knew she lived alone with her teenage daughter. Everyone in town knew her old man had abandoned her, walked out leaving her high and dry with a kid to bring up by herself. Chester didn't give a hoot about that, but he did admire the man's guts. If the marriage wasn't working out, at least the fellow had the gumption to get the hell out. But that was of no matter to him, really. He just admired a man who got done what needed to be done. And hadn't Chester accomplished a similar thing? Yes, he had, years ago, when he had shot Herbert Flack dead. Chester puffed up for a moment with unbridled pride. *Cocksucker deserved what was coming to him.* He envisioned again the image of his father's bloody corpse, permanently burned into the cortex of his brain. It pestered him daily, defying him to forget. *Get the hell out of my mind, old man.*

Chester had other things to think about like the mess he'd gotten himself caught up into the night before. *Jesus, Chester. You should have stayed put on the porch instead of getting involved. Now you have the cops, and that arrogant George Murphy nosing around, asking questions.* Well, he had told the officers and the detective all he knew, what he'd seen. Every one of them could go to hell for all he cared.

The road on which Chester drove curved left and then right at intervals that were so short, Chester grew dizzy. The fact that he was speeding as usual clearly contributed to his unease, but he couldn't help himself. Habit. Besides, driving helped to free his mind, although, for some reason, today it wasn't working so well. He kept remembering the moment he sighted that mangled sports car – the steaming radiator, the blue and white BMW emblem, and the smell, the rank mixture of sweet perfume, booze, and pungent perspiration all mingling together. *It was enough to make me sick.* His face skewed as he recalled the stench that had permeated the scene.

And what about the driver, or a passenger - maybe more than one – who had vanished into the night, just like that? Were there injuries? He hadn't seen blood. He'd heard the noise of a shrill engine as a truck almost ploughed into the crash site though. Loud. Why had such a vehicle appeared right on the heels of the accident? The truck couldn't have been stopped more than a minute before it was gone again zipping away like a phantom into the night. Chester had glimpsed only the back end of the vehicle after having escaped his vantage point behind the old oak, but he'd heard it, the metallic, knocking roar of the diesel engine clear in his mind, almost as though it was real even now. And then, astoundingly, it was, the sound physically present, a roar not four vehicle lengths in front of him. Chester was driving much faster than the person in the truck and in only seconds he was upon it, only feet away. He slammed on his brakes. *Shit. Nearly rammed into the motherfucker.*

An unwelcome, physical sensation washed over Chester as his truck slowed. He began to sweat and his heart raced. *Fuck.* He tightened his grip on the steering wheel and stared at the driver ahead. Was it a man or woman? Long hair. He could see that. The person sat high in the seat, however. Tall. Whoever it was, was tall and more widely shouldered than most women. *A man. It has to be a man.* Chester was a bit mesmerized by what he was observing, patently staring until he caught the driver's eyes in the rear view mirror. Deep set and wild they were, and he had spotted Chester behind him as well. The man raised his fist as though in anger and roared ahead and around the next curve before Chester could gather his wits. *That was the same truck. I know it. Shit. Should have gotten the goddamn license.* The fact was, however, that he hadn't even noticed if a license plate even existed. No, his attention had been riveted on the man's eyes, mad and fearful, a feral animal's glare that had made Chester feel strangely threatened. *Jesus, Chester!*

For a rare expanse of time then, Chester Flack drove slowly, so slowly in fact, that he arrived at work late for the first time in his life. Victor Conti, his scowling supervisor, stood at the gaping door of the vineyard warehouse. His hands were on his hips and his stocky legs were spread wide. When Chester pulled into a parking space nearby, the man eyed him suspiciously. He did not look pleased.

"Truck broke down," Chester lied. "Got her fixed though."

Chester's boss said not a word. Instead, his response was to spit a huge wad of tobacco into the dirt path directly in front of Chester who stepped over the vile sputum without looking up.

"Hell of a day this is turning into," Chester muttered to himself when he was a few more feet away from the man. *Christ, first that maniac on the road, and now this ass wipe's attitude. Keep your head down, Chester. Get to work.*

Fortunately for Chester Flack, working hard always had been a salve for him. Whether it was at the winery or on some project at home, he was able to force himself into a realm of conscious concentration that enabled him to focus and forget. When work was done, however, life's demons (and he had more than a few of them), bore in and tormented him unmercifully. Of course, Herbert Flack's murder resided like an anvil deep in his gut. In no way could that be expelled. Nor was his mother going away any time soon either. Chester could imagine the old woman would live to be one hundred or more, and having lied for him, having covered for his impetuous action that had killed her husband, had an uncanny control over every aspect of his life. He was saddled with her. Chester supposed that her constant presence, her unwavering loyalty, and her uncompromised, motherly love was the reason why he never had been, in his entire life, with a woman. At forty-eight, Chester Flack was still a virgin. Oh, it wasn't that he hadn't fantasized about having a go with one woman or another, but who'd have him anyway? *I'm sure no prize - ugly as a bucktoothed goat.* Whether it was so or not was irrelevant; it was true because Chester held it to be.

From childhood, he had been different. He believed it; everyone else knew it. Never in his life had he fit in, not in school, and certainly not in any social situation. Instead, by his own making, he had constructed an invisible shield around himself and he would let no one in, except, on occasion, he had to admit, his mother, Bertha. And he owed her too. When he was floundering after leaving high school, having no idea what to do with his life, she had sat him down and demanded he listen.

"Get yourself a job, Chester. I know you can't stand a soul in the world but you're going to have to work with people sooner or later. You can't sit around here all day, every day. Hunting up in the foothills all the time like you do is going to get you nowhere. Besides, we need a little money around here. Now march your ass down to one of those canneries and get yourself a job."

Seven canneries rejected Chester in quick succession, but when Bertha herself beat a path over to Bending Vine Winery, one of its vineyards of which butted up against her small plot of land, things changed. She never would confess to the details of the conversation that had transpired between the manager and her, but she must have been convincing. When she came home that day over thirty years before, Chester had a job.

"You start tomorrow. Buck up, Chester. Make yourself presentable."

He had combed his hair flat, lacquered it with Vaseline, brushed his teeth, put on clean trousers and work shirt, and set out down the road in his then-new, red, pickup truck to the first and last job he would ever have.

After more than thirty years he had not moved up in the ranks but, instead, was content to work in relatively solitary confines doing redundant chores he was assigned: lifting bulk grapes onto the conveyor, connecting pumps, running the agitator, and more often, cleaning and sterilizing fermenting tanks. He stacked boxes, piled pallets with medal hoops and oak barrel staves, and swept the concrete floor of the building every, single day. Though other workers came and went, Chester became a mainstay, content to perform his duties with mute compliance. He interacted with no one and others acquiesced to his aloof and self-conscious demeanor that delivered a silent message: *Stay away. Don't want a thing to do with anyone.*

The years had passed quickly with few conflicts to interfere with Chester's simple life except for the random intrusions onto his mother's property by obnoxious adolescents who had nothing better to do in the sleepy, farming community other than to harass him, and of course, his old mother, *the witch.* Those incidents made Chester's blood boil, but he had learned to brandish his trusty rifle, leveling it directly at a kid or two, and hiss every profanity he could think of until they high-tailed it down the dusty, dirt driveway to the road. And when it was all over, every time it was over, Chester was overcome with a feeling of satisfaction, for his plucky nerve, but more so for his self-control. *I've killed a man. Wouldn't take much effort to do it again. Little motherfuckers.*

⌘ ⌘ ⌘

When Chester's day of work ended, he drove home the way he had come. It was a conscious decision. For the entire day, he had not been able to stop thinking about the man in the roaring truck. Who was he? It was the eyes, those wild and disturbing eyes that Chester could not forget. They were haunting. *Shit.* Chester's stomach churned. *I have another goddamn dilemma. Should I tell George Murphy I saw the truck again? Does he need to know the driver was a man, a man with long hair, a man with creepy eyes? Jesus, Chester. Here you go again.*

CHAPTER FOURTEEN

FLO

A tall, pimply-faced, young police officer appeared at Flo's door not thirty minutes after her call. He shuffled onto the porch noisily, cleared his throat, and began, "Yes, Mam, name's Officer Sanchez."

"Flo, Florence Gray," she replied. Her hand shot up to cover the black mole on her cheek.

"I'm following up on your call to the police this evening," the officer continued. "You stated that your home was vandalized?"

"Yes. Yes, it most certainly was," Flo stammered nervously, and in that instant wished she had had the self-control to have waited a bit before informing the police of the break-in. She wasn't sure why though. And then, just as quickly, she understood. Simply having a man on her doorstep, someone other than her Randall, was disconcerting. It didn't seem normal; she was use to her solitude. She bit her lip and tugged on her long, dark and silver-streaked hair that had loosened from its bun and hung nearly to her waist. She glanced up at the policeman's deeply set, brown eyes but did not hold contact.

"May I step in, Mrs. Gray?" Officer Sanchez asked.

"Oh, yes, yes, of course." Flo stepped backwards, bumping as she did into an end table. The lamp wobbled precariously with her touch.

"Oh, goodness!" she muttered, grabbing the lamp with both hands to stop the bobbling. "I nearly knocked the darn thing over." She looked at Officer Sanchez once more, sucked in her breath, and continued. "Sorry. I'm just so damned upset about this mess."

"I can imagine you are," the man agreed. "Perhaps you can explain to me what happened."

He sat gingerly on the edge of a straight-backed, wooden chair, just as Flo flopped onto the couch and began to talk. She took her time, halting to clear her throat at moments when her words seem to gather like thick mucus there, strangling.

"Well, to tell you the truth, I'm not certain what happened. I was out for a walk this afternoon. I chatted with my neighbor, Susan Wallis. She's a teacher in town. Talked with her about the shooting at the high school. See, I'm a custodian there, and was on duty when that awful fiasco began. Can tell you I was scared half to death like everyone else over there, and shocked. See, I knew the teacher that did the shooting. Cleaned her room every evening. So, well, you see, officer, I run on an even keel. I don't get shaken up too easily, but, well, I was pretty upset to think that a crazy person, sorry, but I guess she was, was ready to snap right there in the midst of all of us. Gives me chills to think about it."

Flo stopped for a moment and swallowed. She scanned the ceiling from one corner to the other, as if searching for more words, before continuing.

"Actually had myself a good cry yesterday. So, you see, I guess I was pretty troubled about the whole shooting thing, and tired. Came home from my walk, had a bite to eat, and sat down with a glass of red wine and a book. To tell you the truth, officer, I don't remember falling asleep, but I must have been practically comatose, because I didn't hear one, single thing. Had a nightmare though. I remember that. Woke myself up with a scream. That's when I saw my front door open, wide open. I heard some noises. Somebody yelled, and then I heard a car or truck, some kind of vehicle, drive off."

Officer Sanchez had been jotting a few notes, but looked up when Flo stopped talking again. "Is that all?"

"Oh, no. There's more."

"Well, well, I jumped up, slammed the front door and noticed my wine glass had been knocked over, wine spilled all over the place. I was scared all over again. Some person, someone unbeknownst to me, had to have been in here, with me sleeping. Probably stood right over me and I didn't hear a damned thing."

Flo's face had flushed red and she stood abruptly. She grabbed her upper arms with her hands, crossing herself protectively. "Come on. I'll show you."

She led Officer Sanchez down the dim hallway to the room that had stored Randall's paintings and drawings since the day he had died. She pushed open the door, flicked on the light, and stepped aside.

"This. This is what somebody did to my husband's work. This is what they did. This is what they did," she wailed for a third time, "while I was sleeping."

Flo's eyes grew glassy with tears and her voice dropped to a whisper. "Who would have done this? Randall's dead, and even when he was alive he didn't have an enemy in the world. All he wanted to do was paint. Paint. Paint. Paint. Why, look at this mess. Why would anyone do this? Poor Randall."

The young officer shook his head. He did feel sorry for the poor, little woman beside him, but retained his composure. "I'd advise you not to touch anything in this room, Mrs. Gray. I'll have someone come out and dust for fingerprints in the morning."

She left the light on, pulled the door closed, and said, "Well, there you have it."

"I'm sorry, Mrs. Gray," Officer Sanchez offered. "I know this has been a frightening invasion of your home, but we'll do everything we can to find the vandal. Do you believe you'll be all right here tonight? Do you have someone who could stay with you, somewhere you could go?"

"No. No. Neither. I'll be okay. I don't want to leave the house anyway and I like my privacy. Whoever was here came and went. I don't think they'll be back. I don't have anything of much value."

"Well, Mrs. Gray, I'm going to ask you to come down to the station Monday morning so that I can compile a more formal report. Nine o'clock?" Sanchez asked.

"That's too late. I have to work. Look officer, I'm up with the chickens. I'll be at the station early, before school starts, five or six. Don't think I'll be sleeping much for a few days."

"Okay, then. Come on over when you can. I'll be there. Shouldn't take more than an hour. In the meantime, look around to see if anything is missing, stay out of that room back there, and try to recall the events of the evening one more time. If you've forgotten a detail or two, we'll go over them when we meet again. Are you sure you are all right?"

"I am. I need to sit quiet now. Never talked so much in my life." Flo knew that to be a fact.

⌘ ⌘ ⌘

After the officer had departed, Flo wrapped herself in the afghan once more, and lay on the couch, staring at the door that had been bolted twice from the inside. "Think, Flo Gray. Think. Have you missed anything?"

She suddenly bolted upward, her eyes scanning the room, and her heart sank once more. Missing from its permanent position against the corner of the fireplace was her father's guitar, the only item of value he had owned when he had been killed years before. Flo had cherished the instrument, often holding it across her lap as her father had, and remembering his voice filling their humble home with lovely sound, the resonance as clear in her mind as if he were actually present in the room. She sighed deeply, angered, sad, and burdened with memories, for she found herself mourning, yet once again, the loss of the only two men she ever had loved.

Though she wanted to scream, her throat tightened, silencing her. She stood very still. *I'm not going to cry. I'm not going to cry. I'm going to find out who did this, one way or another.* Flo determined in that moment that the intrusion, the vandalism, the robbery, all, would not defeat her. She would not let that happen. No. She gathered her wits, picked up her cell phone and began taking photographs of the interior of her entire house. Defying Officer Sanchez's request, once more, she opened the door where Randall's works had been stored and took a photograph of every damaged painting, the empty wine bottle, and the soggy, mangled drawings heaped in a corner. Had she had the means, she would have bottled the stink that had settled there too, for mingling with the aroma of red wine was a pungent odor of strong whiskey, beer, and sickeningly, sweet perfume.

By the time she had finished, her resolve was firm. With or without the help of the police, she was determined to find the person who had defiled her home. She would be no one's victim ever again.

CHAPTER FIFTEEN

GEORGE

After over twenty hours on the job, George drove home. He wanted nothing more than a hot shower, a bite to eat, and sleep, in that order. The house was dark, except for the lone, front porch light that lit the walkway, and enabled George to unlock the door with little effort. *Guess Angie's out with Willard somewhere. It's still early. They'll be here soon.*

Once inside the house, George trudged slowly up the stairs to his bedroom, stripped off his clothes, and within minutes stood in the shower, warm water peppering his body. As steam filled the stall, he began finally to relax. He thought back over the prior, twenty-something hours that had begun with his chief's urgent, phone call, followed by interactions, one after another with folks who unwittingly had become ensnared in the fringes of a criminal investigation. A few, unfortunately, without having an option, were caught right smack in the middle

George recalled going to the run-down, stucco home of crazy, reclusive Chester Flack and his poor, old mother who seemed to be barely hanging on. George had been wary of speaking with Chester, who in the past had been confrontational and uncooperative, but their conversation had been civil and Chester had been accommodating, supplying enough information to give teeth to the investigation into the case of a now-missing, young girl.

George also reflected about his meeting with the Wallis woman. *Susan.* Although, panicked and a bit emotional, Susan Wallis had been pleasant and as helpful as she could be under the circumstances. Without a doubt, Susan Wallis had her hands full with her daughter, Jenny, who clearly had been accosted and harmed by someone who at this point was an unknown. That situation, in itself, was likely an element of the greater, more pressing crime - the fact that Courtney Taylor was missing. *How does it all fit together?*

Susan had been able to supply some relevant information, more of which George hoped to obtain when they met again, but her daughter, Jenny, had been able to offer nothing. She had been down for the count, passed out cold. Regrettably for George, the planned meeting with Susan and Jenny for this day had to be postponed as well.

"Jenny is much too sick . . . still," Susan Wallis had admitted when she had phoned George mid-day. "She's been awake, on and off, but that's it. She won't eat. Won't talk. I managed to get her to her own bed, but she refused to let me help her undress. She collapsed onto her bed, pulled a blanket over her entire body, and groaned something incoherent before she fell asleep again. All I can do is keep an eye on her."

"Yes. I wouldn't leave her alone," George had advised. "And, please, call when there is a change. Will you do that?"

"Of course. Of course, I will." Susan's voice had been barely audible. And there had been no *good-bye*.

George felt a twinge of sorrow. Any meeting would have to wait. His thoughts switched from Susan to Jenny. *How much alcohol did the girl consume anyway? What details, if any, will she be able to provide? And what if she refuses to cooperate at all?* George could only hope that Jenny had not completely blacked-out critical details and would remember what happened the night of the accident. She was the one person, in George's view, who could provide the greatest insight into what had led up to the disappearance of Courtney Taylor. At this point, George only had access to Courtney's car, a small BMW that had been hauled away from the country highway near the Flack house to a secure site adjacent to the police station for inspection. *It's going to be a waiting game.*

⌘   ⌘   ⌘

What a sharp contrast in civility and respect Susan, and even Chester, had been compared to Bennett and Jill Taylor who, clearly agitated and exhausted, had stormed into the police station early that morning. Bennett in particular, had been ready to mow down anyone who got in his way.

George had been sorting through files at his desk and sipping coffee when the couple arrived. The fact that the two were angry, anxious, and fearful was an understatement. The latter two emotions were clearly understandable – their daughter was missing - but anger? In George's view, the rage that Bennett, in particular, displayed simply was out of place. It was not going to solve anything, and, in fact, complicated matters.

Upon entering the station, Bennett had marched directly toward Janice Cochran as though she were the enemy and had slammed his fist down on the counter above her desk so hard that her cup of hot tea toppled over spilling the scaling liquid onto her hand and nearly saturating a stack of paperwork. Bennett was oblivious to the mess he had created, and insensitively ignored the fact that Janice was grasping her hand in obvious pain.

"I'm Bennett Taylor. Bennett Taylor," he repeated, nearly shouting and emphasizing each syllable of his name as though Janice were deaf. "Where's the chief?" he demanded. "I want to see him now."

"Chief Garza is not due in until later this morning," Janice replied tersely as she rubbed her blistered hand.

"Not in? Not in? My daughter is missing, kidnapped, injured maybe, God only knows what, and he's not in? What the hell? Does he not know who I am?" Bennett's face had grown deep red with his rage and he shook his fist menacingly not two feet away from Janice's face.

She retained her calm. "The Chief was here all night, just like the rest of us. He went home to freshen up and will be back soon."

"I want you to get on that phone and call him now. Now. Tell him my wife and I are here and he'd better get his ass down here pronto."

Janice bristled. *I'll do no such thing. Not for this jackass.* "Have a seat, Mr. Taylor, Mrs. Taylor. I'll notify Detective Murphy that you've arrived."

"You expect me to sit? You expect me to sit and wait like some peon? I am Bennett Taylor. I don't wait for anybody. I practically own this town." Bennett's face was scarlet and his mouth had twisted into a vulgar snarl.

"You've made it perfectly clear . . ." Janice coolly began, but she was interrupted by George Murphy who had over-heard the commotion.

"I've got this, Janice," he said as he stepped out of his office. With obvious concern, he glanced quickly at his friend, Janice, but strode toward the access door to the lob-by. When he reached Bennett and Jill Taylor, he extended his hand.

Bennett snubbed his gesture and instead shoved both hands into his trouser pockets. Though George was a bit taken aback by the man's rudeness, he ignored the slight. "Mr. Taylor. I'm glad to see that you made it here safely. We have a great deal to discuss. Please come into my office. I'm Detective Murphy. I've been assigned to this case."

Bennett studied George inanely for several seconds be-fore brushing past him as though he was invisible, and leav-ing his wife, Jill, gazing around the lobby bewildered.

George extended his hand and motioned for her to fol-low, "Come into my office. Have a seat. Could I offer you a cup of coffee?"

Bennett did not let her respond. "Coffee? We don't want any damned coffee. We want our daughter. That's what we want. Coffee? For Christ's sake, what is wrong with you peo-ple? And how is sitting in this ridiculous office going to lo-cate my kid? Tell me that Murphy!"

"Mr. Taylor, we are doing our best. As the primary Family Liaison Officer and detective in this case, I already have taken the initial steps necessary in order to locate your daughter."

"Yes, and what the hell is that?" Bennett had not taken a seat, but instead was pacing back and forth in front of George's desk. His hands were knotted fists.

Disregarding the man's truculent behavior, George continued, "Officers currently are searching areas nearby the crash site, all local police agencies as well as the state police have been notified, and we have conducted a number of informal interviews with more formal inquires to follow. A brief press release was issued, but we have been waiting for your return so that relevant details can be added. We need your cooperation, Mr. Taylor. We're not your adversaries."

"What is it you need to know?" Jill Taylor managed to ask. She had been looking intently at George, while sitting on the edge of her chair. Her shoulders were hunched and pulled forward slightly; she clearly was aware of the fury behind her. George watched Jill's hands reach for each other. She clutched them together as if in prayer.

"Keep quiet, Jill," Bennett snapped. "Let Murphy do his job."

Jill's cheeks flushed crimson. She flinched noticeably at the sound of her husband's scolding tone, but she did as she was told. Jill offered not one additional word. The hostility exhibited between the missing girl's parents did not go unnoticed by George Murphy. *Is this the norm?* He had to wonder. Had such obvious antagonism between Bennett and Jill played into their daughter's accident in some way. He was not placing blame. How could he? The Taylors had been miles away when Courtney crashed her car, but had they, George wondered, in some enigmatic, remote way, been right there with her?

⌘ ⌘ ⌘

The interview with Bennett and Jill Taylor lasted for over an hour. Jill was quiet, having been silenced by her husband.

Ironically though, despite his obvious insistent and belligerent need to maintain control over the inquiry, Bennett inadvertently revealed to George Murphy much more than he actually realized as a result of some of his comments.

"She's eighteen," Bennett responded tersely when asked Courtney's age. Almost immediately though, he launched into an angry outburst. "She turned eighteen on February twenty-eighth. God. I'll never forget that horrible night in February when she was born. Barely got Jill into town. It was colder than shit . . . slippery, wet roads. Fog. Kid was born at that pitiful clinic downtown. Couldn't make it to a real hospital. What a nightmare. From the word *go* Courtney hasn't made life easy."

"She attends Hollow Vista High School. Could have gone anywhere, to an elite, private school somewhere where she'd get a decent education, but no, she'd have none of it. Threw tantrums for days. Screamed obscenities. Refused to eat. Finally Jill and I gave in. 'Well, to hell with it! Go to that crummy high school. Be ordinary!' I told her. She's supposed to graduate next Friday, but now she's screwed that up too."

"Yes, she has a cell phone. What kid doesn't? Jill, get Murphy the number. Yeah, and she has a computer, laptop, tablet. You name it, and she has it. Kid's on social media from morning until night."

"Yeah, everything should be at home, except for her cell phone. She doesn't take a shit without that with her."

"I have no clue what she was wearing. We weren't around . . . obviously." He shot George a nasty look. *What an inept piece of dung.* "Her friend, Jenny Wallis, might know. Those two have been inseparable for years. Don't know what Courtney ever saw in the girl. Her poor mom's a teacher. They don't have much; live in one of those little, stucco houses that butts up against a vineyard, edge of town. So, no, we wouldn't know what Courtney was wearing. No doubt it was something tight and slutty. The way girls dress these days is ridiculous. They're inviting trouble, if you ask me."

"Healthy? Is she healthy? I guess so. She has check ups every couple of years. She's not diseased, if that's what you're insinuating. Jill did make sure she was put on birth control years ago. Damn good thing too. We sure as hell didn't want that problem. Girls these days serve it up on a platter, from what I hear."

George scowled at the comment, but Bennett took no notice. Instead, he attacked the next question.

"Does she do drugs? Our daughter? She absolutely does not. She knows she'd get her ass beat if we found out she was into drugs. Probably smokes pot, but that doesn't count. Pot's like beer these days, isn't it? Kids live for it. A few adults do too, I would imagine."

Bennett actually chuckled. Then he took out a white handkerchief and noisily blew his nose before addressing the next question that set him off again.

"What do you mean, 'What's her mental state?' She's a normal, moody teenager. She pouts and cries when things don't go her way and is euphoric when she does what she wants and she usually manages that. Hate to say it, but she's pretty much a spoiled brat. Jill's done a great job of creating that monster. And she's not depressed or suicidal, if that's what you're suggesting. She doesn't have an eating disorder either, like I've read some girls do, though she's nice and slim. Keeps herself in great shape. Takes after her old man." Bennett threw his shoulders back and smirked arrogantly as if he had forgotten suddenly why he was in the room.

George glanced at Jill Taylor whose face had grown pale. She soberly bit her lip. George wished he were a mind reader. *What is she thinking? Not one word from her. How can she stay silent? Does Bennett have that much power over her?*

The questions George had asked were routine. He would have made the same inquiries in any missing person situation. It was protocol. Bennett's responses, however, had George's head swimming. What loving father would talk about his daughter as Bennett Taylor had, especially at a time like this? Courtney had been involved in an automobile accident. She was possibly injured, perhaps hurt badly, but more to the point, she was gone. Vanished. *Where is she? We need to find her and soon.* George swallowed hard for suddenly he was overcome with queasiness. His head ached.

"Look, Mr. and Mrs. Taylor," he finally said, "I appreciate your input this morning. It's been helpful, but we will need more. I'd like to see Courtney's bedroom, look at her computer, and check her emails. Another officer and I will be by your home in an hour. I am assuming you both are going home now."

"That wasn't the plan, actually," Bennett replied, as though harboring a secret, "but we can make that happen."

"That would be good, very good. The sooner we are on this, the better."

It had become very clear to George that Bennett Taylor was the type of man who would challenge him at every corner, on every issue, if only to maintain the upper hand. *Can't let that happen. If the Taylors have any hope of seeing their daughter again, I cannot let that happen.* George was locked in, focused once more. He had one mission – to find Courtney Taylor.

⌘ ⌘ ⌘

George met with the Taylors again for the second time early that afternoon. Bennett and Jill Taylor escorted him and the police department's new-hire, Officer Sanchez, up the stairs of their sprawling, two-story estate to Courtney Taylor's bedroom where the officers made a cursory appraisal of what was there before asking her parents to leave them alone to investigate further.

"If you think I'm going to leave you alone in this room to rummage through my daughter's belongings, you have another thing coming!" Bennett protested.

In haughty defiance of the detective's request, he squared his body and widened his stance. His chest rose like that of a cocky rooster, his mouth twisted angrily, and blotches of scarlet emerged on his neck and cheeks.

Jill shot a look of disgust in her husband's direction and cleared her throat nervously, but said nothing. She then turned like an obedient child, and with her shoulders slumped forward as though she bore the weight of the world, shuffled out of the room into the hallway. George watched her from his vantage point just inside the room. She wandered down the long hall, her head tilted awkwardly to one side as if she were too exhausted to hold it upright. As she moved away, the slender fingers of one hand lightly touched the wall at intervals, presumably to balance her unsteadiness; in sharp contrast, however, with the other hand, she formed a fist and seized a chunk of her blond hair that lay in tangled clumps inches below her shoulders and yanked hard. George could not have articulated why he had taken note of her behavior, but he had. It was the disparity between Jill Taylors's obvious carefulness, on the one hand, compared to her ostensibly punishing herself, on the other, that struck him as odd.

At the double doors at the end of the corridor, she turned abruptly and glowered at George as though he were the perpetrator of the crime that he was trying to solve. It was an alarming and sobering moment to be the recipient of such a look, a glare that embodied an unwarranted air of unrestrained hate. And why had she directed it toward him? Or had she been focusing on Bennett instead? *There's a mountain of emotion beneath her façade. That woman is harboring some deep-seated anger.* George could not help but privately speculate about her, but he let his thoughts go for the moment and turned his attention to Bennett Taylor.

"Look, Mr. Taylor, again, let me make it clear that we are not your adversaries here. We're on the same team. We are simply looking for clues that might give us some idea about where to search for your daughter. What places did she frequent? Who were her friends? Had she had contact with someone she did not personally know? Privacy in our search would be helpful. We could wait for a warrant, but that could take days. We don't have days to waste. Surely you can understand that. I can promise you nothing will be removed from this room without you being informed."

"Without my permission, you mean," he shot back.

"In this case, Mr. Taylor, I don't need your permission." George looked at Bennett straight in the eye. He did not waver. Bennett held the stare for a brief moment before turning on his heel, without uttering another word, and marching out the door in the direction his wife had gone.

George looked at Officer Sanchez who had stood by without a sound, observing. "Good job, Sanchez. Let's get busy."

Courtney's room was a mess. Empty water bottles were heaped in an overflowing garbage can and crumpled bits of paper had tumbled onto the floor. Assorted fashion magazines were scattered across the bed that had not been made up properly. The bedspread simply had been pulled over rumpled blankets and sheets beneath. A least ten throw pillows of various sizes and shapes had been tossed haphazardly against the mahogany headboard. Several textbooks and notebooks were in a cluttered heap next to an end table. A gauzy red scarf had been placed over the lampshade of a porcelain lamp and beneath it were scrunched tissues, a half dozen empty, miniature bottles of cheap wine, and a half-filled container of Advil.

George shook his head. This was the antithesis of his daughter, Angie's bedroom that always was neat and tidy. "Wow," he said. "Hard to know where to look first."

"You check the bathroom, Javier, and I'll go through drawers, the closet, and the desk over there. Let me know if you see something that might give us a clue or two," he ordered.

Officer Sanchez departed through an opened pocket door into the bathroom while George began his search. Drawer after drawer seemed a duplicate of the one before. All were crammed with clothing, little of which was folded neatly. Small drawers contained socks, frilly panties, and lacey bras. Larger ones held camisoles, t-shirts, sweaters, leggings, and jeans. The walk-in closet was equally jammed with clothing and other items – skirts, jackets, blouses, prom dresses, sweat shirts, no less than a dozen leather purses, several backpacks, and at least fifty pairs of shoes and boots, the footwear interestingly lined up neatly in a row at the bottom of the closet. Nothing appeared out of the ordinary, except for the fact that Courtney could have worn a different outfit every day for a year. No exaggeration.

The desk held a new iMac computer, a printer, router, and a basket of USB connectors and cords. Beside them lay an iPad, MacBook Pro laptop, and a Kindle, all plugged into sockets nearby. Post-it notes were abundant, one piled on top of the next, and all with a random word or two scrawled there. George gathered a few scraps of paper that had phone numbers on them. He would have Jan check on those. The drawers of the desk were filled with myriad supplies – pencils, pens, note pads, and the like. Most looked as if they seldom had been touched, and some items were still in the original packaging. In the bottom drawer, George was surprised to find a small, brown, teddy bear and a bright pink, stuffed rabbit, carefully tucked in on a soft, blue towel. George lifted them carefully, examined them for a moment and then set them back. He had to wonder why a teenage girl, on the verge of adulthood, had kept these vestiges of childhood. His throat tightened. Probably not ten years prior, the little stuffed animals, gifts quite likely from someone special, would have been displayed in plain sight. Of the countless toys she must have had, why had Courtney kept those two? George gently closed the drawer. He had to wonder. *Maybe a small part of this girl didn't want to grow up at all, and especially so fast. Had she considered her choices? Had she any idea in which direction she was going, and more importantly who cared?* The overbearing manner of her father combined with the mercurial demeanor of her mother had him perplexed.

"Focus, Murphy. Quit speculating." He knew he needed to concentrate on the most important challenge at hand – finding Courtney Taylor. It was not going to be easy. *Where in the devil is she?*

George checked his emotions. *Have to keep this on a professional level.* The warning was stern and very real, but for George, adhering to own counsel would be difficult. He understood this fact at the deepest level for his own daughter, his Angie, was exactly the same age as this missing girl. And Jenny Wallis was too. All were classmates. All were set to graduate, to set out the gate, and to make their ways. One wrong turn, however, one dubious choice had altered Courtney's course, and perhaps that of a few others. *How is it that life can shift lanes so quickly?*

And in that moment, the words of George's father came back like a slap in the face, "Get on track, George. Stay focused, because no matter what you may think, life is not a through street."

George had had more than enough experience to back up the veracity of his father's words. He had never forgotten them.

⌘ ⌘ ⌘

When George was satisfied, he and Officer Sanchez left the Taylor residence, but not before advising Bennett and his wife to leave Courtney's bedroom untouched.

"The investigation is far from over, and it is quite likely we will need to come back," George told them.

This time Bennett simply shook his head, understanding. His agitation had shifted, it appeared to a state of dull acceptance. Jill stood silently beside him, grasping a wad of tissues. Her face was pale and sober, her eyes red-rimmed. Clearly she had been crying, and perhaps, George considered, for more than a few reasons. He was truly sad for her.

The only item George carried out with him that afternoon was Courtney's laptop computer. A perusal of her emails and her social media pages would be performed at the station, and unfortunately, that would take a bit of time with dubious results at best.

CHAPTER SIXTEEN

SUSAN

Susan was jolted awake by a wretched moan. *Oh no. I fell asleep.* It had not been her intent to sleep, but she obviously had. Through the window she could see that already the sun was low in the sky. Almost a whole day had passed and Jenny was finally beginning to stir again. Susan's eyes blurred with tears as she looked at her daughter whose face was colorless save for her parched lips that had taken on a bluish-purple hue. Jenny had moved hardly at all for a day, having cocooned her body with a thick blanket before falling into a deep, stupor-like sleep. With great effort Susan had guided Jenny from the couch to her bed earlier that morning. Jenny had not wanted to be touched, but she had been unsteady and confused, staring wide-eyed for seconds seemingly puzzled by her surroundings. And though she physically protested, pushing her mother away from her, Susan persisted and finally was able to flop her onto the bed. Jenny had looked at her mother gravely, before wrapping the blanket tightly around her and falling sideways with a painful groan. She had lain in virtually the same position for hours. But now, she was stirring.

Susan stood up and gingerly tiptoed to the bed. She sat on the edge and placed her hand on Jenny's forehead. Her skin was cool, clammy, her breathing so shallow that Susan had to lean in to hear. Sweat had plastered Jenny's bangs to her forehead and Susan pushed them aside before she spoke, "Jenny?"

She had no idea if a response was forthcoming and held her breath in anticipation. *Please, be okay, Jenny. Talk to me. Tell me what happened. Who did this to you? And where is Courtney? Please, Jenny, wake up and talk to me.*

Questions swirled in Susan's mind, but she needed to be careful. She said nothing more than Jenny's name and then waited. And she waited longer, until at last Jenny opened her eyes.

"Mom," she whispered. "Water."

Susan quickly opened the bottled water that she had placed earlier next to the bed. "Here, let me help." She pulled Jenny forward and stuffed two extra pillows behind her back so that she was sitting. This time, Jenny did not push her away. Though she handed the bottle to Jenny to hold, she held it as well, just in case Jenny was too weak to manage it, and in that instant, she was taken back in time to the days when Jenny was an infant, clutching a bottle of milk, and nursing contentedly.

Oh, mother, how did I arrive at this place? The woeful query, with unexpected clarity, played once again in Susan's head.

⌘ ⌘ ⌘

Jenny sipped the water tentatively, as if she were uncertain it was safe to drink, but finally managed a gulp. Unfortunately she gagged on the liquid and it spewed from her mouth onto her chin and neck. She grabbed at her throat, grimacing in pain. The abrasion on her neck had oozed open once more and when she drew her hand away her fingers were smeared with blood. She stared at her hands as if they were not her own, turning them first palms up, and then down.

Susan watched bewildered. "Jenny?" she asked once more.

Jenny uttered two words, "Oh, Mom," and as she had two nights prior, she began to cry.

Susan scooted farther onto the bed. She had never felt so helpless, but knew she would not leave her daughter's side, not for one minute, not now. She placed her hand gently on her arm. This time, Jenny allowed her touch. "Oh, Jenny, honey. What happened? Can you tell me what happened?"

"I don't remember. I can't remember."

Susan held her breath. *No. She has to remember. She has to remember, for me, for George Murphy, and for Courtney. Oh God, how am I going to tell her about Courtney?*

"It will all come back to you. It will. It will, in time." In reassuring Jenny, Susan was quite clear that she was trying to convince herself as well. *What if she doesn't remember? What then?* She closed her eyes against the veracity of that possibility, and then she spoke once more. "Let me help you up, honey. I'll run a warm tub and you can soak for a while. You'll feel better after you've cleaned up. And maybe you can eat something. A bowl of soup, maybe?"

Jenny nodded. She had stopped crying and had scooted into a sitting position, her feet now touching the floor. "Bathroom," she said.

"Of course," Susan replied. "Of course. Let me help you." She held Jenny as she wobbly stood. "You okay?"

"A little dizzy," she said. "Thanks, Mom."

"Okay, here we go." Arm in arm, the two women walked slowly from Jenny's bedroom to the bathroom. *Progress. Maybe we're over the hump.*

After Jenny had settled finally into the bathtub of soapy water, Susan took a soft cloth and gently cleaned the abrasion on her daughter's neck. Jenny did not protest but rather tilted her head sideways and mumbled another *thank you.* Once she was satisfied that the wound had been thoroughly cleaned, Susan gathered her daughter's ripped blouse and dirty jeans, and placed them in a plastic bag. She was not certain why she did so, but it was almost instinctual. *Maybe the police will want to examine them. Who knows?*

She had just set the bag aside in the hallway when her cell phone rang. She grabbed it from her pocket and checked the caller's name: George Murphy.

"I'm going to step into the hallway and take this call," she whispered, as though it were a secret.

"It's okay," Jenny replied. "I'll be okay."

In the hallway, with her back pressed against the wall, Susan pushed the cell phone talk button. "Hello?"

"Oh, hello, Susan. It's Detective . . . it's George Murphy. I was just checking in."

"She's awake."

"Great. And she's feeling better?" His voice sounded genuinely concerned.

"She is, but there is one thing," Susan disclosed, apprehensive of the response.

"What's that?" George asked.

"She can't remember what happened," Susan stated matter-of-factly. "She can't remember a thing. Nothing."

Following a second of silence, George responded. "I'd like to come by, Susan, if I might. Maybe I can assist her in recalling at least a few details. Time is of the essence now, Susan. You have to know that."

"Of course. Come over. We'll be ready."

"See you soon," George said, suddenly anxious.

"Yes, good-bye for now, then, George."

⌘ ⌘ ⌘

George Murphy drove slowly down the dirt lane that led to Susan Wallis's front door. It was dusk. The sun had ducked behind the vineyard hillside that bordered the road to the right; a line of scraggly pine trees dominated the left, all the way to the front yard. The remaining light of the day played eerily on the branches that trembled in the cool, evening breeze. In a rustic, bucolic way, the place was very inviting.

It had been an exhausting day, and yet George was strangely energized at the thought of seeing Susan Wallis and her daughter, who hopefully could provide him with some much needed information as to what had transpired the night before when she and Courtney Taylor had ventured, undoubtedly, into a nightmare.

As he pulled closer to the house, the beam of his headlights slid across the wide, front veranda alerting Susan that he had arrived. From inside the house, she flicked on a porch light and opened the door. It had been ajar when he had stepped out of his car, but was opened wide as he approached the door.

Susan welcomed him with a wary smile. She was a bit taller than he had remembered and slender. She wore skin-tight jeans and an oversized sweatshirt bearing the emblem of the University of California at Berkeley. *Did she go to school there?* Her long, dark hair fell below her shoulders in soft waves. She grabbed nervously at the tips as he advanced toward her. *She looks too young to have an eighteen-year-old daughter. Pretty.* It was true. Susan was pretty, naturally so.

"Thanks for letting me come by on short notice, Susan," he began.

"Of course. No problem. I know you are anxious to see Jenny. Come in. She's upstairs, having soup and crackers in bed. I'm afraid I'm spoiling her, but I'm just so relieved she is awake." She paused. "Come this way."

George closed the front door, secured the lock, and followed Susan to the stairs. When they were half way up, she stopped and turned. "I'm afraid she hasn't told me one thing about what happened. I haven't pressed her."

"I believe that's wise," he replied. "And she does know that I'm here to talk to her, to ask about any details she can remember?" He turned his statement into a question.

"Yes, I told her. She knows. I hope she will be able to remember . . . something, anything. Do you think if she recalls one simple facet, the rest will follow?"

"I don't know. If she has simply emotionally blocked out what happened, she could remember eventually, maybe right away, I suppose, but if she was intoxicated, really drunk, and actually blacked out, well, that's a different story."

Susan looked at him quizzically. "How so?"

"It's an odd phenomenon that I learned about when I was in the academy," he said. "Passing out from drinking is one thing. Blackouts are different and are caused when a person actually develops alcohol poisoning from drinking way too much. See, alcohol poisoning can result in a form of amnesia. Part of the brain, the hippocampus, creates memories, but if that area is poisoned as a result of extreme intoxication, it does not function normally and no memories are created. So, in effect, the person hasn't forgotten anything. I know that sounds bizarre, but apparently it's true."

"That is so weird." Susan cocked her head, ruminating on the concept.

"The point for law enforcement officers like me, I guess, is that we be aware that maybe, just maybe, a person who has blacked out is not being obstinate or is not lying about remembering. Maybe there simply are no memories to be had. Crazy, I know, but in some cases it's true. So we'll see with Jenny. Obtaining any information at all may take a little time and more than one session with her."

Susan leaned against the bannister of the stairs and was silent for a few seconds before replying. "It's a conundrum isn't it? If she remembers something horrible that happened she'll in essence live it all over again and that could be horrible for her. At the same time, she has to remember. She just has to, so we can find Courtney."

George honed in on the pronoun *we*, and in that moment knew Susan Wallis's support for him and the investigation was absolute.

"Let's go see if Jenny's up for talking," he said gently. "And don't worry. I'll take it slow."

⌘ ⌘ ⌘

Jenny had finished her soup and was nibbling a cracker when Susan entered her bedroom with George Murphy right behind her. Jenny's face was still pale, but her upper cheeks had gained a tinge of pink, likely the result of sipping the hot soup. Her hair, long and copper colored, fell about her neck obscuring the angry gash George remembered being there. He would mention it, in time.

"Jenny," this is Detective Murphy. "He's here to ask a few questions about what happened when you were out with Courtney this weekend."

"Hi, Jenny," he said, extending his hand to shake hers. It was ice cold. She gazed at him with dark, tired eyes, not looking away when he greeted her. *Maybe she wants to talk. Maybe she's ready.* He was hopeful.

"Hi," she replied. "Nice to meet you, I guess. Am I in trouble?"

"Not with me," he answered, glancing quickly in Susan's direction as he did. "I do need to ask you some questions, though. You were pretty drunk last night so it wasn't possible then."

"Man," she began. "I've never been so damn sick. I guess Courtney and I drank more than we thought." At the mention of Courtney's name, Jenny's face blanched. "Oh, shit. Courtney." An uncomfortable shiver gripped her and she had no clue why. *Poor Courtney. I hope she is okay. Hope she's not as sick as I've been.* She pictured Courtney's face, pale and ashen, and her body, prone on her bed in the midst of the throw pillows always piled there. She'd be safe at home, just as Jenny was.

George glanced apprehensively at Susan before doing the one thing he dreaded most – telling Jenny that her best friend was missing. "So, Jenny, I need to tell you something."

"What?" Jenny asked and she shivered once more. "What's going on?"

"Jenny, your friend, Courtney, is missing. She disappeared after the accident. Do you have any idea where she might be?"

"What? What are you talking about? What accident?"

"Courtney crashed her car last night, and I am assuming you were with her. Were you?"

Jenny stared at George as if he were insane. She then knotted her fingers into her palms and pressed her fists onto her cheeks. She squeezed her eyes tightly shut, and in the darkness searched, searched for something, anything. And remarkably she found it - the memory. She remembered.

"Yes," she said weakly. "I was there. Courtney was speeding, and a car, a truck, one or the other was coming up on us. 'Get the fuck out of here, you bastard!' Courtney was yelling. She kept looking in the rear view mirror, instead of at the road. And then it was there, a sharp turn. I heard her yell, 'Shit!' I screamed and then the car crashed, hard. I faintly remember lunging forward. That's all. Nothing else. Nothing after that moment."

George knew he had to pry more. He was gentle. "Do you think you'll be able to answer a few questions, Jenny? I need your help. We need your help, so we can find Courtney."

"I'll try." Tears had welled in her eyes.

"Good. So Courtney is your best friend? How long have you known her?"

"Forever, kindergarten, probably. We've gone to school together for years, but we didn't become best friends until after my dad left." Jenny glanced at Susan and bit her lip. Had she disclosed something she shouldn't have?

Susan rescued her. "My husband, Zach, left us seven years ago. I came home one day after school and he had moved out. He was gone."

George was taken aback by this information, but did not let on. "I'm sorry," he said simply.

"It's okay. We're okay. It was a shock at first and, at the same time, it wasn't. Zach was a restless man. I was aware of the possibility. He needed some space I guess. We've learned to cope," she revealed.

George chose not to inquire further into that personal matter, but instead directed his attention back to Jenny. "So you've been best friends with Courtney for seven years."

"Yeah, guess she felt bad for me, because all of a sudden I didn't have a father, well, not one at home. I think she related."

"But Courtney does have a father," George commented, a bit perplexed.

"She does and she doesn't. He lives there, but he doesn't give a shit. Sorry, Mom, but it's true. Guess Courtney thought we were in the same boat."

George was encouraged that Jenny was talking. Perhaps she would divulge more. "Can you tell me what happened when you and Courtney were out together?"

"Yes. No. I can't remember some things. "

George looked at her inquiringly, but he didn't press her. "Why don't you tell me what, if anything, you can recall about that night? Start from the beginning."

Jenny closed her eyes and tilted her head backwards against the pillow. She said not one word for a full minute. George sat down gingerly on a chair Susan had placed close to the side of the bed. He shifted slightly, waiting. Susan inched her way to the foot of the bed, finally sitting on the edge. The shifting of the mattress appeared to draw Jenny back.

"So, what do you remember?" George asked.

"We were at Courtney's all afternoon, just hanging out. We were looking at magazines, and talking about fashion shit and guys. We were trying to decide what we wanted to do to have a little fun." Her voice had grown stronger.

"You mentioned guys. Anyone in particular?"

"Not really. There's this guy, Cole Jackson, who keeps asking me out. Not interested though. He's a wrestler. Good, too, but he creeps me out." Jenny was speaking to George, but her eyes were on her mother who absorbed the news without flinching.

"Anyone else?"

"Oh, yeah, Jimmy, of course."

"Jimmy?"

"Yeah, Jimmy Nelson. He's crazy in love with Courtney, but they're like best friends. They grew up together practically like brother and sister. Their parents are best friends too and, well, Courtney and Jimmy were always shoveled off with nannies together when their parents took off on trips and shit. At least that's what Courtney's told me. They grew up in two different houses, but it might as well have been one to hear Courtney's stories. So, they've been together pretty much every day of their lives."

"And was Jimmy Nelson with you girls at all the night you and Courtney were out?" George knew he needed to talk with this kid.

"No. That's the thing. Courtney said Jimmy had been trying to get all over her lately, you know, and like, shit, she's not ready for that. So she wanted a break. It was girls' night out."

"And?"

"Well, I figured we'd end up at Jimmy's place sooner or later. We always do. He watches every move Courtney makes, and, shit, to tell the truth, he's saved her ass more than a few times."

The fact that Jenny was being so remarkably candid in speaking with George surprised Susan, who knew her to be evasive at times. She often had been afraid that Jenny gave her half-truths or told only part of a story.

"And how is that?" George asked, his question redirecting Susan's thoughts.

"It's like, Courtney's alone a lot. Her parents take off and leave her at home. They buy her all kinds of shit but hardly even talk to her. She gets pissed off, wants to pay them back, so she steals their booze and takes off in her car, driving anywhere to get away. Funny thing is, she always ends up back with Jimmy cause he's flippin' family. She either finds him, or it's the other way around."

"But he wasn't with you and Courtney Saturday night?" Again, George's statement became a question.

"I don't think so." Jenny's eyes beamed to the ceiling as though she might find an answer there.

"So, you don't remember."

"I don't remember seeing Jimmy," she said, "but, shit, maybe we did. I'm sorry. I'm sort of confused."

"Jenny, start, if you will, at the beginning of the evening. You were at Courtney's house until when? When did you leave? And where did you go?" George nudged.

"We left around six, I think. We took some beer from the fridge and Courtney gabbed some booze. Yeah. I remember. She said her dad had bought a shit load of booze for him and his friends for her graduation party. That's supposed to be next Saturday. She said he wouldn't miss a couple of bottles."

"So you left in her car to drink." It was a pointed statement.

"Yeah. Yes, sir. Pretty dumb, I guess."

Jenny stopped talking and held the palm of her hand against her temple as if in pain. Finally she began again. "We started out and the first thing that happened was she got a flat tire. Her car wouldn't steer right and she was pissed. She had to drive a couple of blocks on a flat tire to that old service station right at the edge of town. Some guy there, who talked his ass off, fixed it for her for a hundred bucks. What a rip off. He was a flippin' creep too – weirdo named Lou. He was fat, big bushy beard. Nosey bastard. We couldn't wait to get the hell out of there."

"Was anyone else at the station? Were there any other vehicles?" George asked.

Jenny tilted her head slightly, thinking. " I didn't see anyone else, but I think there might have been a couple of other cars. Yeah, there were two cars and a pickup truck, a big one, parked. They were all parked to the side."

"But you didn't see any other people."

"No. Just that creep, Lou."

"So, what happened next, Jenny? Can you tell me what you and Courtney did next?"

"We drove around awhile, stopped over at Meadow Wood Park, got out, walked around, and drank a few beers." Jenny glanced at her mother quickly and then, with wide eyes, looked directly at George. "Wait. I remember something. We were at the park and then in the car. We were talking about the shooting that happened at the high school. Freaked us out! Anyway, Courtney started making fun of people at school who were scared shitless, flipping out – kids, teachers, even the janitors. For some reason, Courtney went off on a tirade about one janitor in particular who drives her nuts. It's a little, old woman. She wears her hair in a bun and has a big honking mole on her face. It's flippin' ugly as sin. Her name's Flo something. Anyway, Courtney got the bright idea she wanted to go to Flo's house and mess with her, just for fun. She told me she and Jimmy use to drive by Flo's place once in awhile and harass her for kicks. By this time Courtney was really drunk and talking stupid. This is what happens when she gets shit faced; she does stupid stuff. Anyway, she drove to Flo's place, not too far from here, drank another beer for courage, and then, like a flippin' thief, sneaked into the house."

"Did you go in with her?"

"Couldn't. My head was spinning by then. Knew I had to stay put. I must have dozed off for a few minutes 'cause before I knew it she was back, breathing hard, and kind of giggling and gagging at the same time. I just remember her yelling, 'Let's get the hell out of here.' Courtney had backed her beamer into Flo's driveway, so she just took off, straight out of there, like a bat out of hell."

"And then?"

"She just drove and then, like I told you, we had someone on our tail." Jenny pulled her legs up under the blankets and she stared at George intently. "Somebody started tailing us. I remember now. It wasn't a car. It was a truck. Big. It would come up on us and then back way off and then it would drive up close again. Courtney was pissed. She started driving faster and faster. She was yelling too, 'Get away you motherfucker, you bastard.' She was pissed."

"And then the accident?"

Jenny looked at George, her eyes awash with tears and her face forlorn. "Yes. The crash. I don't remember anything after that. Nothing. The last thing I remember after Courtney's beamer flew off the road and crashed into something hard is throwing up here in the kitchen sink."

Her eyes darted to her mother's face. "Mom. I'm scared. I don't know what happened. And Courtney. Shit. Where is she?"

CHAPTER SEVENTEEN

COURTNEY

The cold awakened her, but she did not open her eyes. If she did the nightmare surely would continue. Instead, though her head ached, she envisioned herself alone, lying on her own bed, her pillows surrounding her. She imagined waiting for her cell phone to ring. It would be Jenny; it would be Jimmy, someone who cared, someone who loved her. She squeezed her eyes together more tightly and rolled slightly, feeling the sharp prickle of straw on her buttocks and thighs. Her arms were free but they were heavy; she could not lift them. And the thirst was back. Intense. Her mouth was dry, her lips parched and yet they were sticky at the same time. They would not part. Her head lolled slightly to one side and as it did a vivid image emerged. It was a mighty waterfall. Torrents of water surged over a rocky outcropping, plunged for a hundred feet downward, and crashed into a wide pool, the liquid angry at the point of impact but slowly settling, tiny waves pushing outward, undulating rhythmically until at last they lapped onto a gravelly shore. She watched, captivated, until slowly the vision faded away into a wash of grey.

I'm so tired, so cold. I cannot move.

As it had the day before, Courtney's hearing suddenly grew disturbingly acute. The rats were still present, skittering under the floor in a frenetic force of activity beneath her. And the horse was there, closer now. Satan. It whinnied, a sound deep in its throat. It was an anxious sound, a sound of sorrow. *Can a horse feel sad?*

At a near distance a new sound began - dull taps - monotonous, repetitive bangs, metal against metal, metal against wood, over and over, the dull and tedious resonance filling Courtney's head until she wanted to scream. She could not, though. She had no voice, no words. Abject weariness won over but before she was drawn back under, a face emerged in her mind. It was a blurry image of her father glaring disapprovingly and it lodged there, relentless and unmoving. She could not escape its intensity.

CHAPTER EIGHTEEN

CHESTER

Chester arrived home after work entering through the back door into the kitchen where a pot of pinto beans and chunks of fatty pork simmered on the back burner of the stove filling the air with a rancid smell. *Reeks like a goddam outhouse.* He slammed his well used and scratched, silver, lunch box on the counter, threw his threadbare jacket on a chair, and crossed the dark hallway into the living room that now, in late afternoon, lay in muted shadows. Shards of sunlight were the only illumination in the room, with one particular patch of yellow elucidating the features of his mother, Bertha, as she dozed in her ancient, rocking chair.

"Jesus, she looks like death warmed over," he mumbled. Though his voice was barely audible it was enough and the old woman stirred and started.

"What the hell, Chester. Don't sneak up on me like that. You're going to give me a heart attack and push me clear over to the other side."

If only. It was a hateful thought. Chester knew it, but it played in his head more often than not. *She's going to live forever.*

"Stinks in here," he announced, ignoring his mother's complaint. He opened the front door and began fanning the air with a newspaper as though that was all it would take to freshen the place that smelled of dirt, mold, and an old, old body on the verge of giving in to the inevitable.

"For God's sake, Chester, close the door. You're letting in flies. There was a hatch of the boogers somewhere near the porch this morning. Haven't been able to walk outside without getting swarmed by the little fuckers."

"Mother!" Chester seldom ever had heard his mother use profanity except for moments in years past when she had spoken in disdain of her husband, Herbert. *Herbert Flack - one dead motherfucker.*

"Well, it's true. They're a damned nuisance," she retorted in a voice that in recent years, had become permanently hoarse, grating, and to Chester, irritating as hell.

"Something must have died out there," she continued. "Under the porch. Maybe a possum, rat, raccoon, or some other varmint is rotting out there. Any decaying carcass would be fly heaven."

"Dinner's cooking by the way," she added ludicrously. "Another half hour and it'll be ready. Cooked up some pork and beans, one of your favorites. I'll whip up some cornbread."

"Hungry," Chester replied. "And so tired I could sleep standing up."

Chester had latched on to the many clichés and adages that laced his mother's vernacular and used them as though they were his own. They had lived together for forty-eight years. It was no wonder. And though a day might pass by without a word between them, they could finish each other's sentences if need be. In some ways it made life simpler, and in others, well, in others, it was an uncontrolled conflagration in Chester's gut.

⌘ ⌘ ⌘

After a silent dinner, both Chester and Bertha retired to their bedrooms. Though Bertha might have welcomed a bit of conversation, having been alone all day, she was sensitive to Chester's moods. *Something's whipping around up there in that boy's mind. Reckon I'll let him have at it.* Bertha had a keen grasp on Chester's ever-changing disposition and was fittingly wary of it. Her self-protective instincts in regard to her son were buoyed by her belief that she knew him better than he understood himself. She smugly had confidence that she could see *it* coming.

Bertha and Chester had traveled a long road together, a journey that had twisted and turned from the time of Chester's infancy. Experiences, especially those connected to the dark side of humanity, had knotted them, mother and son, into a tangle of love and hate that could not be separated. It was an absolute truth. Both, desperately dependent on one another, lived with those paradoxical emotions churning inside.

Bertha looked at Chester with sad eyes, her own feelings suddenly maudlin. The growth of her boy, her Chester, had happened so quickly, the years sprinting by, and he was a man now, an aging man. *Why, Chester never got married, did he?* Bertha's befuddled musing surprised her and she lowered her eyes as if in shame. *Wonder why? He's a good boy. He's come through all right. Hasn't he?*

To some degree, she was correct, although, due to choices of his own, the quality of Chester's life was dubious at best. He had learned, through experience and time, to invest in not one single person, save the mother who had protected and defended him for a lifetime. From childhood, he purposefully had distanced himself from every person he could, and as a result, discovered that without exception, others reciprocated. He had not a friend, or enemy, for that matter, in the world. Nor did he want one . . . or the other.

Therein lay his current dilemma and the unmitigated reason why, on this evening, he needed to be alone. He had to think. With little time to spare, he had to sort out a solution to an unforeseen, vexing quandary into which a longhaired man with evil eyes, without provocation, had snared him.

⌘ ⌘ ⌘

Alone in his room, Chester, fatigued and agitated, lay on a bare mattress with a thin blanked pulled up to his chin. As was normal for him, he went to bed fully clothed. This habit allowed for a quick get-away if his nighttime pacing called, and this night, the probability was high, for his thoughts were a hornet's nest. *This fucking day went to shit from the beginning. Goddammit.* When he closed his eyes every, single happening that had occurred throughout the day became a scrambled frenzy in his mind. He tried with all his might to force sleep, counting imaginary signposts along an imaginary highway; he said the alphabet backwards; he ground his teeth. *Shit.* Finally he fell into a fitful slumber but it was short-lived as his sleep often was. Awake again, he stared into the darkness until his eyes burned and he began to perspire, rivulets of sweat sliding down the sides of his face. *Fuck.*

Chester flung off the blanket, stood up at last, and as he had for countless nights before, began pacing. He walked the length of his bedroom several times, back and forth, back and forth, but within minutes the walls of the room drew in on him. He was suffocating.

He stepped into the hallway where his pacing continued for an hour, two, three, and more until he was numb with exhaustion. He leaned his aching body against the doorjamb of his bedroom and remained motionless until his mind finally cleared. *There isn't a fucking choice.* He was resolute. Though moral fortitude had never been Chester's forte, for a reason, unclear even to him, he knew he would find Detective Murphy. He would find him this morning, as soon as he could, and he would tell him; he would tell him exactly what he knew.

Chester trudged farther into his bedroom, grabbed fresh, wool socks, slid on a pair of worn, work boots, and threw on a clean shirt. He then turned three times in a circle like an anxious mutt before stomping to the front door. The racket he had made was the least of his concerns.

"Be back," he yelled in the direction of his mother's bedroom, and he was gone.

Once outside, he looked toward the horizon. The sun had not risen yet, but he could see that the sky was lightening to a cloudy day. He hustled quickly to his old pickup. The vehicle's rusting door screeched as he pulled it open. "Christ," he said out loud. "This fucking thing is falling apart."

The truck started though, the engine turning over on the first turn of the key. Chester revved the motor several times before he pulled away from the house and down the dirt and gravel driveway to the narrow, county highway that led into town and to the police station. He knew what he must do, indeed, what he would do, despite his abhorrence to speaking once more with a cop he detested.

As he sped down the highway, fumes from the gasoline engine filtered into the cab making Chester a bit nauseous. His dinner had not settled well; his stomach was bloated and it churned painfully. He squirmed uncomfortably on the bench seat, rolled down the window, and let out one, long, raspy fart that temporarily eased his discomfort.

"Ah," he muttered. "Better."

Chester's truck screeched to a halt two miles farther down the road virtually at the front door of the police station. The place already was a haven of activity. Several vehicles were parked outside, and a young, police office was standing on the steps of the building chatting with a short woman whose head awkwardly was tilted back and nested onto her upper back so that she could see his face. The man towered over her. *That's Flo Gray. Wonder what she's doing here so early in the morning.* Chester recognized Florence Gray at once. For years, she and her husband, Randall, had lived not a half mile away in a stucco cottage, a carbon copy of the one he shared with Bertha; that is, until old Randall up and died from some kind of cancer, he believed. He didn't know why he had become privy to that small detail, but it likely was a rumor his mother had brought home from the nondenominational church in town. Chester was convinced that that holy place was a hotbed of gossip and he had told his mother as much, but she had shushed him, more than once, and snapped, "Chester, you're just plain full of the devil." Chester was right though; he knew it in his gut.

Once parked, he opened the door of his truck, swung his legs around and hopped to the ground, passing gas noisily as he did. The officer's eyes turned toward him and he held his gaze until Chester brushed past him and Flo Gray into the lobby of the station. He could not have known that behind his back, Flo Gray eyed him curiously. *What's Chester Flack doing here?*

Behind a glass partition and a wide counter, a woman who in Chester's warped opinion looked ready for a date with the coroner, sat shoving chunks of a fat muffin into her mouth. Chester smirked. *Can hear Mother now – "Why, she's as old as the hills. Got one foot in the grave." – as though Mother has room to talk.*

Janice Cochran, the woman at the desk, looked up at Chester quickly, chewed heartily as she did so, and swallowed before addressing him. "Yes?"

"Name's Chester Flack," he said, "Need to talk to Detective Murphy if he's around. Believe I have some information he could use."

"Information?" Janice asked.

"Yeah. I talked to Murphy a couple of nights ago about a car crash down close to the road leading to my house. Came upon some new info he'll want to know." Chester crossed his arms across his chest and scowled at the woman.

"He arrived here only a few minutes ago," Janice said. "Let me check to see if he's available. Have a seat."

"I'll stand."

Chester easily could have sat down, if for no other reason than to ease his aching legs and tired body, but the mere choice of being obstinate gave him a moment of simple pleasure. *Screw her. I hate people like her. Real quick to give orders for no good reason other than to be bossy.*

Janice disappeared into the bowels of the office and returned ten minutes later with Detective Murphy in tow. She had determined very quickly that she was not about to let Chester Flack, a man she had never laid eyes on, into the station beyond the lobby, even into the holding room. Detective Murphy would have to identify him first. Janice had been a cornerstone at the police station for eons and had an eye for unsavory characters like this Chester Flack fellow. She prided herself on being nobody's fool.

Chester smirked when he saw George Murphy. *I hate that son-of-a-bitch.*

"Morning, Detective," he said, "I came upon some information yesterday, just by chance, that I think you might want."

"Good morning, Chester. What do you have?" George asked. He wasn't convinced he could trust a thing Chester Flack had to say after their previous interactions.

"Rather not tell you the details right here," Chester asserted, gazing around the lobby as though it were swarming with people. The fact was, that it was dead empty.

"Yeah. All right, Chester," George said, "Come on through the door on your left. I'll unlock it."

Chester moved slowly through the opened door and looked around nervously. His eyes darted to every corner and he wiped his hands up and down on the sides of his trousers. His stomach gurgled. Never in his life had he wanted to be in a police station, not for any reason, and although he might have wanted to credit the sheer fact of his presence here to fate, he knew differently. A conscious decision had landed him right smack in the middle of the place.

"Follow me, Chester," George ordered. "We'll talk in my office."

George Murphy's office was small. A singular desk, piled high with files and stacks of loose paperwork, dominated most of the room. Bookcases, filled with binders and thick books, lined three walls. Two wooden chairs with broad arms were positioned in front of the desk, and behind it was a high-backed, leather office chair – George's, of course.

"Take a seat," George told Chester, "unless you'd rather stand."

The option gave Chester, who relished being contrary, the chance to sit. He flopped into the chair, placed his hands firmly on the flat arms, and after exhaling a long breath of air, opened his mouth. No words escaped though.

"What do you have for me?" George was blunt. He had no time to waste.

Chester cleared his throat and began talking. "Yesterday, I saw the truck. I'm sure of it. I could tell by the sound. It was exactly the same engine roar that I heard after the crash. Loud. The fucking thing's a diesel for sure. Came up on it on my way to work yesterday morning."

"And you're just now getting around to telling me this?" George was irritated that perhaps relevant information had been withheld, even for a short time, but he knew to watch his step with this guy. Chester would freeze him out in a split second. "Look, glad you came in. Tell me more."

"Well, I wish to hell I'd never been outside the other night to hear that damned crash. Then I wouldn't have to be here now, involved in something I don't want no part of. But it happened, and I'm suffering the consequences." Chester was having difficulty controlling his angst. His face flushed crimson and he began blinking incessantly.

George pressed, "I know, Chester, but you were there, and now, well, you're doing the right thing to come here. Where did you see the truck?"

"I took the long road to work this morning, down Bending Vine Road, you know, that twisty ass road that goes behind the vineyard next to my place. Was driving round those curves."

And speeding. George knew that to be a fact.

"I was thinking about the accident, and the sound of that truck for some reason. That roar had been stuck in my head like a bad song. I could hear it as plain as day. And then, goddamn it, it was there. I wasn't imagining anything. It was right there in front of me. Right there. Almost ran into the damned thing." Chester's voice rose.

"You almost hit the truck?"

"Yeah. Slammed on the brakes inches from the bumper. Driver shook his fist and glared at me. I could see the eyes, evil fucking eyes. Dude had long hair. Ponytail. Thought it was a woman, maybe at first, cause of the long hair, but the dude's shoulders were wide, and whoever it was, was sitting high in the seat. Had to be someone tall. It was a man with long hair, and the most evil fucking eyes I've ever seen."

Chester stopped. He leaned back in his chair. "Then the guy sped off. Left me in the dust. But I heard that engine roar. Same one. I'd bet my last dollar. I don't mean to tell you, I was shook up. Those awful eyes. So, I just drove off to work, slow. Honest to God. Was late to work too, but that's another damn story."

"You didn't see anyone else in the vehicle?"

"No, and I didn't get a license, either. Thought about that too late. Oh, but I saw the make, plain as day. It was a Ford – a black, Ford pickup with a diesel engine. I'd stake my life on it."

George leaned forward. "Thank you for this, Chester. You did the right thing by coming here. You did. It's not a lot, but at least we know the truck is in the vicinity and we have a make. We'll be on the look out."

George looked at Chester steadily for a few seconds before asking one last question. "If this man is located, Chester, could you identify him?"

"Only by the eyes. If I could see those eyes, I could. I'll never forget those evil, fucking eyes in my life."

CHAPTER NINETEEN

FLO

Flo kept her promise. She was parked in front of the police station before the sun had risen. Though she had not slept all night, she did not feel tired; rather she was strangely energized, determined to find out, one way or another, who had slipped into her house in the dead of night to vandalize and steal. She was deep in thoughts that had her walking through her home once more, looking into every corner, mourning once again the damage done to Randall's artwork, and finally settling on the empty space where her father's guitar had sat for years. Sadness gripped her; her throat tightened and her eyes burned with tears. *Come on, Flo. No more crying. That'll get you nowhere, and fast.*

The station was creepily silent that early in the morning, but Flo imagined that within an hour or two it would be bustling. The officers in the tiny Hollow Vista Police Department likely had not had to address quite so much criminal activity in years. The invasion of Flo's home was a paltry offense compared to the recent murder of a prominent realtor in town, followed in only days, by the horrifying shootings at the high school, but the fact that some unknown person stealthily had entered her home in order to vandalize, in Flo's view, was cause for concern. She was astute enough to realize that her anxiety had been heightened not only because of recent crimes, but because the home invasion had been a direct affront to her personally. And she was incensed. *Of course, I should be upset. Who wouldn't be?*

What Flo could not possibly have known at that moment, however, was that her sense of unease would be exacerbated even further when she learned the news of an apparent abduction of a high school senior - smug, little Courtney Taylor, whose ongoing sneers and snippy remarks directed for some absurd reason at Flo, had not gone unnoticed. Though by no means did she appreciate the abuse, in time, Flo had learned to ignore the girl's obvious immaturity. It had not taken long for her to deem Courtney unworthy of her worry.

⌘ ⌘ ⌘

Flo finally stirred from her musings and focused on the sole reason for her being at the station so early – to complete the formal report about the vandalism, and moreover, to inform Officer Sanchez that she had been robbed as well. She stepped from her car, locked it quickly, and ascended the steps of the stone and stucco building that housed the police department, the coroner's office, and a tiny, transitional morgue. Shivering slightly in the cool, morning air, she glanced upward searching for a brightening sky.

Instead, she saw only a sheath of laden, grey clouds that completely obscured the rising sun. *Odd. It's usually sunny this time of year.*

She pushed open the heavy door and walked slowly into a dimly lit lobby. Behind a thick, glass partition and a wide counter was an empty desk. *Where is everyone?* Instantly, as if in answer to her question, Officer Sanchez appeared, looking remarkably fresh and rested. *Well, at least he must have gotten some sleep.* Officer Sanchez acknowledged Flo with a wave of his hand and motioned for her to go to a door at the left of the entryway. By the time she began moving in that direction, the door swung open and she was face to face with the young officer who had made the initial report.

"Come in, Mrs. Gray," he ordered politely. "We'll talk in one of the small, conference rooms."

Officer Sanchez already had prepared a preliminary, word-processed report based on the information he had taken the night of the incident. Flo had only to verify its accuracy and add the one significant detail that clawed at her emotions – the theft of her father's guitar.

"I noticed it gone after you left," she told the officer before adding more. "My father played that old guitar almost every night when I was growing up. He'd come home from hours at the cannery and he would pick it up and hold it like a baby. He'd strum a few cords, tune it a bit, and then play. And he sang too. I'll never forget." Flo's eyes were glassy and she felt again a profound shudder in her chest.

"What was the value of the guitar, do you suppose?" Officer Sanchez asked, professionally sidestepping Flo's sentimentality in order to address the issue at hand.

"I really have no idea," Flo answered honestly. "I don't think it was worth a lot monetarily, but it has tremendous sentimental value to me. It is the one item of value my father had when he was killed years ago. We were poor. It was a luxury for him. He loved that old guitar, and I cherished it."

Flo's face grew slack with despair and her lips quivered. Her hand shot up to cover the huge mole on her cheek and she held it there, until at last she spoke once more. "I suppose whoever destroyed Randall's artwork took the guitar too."

"Maybe," Officer Sanchez said quietly, not committing to agree.

"Maybe?" Flo was confused.

"We'll need to investigate further. It's a possibility the vandal took it, but, then again, someone else may have stolen it," the officer proposed.

"How could that be? Are you suggesting that another person came into my house? No. That's not possible." Flo looked around somewhat frantically. "No."

The mere suggestion that more than one individual could have entered her little house, her special, private, space, while she had been sleeping, horrified her. She felt more than violated; she felt exposed, and though thankfully unhurt physically, in Flo's mind, she had been preyed upon in a most disturbing manner.

"I'm not actually implying anything," Officer Sanchez said, backing quickly away from his initial, mild assertion. The last thing he needed was for Flo Gray to become hysterical. "We have to keep open to any and all possibilities though, just as a precaution. And realize we'll be dusting for fingerprints today. The more information we can gather and the more we consider all angles, the better."

Officer Sanchez's eyes beamed to the ceiling and in that instant his mind took him back to the first days of his career and to Detective Murphy's sage advice: *Don't go into any situation, Sanchez, no matter how insignificant it may appear, wearing blinders. Keep you eye on the road but realize that life is not a through street. Investigations are just like the lives we're living. They have divots and potholes, twists and turns. Don't let yourself be blindsided.* Javier Sanchez had taken Murphy's counsel to heart. He applied it every day.

Flo looked at the young man steadily. *Smart.* "You're right, Officer Sanchez. Thank you."

"You're welcome, Ms. Gray, and thank you for being so prompt this morning."

Flo glanced quickly at the clock above the door of the conference room before standing to leave. She had fifteen minutes to make it to the high school on time. As she turned toward the door, the space was filled with the hulking figure of a tall man.

"Ms. Gray?" George Murphy asked.

"Officer," he added, nodding at Officer Sanchez.

"Yes," Flo stated, her voice hushed.

"I'm Detective Murphy," George said, looking directly at Flo Gray. "George Murphy. I have some information regarding your case. Would you mind sitting back down for a few minutes? It shouldn't take long."

CHAPTER TWENTY

GEORGE

Reassuring Jenny Wallis that the search for her friend, Courtney, was a top priority and that, yes, she would be located, was not easy. George understood her uncertainty at the deepest level, although he would not admit that to anyone. Rather, he simply observed Jenny helplessly as she cried. Her reservoir of tears seemed endless, but finally with her mother's gentle coaxing, she settled down.

"I'll be going now," George said quietly to Susan, but before she could answer, Jenny spoke.

"Cold," she mumbled. "Really cold." Despite the warmth of the house, Jenny had begun to shiver.

Susan retrieved an extra blanket from a hall closet and tossed it carefully over her daughter. She then tucked it around her, leaned in, and kissed her on the cheek. "Go to sleep, honey. Things will be okay. We'll know more tomorrow."

Her comment was ridiculous, and she knew it, but, like a little girl, Jenny responded. In moments she had drifted to sleep with only an occasional involuntary whimper deep in her throat breaking the silence.

Susan looked at George woefully. Her dark, brown eyes shined with tears, but she managed a tiny smirk at last. "Let's go downstairs," she whispered.

George followed her down the staircase to the landing below where they stopped and gazed at each other awkwardly. He could feel a blaze of warmth on his neck and he clumsily slid his hands into his jacket pockets. He felt as if he were twelve.

"Would you like tea? Coffee?" Susan asked and then quickly said, "Oh, maybe I shouldn't have asked that since you essentially are on the job. Is it against the rules for you to have a cup of coffee?" She blushed.

George had been about to say no to her offer, but despite knowing he should leave and go home, if for no other reason than because he was exhausted, changed his mind. "Well, sure. Why not? A cup of coffee sounds good. It's been a long day."

Susan smiled. "Good. Come on."

She led him into the kitchen, motioning for him to sit. It was the second time he had sat at Susan's kitchen table and though he could not ascertain why, he felt absolutely comfortable being there.

"Thanks, Susan," he said, scanning the space around him. A refrigerator, stove, and counter area lined one, deep burgundy colored wall. The opposite wall, directly across, had been painted beige and was dominated by a large, currently-shaded window; below was a double sink and additional countertops that were adorned with various bottles and canisters, a few potted plants, and books, lots of cookbooks, a few brand new looking, and others obviously well used. Despite the array, everything appeared to be in its place, clearly in an intentionally arranged order. George and Susan had entered the kitchen from a narrow hall that separated the living room from the cooking area; a wooden, kitchen table had been placed near the entry of the room, and beyond that was a butcher-block cooking island. In the center of the back wall of the room was a glass-paned and wooden door that led to a partially screened-in back porch. Must be beautiful out there on warm, summer nights.

"This is really a nice room. Cozy," George offered.

"Well, it's far from fancy, but it is home. I've spent hours in this room, cooking, making plans for my classes, or just looking out the window at the vineyard. I've always loved how a vineyard changes colors with the seasons, how after a dormant winter, the vines leaf out in spring, grow lush in the summer with bunches of grapes dragging down the branches, and then in fall . . . those vibrant colors . . . red, orange, burgundy." Her face was a visage of someone far away, or wanting to be until suddenly she gained command. "Oh, I'm sorry. I didn't mean to go on a tangent." She smiled.

"Don't be sorry. That was nice. I've always loved this countryside too," George agreed.

"Did you grow up around here?" Susan asked, setting a steaming cup of coffee in front of him.

"No, actually, nearer Monterey. My folks worked in canneries there. Retired now, both of them."

"Oh, so you're here because you were hired by Hollow Vista PD?"

"Yes. It was my first job. Been here ever since. Can still remember my father saying, 'Get an education, George. Get a profession. If you don't, you'll end up working in a cannery and you won't like it.' It was good advice. I've always enjoyed police work, especially when it leads into investigations, like this one. I have to admit though that lately, what with the murder of Sherry Mitchell, you know, the real estate agent in town? Well, that, followed by the shootings at the high school, and now Courtney Taylor's disappearance or possible abduction, well, it's been all-consuming, to say the least."

"I can imagine. Don't know how you do it."

"And what about you?" George asked.

"What? What about me?" Her reply was a question.

George offered a half smile, nodding his head from side to side as if amused. Clearly he and Susan thought about things very differently – he in a very linear manner, one step at a time, eyes on the road, and she, circuitously, with her mind seemingly meandering every which way. How does she stay on course?

"I mean did you grow up here?" He grinned. "Your turn."

"Oh, yes. I did. Born here. My mother was of Yokut lineage, the Yokut tribe having lived in this part of the country for generations. She was very proud, very astute, and insightful . . . seemed to sense things before they happened. I miss her like crazy. Rachel was her name. My father died when I was an infant. Sadly I don't remember him, but my mother told me many tales, so I have that. Mama died sixteen years ago, when Jenny was just four. Zach . . . that was my husband . . . managed to stay around for six or seven more years and then he left one day . . . when Jenny was eleven. It's been the two of us ever since."

George did not offer any further information about his personal life, but had been struck immediately by how his life paralleled Susan's, both parenting teenage girls alone.

What was the chance of meeting someone who had been walking the same path?

"I'm sorry for your losses," he said.

"It's okay. Really, it is. Losing my mother was crushing. We were so close and she adored Jenny. As for Zach . . . well, his leaving stung at first, but I wasn't surprised, really. Somehow I knew he'd be gone one day. He was restless . . . had a hard time settling down. I see now it was for the best. A lot of years have gone by. I'm content." She smiled the tiniest smile. "Jenny, on the other hand, well, I'm afraid she's like her father was, a bit edgy, and, unquestionably, wanting more excitement than little Hollow Vista has to offer."

"Thus, the shenanigans with Courtney Taylor," he added.

"Yes. But this time, it looks as though they stepped over the line." Susan drew a loose fist to her cheek and she seemed to stare at nothing.

She's searching for answers. We all are. George leaned forward. "We'll solve this. We will." He was not at all certain this was so, but the words were out there.

"I want to believe," Susan said. "I have to. Thanks, George. Thanks for being so kind to Jenny and thanks for staying for coffee. I appreciated the conversation."

"Me too," he said, standing up. "Better get home though. Need a few hours of sleep."

"Yes."

Susan followed George to the front door. "Good night, George."

"You too," he said softly. "Lock up, now. Get some sleep yourself."

She nodded. They looked at each other for too many anxious seconds before she simply said, "Take care, George. See you soon?"

"Of course. I look forward to it." He turned and walked quickly to his car. Once inside, he sat very still for a moment, his heart pounding disconcertingly as it had not done in many years.

CHAPTER TWENTY-ONE

SUSAN

The thick, wooden, front door had been closed for several minutes but Susan continued to stand with her back to it, her hands at her sides, palms flat against the coarse oak. She had been listening. George Murphy's heavy steps as he descended from the porch had been followed by the opening and closing of a car door and then silence. An extended interval lapsed before the engine finally turned over and she heard the crunch of tires on her dirt and gravel driveway. *Why did he hesitate? Is he thinking what I am? Oh, don't be silly, Susan. He's a professional, doing his job. That's all.* Though she reasoned with herself, her senses did not oblige, and she was left feeling a bit lightheaded. *Enough. That's enough.*

Susan glanced sharply around her living room in an effort to refocus. She loved it there. A stone fireplace dominated one wall and was flanked by wide, floor-to-ceiling bookcases on either side, each filled to capacity. The volumes were organized in an engaging horizontal and vertical arrangement that allowed for several photographs and complexly designed, woven baskets and clay bowls, crafted by indigenous people of the region, to be displayed as well. Above a sturdy, roughly hewn mantle hung a large, intricately designed, feathery wreath that Susan had created herself using nettles, bird feathers, pinecones, stringy fronds from bunchgrasses, and other natural materials she had collected for years when she hiked the nearby hills. When Zach had left with his guns, Susan had removed and dismantled the gun rack that Zach so adamantly had insisted be the focal point of the room and had replaced it with the wreath. It was a simple transition but it loomed larger than she might ever have considered. Her own creation, fashioned and formed with tenacity and care, had initiated a healing process; it had allowed her to focus on what was beautiful in life rather than what was ugly, as Zach's ever-present anger and edginess had been before his leaving. And, whether she consciously understood then or not, it also had given her an initial, tiny taste of independence. The ingenuous act of hanging the wreath was an exercise in choice, for her alone, and in an odd, inexplicable way, actually had given her silent, unfettered permission to move forward.

Susan stepped away from the door and gazed at the wall before her. Tilting her head, she smiled in smug appreciation before turning in a half circle toward the leather couch - the one Jenny had collapsed onto the night before. Beside it was an end table laden with magazines and a single lamp. The ancient rocking chair that had belonged to her mother, Rachel, had been placed at an angle near the fireplace and an over-stuffed chair, where Susan loved to curl up and read, was situated in front of the window. Covering the hardwood floor was a large, worn carpet with a dull, multicolored, non-descript design. Susan loved it, even with its thinning patches and frayed edges, for it had been one of her mother's few possessions. Besides, though only an inanimate item, it was one constant that always had remained in Susan's life. She cherished the familiarity of it.

She stood a bit longer, listening to muted, night sounds. The cicadas sang a scratchy chorus, a coyote's disquieting bark echoed from a distance, and the newly budded branches of a maple tree near the front window scraped against the glass as the wind swirled. An owl called. Its raspy hoot figuratively pulled Susan back into the arms of Rachel, her beloved mother.

Oh, Mother, how did I get here? And what will I find down the road? I wish you were here to tell me. I'm a little afraid right now because I have no idea what is to become of Jenny, and of me, for that matter. At the instant the thoughts tumbled through her mind, Susan envisioned the face of George Murphy as clearly as if he were standing right before her. Her heart seemed to skip a beat and she shuddered, disbelieving. *Oh dear, Susan. You can't go falling for a man you don't even know. Can you?* And then, as though Rachel had actually been privy to her thoughts, and was providing an answer, a voice called out.

"Mom! Mom!"

It was Jenny, calling in terror from her room upstairs.

⌘   ⌘   ⌘

Susan stumbled up the stairs, falling at the top . . . hard. Her knee slammed into the back of the top step and her head and shoulder hit the bannister as she fell.

"Shit!"

The tenor of Jenny's voice had been daunting, alarming, as though she were being attacked by someone all over again; Susan instinctively knew she had to get to her fast, but the misstep had slowed her to a stop. She sat still, assessing. Was she hurt? She rubbed her knee first. It was tender to the touch and surely would be bruised . . . and her head?

"Ouch," she said out loud. "A little dizzy."

She scrambled to her feet though and pushed open the door to Jenny's bedroom. The poor girl was shivering again although she was almost fully covered by her blankets. Only one bare shoulder was exposed, revealing Jenny's pale skin and the nasty abrasion on her neck and throat. She was dabbing at the wound with her fingers.

"This," she murmured. "Somebody did this."

Susan's response caught in her throat. Was Jenny remembering more? She did not want to escalate the trauma, so she meekly replied with a question, "Yes?"

She moved to the side of the bed and sat down, her hand caressing Jenny as best she could. She looked at her daughter's face, a countenance of despair. What a difference it was from Jenny's appearance only days before. Then she had glowed with confidence and determination. She had been ready to move away, to take on the world . . . she and Courtney. And now? Courtney was missing and Jenny was injured, surely both inside and out. She looked like a forlorn, little girl. Susan's throat tightened. The dizziness she had experienced no longer mattered. She waited.

"Mom," Jenny started. "I think a man did this."

"Do you remember him, what he looked like?"

"No." She fell silent again, but her eyes moved from left to right and her head shifted slightly as though she were fumbling through a maze, desperate to find a way out.

Susan lowered her head, remaining quiet and giving Jenny space. She bit her lip, determined to stay silent, but her eyes communicated her concern. As she searched her daughter's face, her head began to throb and a wave of nausea passed over her. Was it the head injury? Was it Jenny's angst? Either, both were ready causes.

"Black," Jenny said at last. "He wore black. A mask. He wore a black mask and a hoodie. Head covered. And it was dark. I don't have a clue what he looked like, but I do know this. He smelled; he stunk . . . bad." She closed her mouth, swallowed hard and stammered, "I'm going to be sick."

Jenny lunged from the bed, dragging a thin blanket with her, and rushed toward the bathroom, but she made it only through the door where she sank to her knees on the tile and vomited her dinner, a slimy mess, onto the floor.

"Oh dear," Susan muttered, stepping forward to rub Jenny's back before pulling her to her feet. "Here, here, honey. Let's get you cleaned up."

By the time Jenny had gained some semblance of calmness and had fallen asleep again, Susan was beyond tired. She knew she should have called George immediately with the details of Jenny's new revelation, but had not been able to bring herself to do it, not until Jenny had settled down, and now it was too late. *He'll be irritated, but I'll explain. He'll understand. I hope he will.* She suddenly was agitated. *I should have called him.* She actually picked up her phone, stared at it blankly, and then plunked it back down on her bed. *No. He'll have to wait.*

Feeling a bit woozy, she wandered back into the bathroom and twice turned in a complete circle as though trying to find her bearings. Finally she placed both hands on the sink to steady her shaky body and stared at her reflection in the mirror. *I'm forty-eight. Look at me. Forty-eight.* Tears slid down her cheeks in tiny rivulets but she made no noise. *Bath. I need a bath.* She ran a deep tub of hot water, sprinkled in lavender bath oil, and after stripping naked, sank slowly into the water in an effort to ease her pain, a hurt that embodied more than her physical injury but a freshly aching heart.

CHAPTER TWENTY-TWO

COURTNEY

The banging had continued for hours it seemed, although Courtney had lost track of time. Her body had grown stiff. She hurt. *Need to move.* She managed to pull herself into a sitting position and stared at her surroundings that were becoming more visible as minutes passed. *It must be a new day. Shit.*

For the first time since gaining consciousness in her stinking confines, Courtney's ability to reason was becoming more lucid. Yet she was completely mystified as to how she had gotten here. *Need to get out of here, one way or another. Where is this place anyway? Who put me here? And why? Shit. Why can't I remember?* She began to panic as she scanned the stall from corner to corner, her head jerking from side to side, up and down.

Finally she managed to stand, pulling herself to her feet by grabbing onto a rickety, corner post. Her legs were weak and wobbled a bit as she put weight on her feet. *Fuck. I can hardly stand.* With the horse blanket wrapped around her shoulders, she carefully began to step around the perimeter of her enclosure. It definitely was a horse stall, filthy and stinking of molding hay, urine, and feces. The nausea that had gripped her had alleviated, replaced by gnawing hunger and intense thirst. *How long has it been? Two days?* She located a bucket of water in the corner; beside it sat a tin pan with three, green apples and a stack of carrots. *Fucking horse food.* She had no choice, however, and bit into one of the apples hungrily. It was cold, mushy and was a putrid peanut brown color inside - a virtual rotten piece of fruit. She spat the partially chewed blob into her hand, looked at it with disgust, and threw it across the stall.

"I wouldn't be doing that, if I were you, missy. You're not in a position to be picky now are you?"

Courtney whirled around so quickly toward the direction of the man's voice that she fell to her knees. He laughed as he stared down at her from his vantage point on the opposite side of the locked gate. "Better get yourself some nourishment, missy, because I'm going to be back for a visit come evening. I want you wide awake this time."

This time? Shit! Courtney glared at the hideous, bearded face. "Don't you come near me," she hissed.

"I can do anything I want," he chuckled, bearing a smirk that revealed wide gaps between sparse, yellow, pointy teeth. "And I'm going to give you all day to think about what that might possibly be."

The man's words hovered in the air like suspended daggers, his intent menacing and terrifying, but before Courtney could utter another sound, he was gone.

She stared at the space he had vacated. All she could see was where the wide planks of a distant, wooden wall met a gabled roof at the end of the barn. Large beams, eight or so feet apart, ran the width of the structure for as far as she could see, but that wasn't far. The place was too dark, and suddenly deadly silent. She crawled to the gate and pulled herself to a standing position again. On tiptoes her fingers could just touch a thick chain that had been wrapped several times around a metal bar at the end of the gate and then connected to a sturdy post at the far edge of one wall of the stall. The hasp of an enormous padlock had been pulled through the links of the chain rendering it taut and unyielding. *Shit. I'm not going anywhere.*

Courtney stood very still, the only movement being her eyes that shifted left and then right before resting finally on the pile of dirty carrots. She moved toward them, snatching one from the top and biting into it. Unlike the mushy apple, the carrot was firm and, to Courtney, at least palatable. She devoured one, and then another, swallowing poorly masticated chunks until her stomach began to cramp. *Slow down Courtney. Slow down and think. Don't choke yourself. What's important is getting out of here.* Instantly she remembered. *There's a hole in the wall.*

She crept like a thief to the far side of the stall, locating the opening that she had discovered when she had first awakened from her drunken stupor the day before, days before. She had no idea how much time had passed.

The gap let in light and was a wide enough aperture so that Courtney could peer through as she had done on the first day she had awakened in this ghastly place. She saw again the patch of earth with the sparse and spindly spikes of dying grass below, and as she had observed before, in the distance, she spied what appeared to be a horse track or perhaps simply a dirt path leading somewhere. Courtney could only imagine where that might be. If the trail in the expanse before her were a horse track, it would be one big oval, perhaps with no outlet at all. She envisioned herself, a captive, clad only in a filthy horse blanket, trotting around in circles forever. No end in sight. Yet if it were a path, it could lead anywhere, away from this nightmare. As she leaned against the wall, Courtney thought only of one place she would wish such a random path to lead . . . home . . . to the house she always had found when she was lost, to Jimmy Nelson's ranch and the residence that had been a welcome refuge for a lifetime She closed her eyes and pictured herself slowly walking on the path at first, and then skipping like an awkward schoolgirl, before running as fast as she could until she was there, at last. Safe.

She sat back suddenly, alarmed and bewildered. *Jimmy. Where is he? Is he looking for me? Why hasn't he found me? What's going on?* And at last she let go. She began to whimper like an abandoned puppy, as her eyes filled with tears. Not one drop slid to her cheeks though. Astonishingly she held back, not giving in to the terror of her predicament; she could not allow that to happen. Instead she focused once more on the rotting wood that edged the opening beside her and began to pick. She tugged and plucked until her fingers were raw and aching, until the hole had widened to a foot in diameter. She pressed her head into the space to see better just as a creature, like a moving phantom, dashed before her, its shadow throwing her into momentary darkness. The sudden movement, so close it was startling, made her lose her balance. She fell backwards onto her bottom, but seconds later, was back on her knees, peering out. Not three yards away, she saw it, the horse that was her barn mate, the broken gelding, whose name she remembered with certain clarity was Satan. The huge, black animal pawed impatiently, its head moving vertically as if it were nodding in concurrence with her plight. She stared at the horse until its eyes lowered, leveling with hers. Satan began to move forward then, step by step until he stopped not a foot from Courtney's head. He snorted loudly, retreated a step or two, and then returned. Courtney reached for Satan's nose, touching the coarse hair with her fingertips and rubbing firmly. "Hey, buddy," she whispered.

In quick response Satan issued a short blow followed by a nicker, the sound deep in his throat. He shook his head as if exasperated by her touch, but did not step away.

"Hey, Satan," Courtney hissed, "Hey, buddy, are you talking to me?" She was reaching for a miracle. "I think we're together in this mess, Satan. You have to help me get out of here. Can you? I promise, if you do, I'll pay you back. I promise, I will. I won't let you down. Satan? Are you out there?"

The horse, his name, a question in her voice, was her only hope, for she felt despondently convinced that not one person in the world had the slightest notion how to find her. Not one.

CHAPTER TWENTY-THREE

CHESTER

As Chester descended the steps of the police station, he felt relieved, as if a proverbial load of unwanted responsibility had been lifted from his shoulders. Unfortunately his exasperating anxiety, the ominous curse that had shadowed him for a lifetime, remained, and in fact, with recent events, had exacerbated to a point that he wished he magically could crawl out of his body. Yet, with the interview over, even that burden seemed lighter. The conversation with George Murphy, Chester assumed, had released him of any further accountability in regard to his having unexpectedly come upon the crushed BMW wedged in a ditch at the end of the lane that led to his house, or furthermore, of observing a random truck barrel away into the night, abandoning the smoldering scene in a flurry of stinking exhaust and screeching tires. Though in reality, Chester had not played a part in any aspect of the actual mishap, he had found himself, at least in his own mind, to be an unwitting accessory simply because of his observations. And that is exactly why, after sighting the truck once again, driven by an unnerving, evil-eyed character, he had shed his inhibitions and done what needed to be done. After the early-morning conversation with the detective, Murphy now had a much fuller description of the truck, a faint description of the driver, and the location where Chester had had his unsettling encounter. Now it was over and Chester could put the ordeal of speaking with George Murphy behind him. The entire situation was none of his business. He was done, ready to get on with his routine, as paltry, he was afraid, as that seemed to be.

He started the engine of his truck, backed out quickly without looking behind him, and nearly collided as he did with an oncoming vehicle whose occupant immediately began blaring the car's horn. He slammed hard on his brakes, lurching forward as he did into the steering wheel. It hurt.

"Shit!" he yelled to himself, and to the other driver, "Oh, shut the fuck up!"

He was angry, first for not paying attention, for almost causing an accident right in front of the police station, of all places, but he was further agitated by the blast of the horn. It was piercing and obnoxious, the driver of the car hell bent, it appeared to him, to want to make a scene, to draw attention. That was the last thing Chester Flack wanted or needed. He had learned after leaving the confines of high school years before that any interactions with other individuals basically did not suit. No. He kept his distance.

He glanced quickly at the person behind the wheel of the car who finally had lain off the horn. The driver was a female, blond, who looked around thirteen. *Should she even be driving?* The girl glared at Chester as though he were a monster, angled her car into a parking spot, jumped out of her vehicle, and sprinted to the door of the police station as though she owned it.

Now I wonder who that is?

And though he could not possible have known it, Detective Murphy's daughter, Angie, was thinking the same of him.

⌘ ⌘ ⌘

Chester arrived for his shift at work five minutes early, and this day, his boss, Victor Conti, was nowhere to be seen. *Thank God. Son of a bitch has been a pain in my butt lately.* Chester wandered into the bowels of the warehouse prepared to continue his chores as usual, with his head down, avoiding conversation with anyone. Several more pallets of barrel staves needed sorting, hoops of various sizes had to be organized, and wooden crates had been set aside for inspection and repair in preparation for the harvest much later in the year. Spring was the time of year when Chester's job was most tedious, for at times he had to search for tasks to do. *The fucking warehouse floor can only be swept so many times.* The exact thought had come to him often, but in actuality, the floor always seemed dirty. No matter how many times he ran a broom over the surface of the concrete, ribbons of cement dust and dirt rose in agitated circles before settling once more. Chester had even embraced the absurd thought that he might in time sweep all the way through the slab and into the soil beneath. "I could dig my own little highway to hell," he chuckled beneath his breath.

"Flack. You in here?" The booming voice of his boss, Victor, bellowed from the gaping warehouse entryway.

Chester was slightly startled to hear his name called and spun around to see Victor Conti eying him. Victor was no taller than five and a half feet and seemed as wide as he was tall, his rotund mid-section bulging over his belt buckle and his thick thighs clearly constrained uncomfortably in tight, denim jeans. He was clean-shaven, completely bald, and consistently as crass and unpredictable as a drunken sailor. He waddled into the warehouse, hands on hips, an unlit cigarette wedged into the corner of his mouth. Chester's body stiffened. *What the hell does that son of a bitch, Conti, want now?*

"Flack, need you to take a truck, one of the stake sides, and head over to the Nelson place. Know where that is?" Without waiting for an answer, Victor continued. "It's outside of town, north. Two estates out there butt up to one another, the Taylor place first, and then the Nelson ranch. Fucking people have more money than God."

Chester stared, wondering the significance of his boss's final statement, but let it go. *Good for them - more money than God. Bet that don't mean shit in the long run.*

"Can't say I know those folks, but I can drive out there. What does this Nelson fellow need?"

"Well, he raises horses, high-end, a couple of thoroughbreds, mostly quarter horses. Seems he wants to downsize though and sell off some of his land on the east side. The parcel he wants to unload borders our northernmost vineyards. Said he's anxious to sell if we're interested in expanding. Land's zoned for agriculture, so it would be a fit if the land's plowable and isn't stripped bare of nutrients. One of our viticulturists will be looking into those details. Sure as hell isn't up to me."

Chester looked blankly at Victor. *Why is he telling me this shit?*

"So, you want me to drive a stake side out there?" he finally asked omitting the word *why*, in effect, revealing his bent toward obstinacy.

"Yeah, yeah. Seems Nelson has an old barn and a run-down pony track at the far end of the ranch. The barn had a shit load of wine barrels, staves, hoops and other various winemaking materials stored there for years. Guess Nelson had pie in the sky dreams of operating a boutique winery of his own, but like a lot of dumb shits, he found out grapes don't grow themselves and wine-making, well, that's a complete other, goddamn story. Anyway old man Nelson says the supplies his workers have salvaged are in good shape. He had a shitload hauled down to the ranch proper and he wants to get rid of the whole kit and caboodle. Thought I'd free you up from the warehouse for awhile to go over and load the crap up."

"Yeah, I can do that. Slow in here today," Chester replied, actually relishing the idea of getting away from his routine for part of a day.

"Good. I'll let him know to be on the lookout for our truck," Victor said, turning on his heels and heading for the main, office building without another word. Chester watched his boss shuffle away with his fat arms, like hefty sausages, swinging back and forth and brushing his wide hips with every step.

Chester was on the road in minutes, the aging stake side sputtering like an old man until it got up to speed. Alone on the open road, the anxiety that had dominated Chester earlier in the day began to subside. Instead of fixating on how he felt, he focused on his driving. Soon, however, he found himself spacing out, thinking of nothing. Through the front windshield, he gazed vacantly at the countryside. Spring in the central valley was astonishingly beautiful and impossible not to notice even for a crusty character such as Chester Flack. Though the sky that morning was a swirl of grey clouds instead of the usual, vivid azure, the countryside itself was awash in color. Winter rains had nourished the hillsides and valleys turning them deep shades of Kelly and shamrock green. Mustard plants abounded on the hills, their yellow, butter-colored, flowers undulating with every, light breeze. Closer to the roadside were purple bush lupines, sweet baby blue eyes, red maids, purple owl clover, and of course, red and golden poppies, bunches of them, sprouting wildly wherever they could grab hold. Not through any conscious effort on his part, Chester had learned the names of countless flowers, bushes, and trees that thrived in the central valley and foothills. His mother, Bertha, unlike his father who had been hell bent on killing any animal in his sight and who thought flowers were for sissies, had badgered him to appreciate nature, and though Chester had made every effort to thwart her efforts to educate him, he had absorbed more than he ever would have admitted.

Chester pulled the truck onto the wide, gravel shoulder of the country road for a moment and gazed over the landscape, feeling overcome unexpectedly with a sense of awe and renewed anxiety. *Why? Why the fuck am I feeling like this now?* The sudden, overwhelming sense of apprehension mystified him. *I'm feeling fucking antsy as hell. Get it together Chester Flack.*

And then it struck him. The scene lain out before him unwittingly had dragged him back in time. For his entire childhood, his mother had forced him on hikes with her to gather wild flowers, especially in the spring. He had grown to hate the treks and her non-stop babbling about one plant or another. Her attempts at interesting Chester in local flora became one more reason to detest her and his flagrant animosity resulted in tantrums and torrents of profanity aimed at his mother, his absent father, and God. From the time he was a small boy he made a mockery of his mother's affinity for nature by stomping to mush the squash and tomatoes in her garden, snapping off buds and blossoms of her beloved roses and dahlias, and hacking at the trunks of the front yard oaks with an axe. Whenever Bertha protested, he resorted to calling her appalling names for one reason, to be cruel. It was an inescapable fact that for the entirety of Chester's youth confusion and anger had reigned and any semblance of self-control was non-existent. His actions were one side of the coin; his manner of communication another.

"Who cares about a bunch of fucking weeds and flowers that are going to be sizzling in the sun or dead come summer?" or "Why waste time digging in the dirt just for a few disgusting vegetables?" He had barked at his poor mother more than once, simply to aggravate her and to impress on her that nothing she could do would penetrate his caustic demeanor and insensitivity. By the time he was seventeen he had made his point clear. *I shot and killed her old man dead, didn't I?*

Chester's breath caught. He did not move. He fixated on a sea of yellow, hillside, mustard blooms until his eyes blurred. *Shit.* In that instantaneous, bizarre moment of clarity, he understood the cause of his rekindled torment. Bertha had sought to instill in him a love for nature's splendor while at the same time embracing the ugly knowledge of her husband's murder and the lie that had bound Chester to her in a most insidious way. The juxtaposition of the two reminiscences, one maddening, the other hideous, had set off this new wave of unease. Chester longed for it to stop. *Living like this is fucking going to kill me if I don't get to somebody else first.*

CHAPTER TWENTY-FOUR

FLO

At Detective Murphy's request, Flo remained in the small room where she and Officer Sanchez had been discussing her case. Though she knew the delay would make her late for work, she complied. *I wonder what this is about. The police have just started looking into my complaint.* Slumping back down onto the hard, wooden chair beside the tiny, conference room table, she noticed for the first time the marred and scratched surface. She wondered how many people, victims and perpetrators of various infractions, had sat in this very place. *Lots of stories, truth and lies, must have been hashed out here. Mine is only the latest.* She clasped her hands together and looked fleetingly at Detective Murphy before casting her eyes on Officer Sanchez's report still resting at the edge of the table. *Wonder if reporting this was worth the trouble. Nothing's likely to come of it.*

"Mrs. Gray," George Murphy began, "Before you arrived this morning, Officer Sanchez shared with me the preliminary report about the vandalism that occurred at your home. I can imagine how disconcerting this is for you. I wanted to allow the Officer to conduct his interview with you first, but told him that I have some information that we believe pertains to your case and the intrusion into you home. I ascertained this information in a round about way, actually, and details have not been fleshed out yet, but I have learned that a young woman, a senior at Hollow Vista High School, is likely responsible. At least, at this time, she is the sole individual who has been implicated."

Flo flinched and twisted in her chair. She swallowed hard before replying. "Who? And why? Why would a teenage girl sneak into my house while I was asleep and damage my husband's artwork? It's irreplaceable. And how did she manage?" Flo paused, her eyes scanning the room as if seeking answers. "Oh dear, I was in such a deep sleep."

George Murphy watched the little woman as she was overcome suddenly with a series of seemingly uncontrollable, nervous twitches. Her hand shot up to her cheek and covered a prominent, black mole. "Who was it?" she asked hoarsely.

"Normally I would be reluctant to divulge a name with the investigation incomplete, but I'm afraid you'll know who it is soon enough because this situation has newsworthy, extenuating circumstances," Murphy said.

"What do you mean, Detective?" Flo was growing confused, her anxiety worsening.

"Well, it appears that the girl in question has disappeared, and quite possibly has been kidnapped," he stated. "An investigation has begun and will be ongoing until, well, until we find her."

"Oh my, that's just awful, Detective, but how is the disappearance of this teenager connected to the vandalism . . . and robbery . . . I might add, at my home?"

"Robbery? Officer Sanchez?"

"Yes, Sir. Mrs. Gray informed me at the very beginning of our conversation this morning that after I had left her home Saturday night, she noticed her father's guitar was missing. Though the actual value of the instrument is unknown, its worth is in the enormous sentimental value it holds for Mrs. Gray who lost her father some years ago. The information regarding the theft has been included in the report." Officer Sanchez gathered the papers protectively.

"I see," George said, drawing out the words as the additional revelation began to churn a maelstrom of queries in his mind. He thought instantly of Jenny Wallis. The girl had not mentioned anything about Courtney stealing a guitar, and surely she would have. Could she have forgotten that detail? It wasn't likely. Jenny had been quite lucent about what had occurred during that portion of the ill-fated night spent carousing with Courtney Taylor, a girl whose courage, bolstered by too much booze, had led to yet another bad choice in an already inauspicious series. *What the hell must be wrong with that girl? Has . . . oh, God forbid, possibly had . . . she no filters, no sense of self-control, no ability to discern right from wrong whatsoever?*

George gained control, silencing his thoughts about Courtney Taylor. "You see, Mrs. Gray, another incident occurred last night, actually very close to your home. After your husband's paintings had been ransacked, the suspect in question had an unfortunate automobile accident - that, followed by indeterminate events, as of yet, not fully probed, that resulted in the girl's disappearance. What we do know is, that in the aftermath of the accident, one of the young women involved was located and is safe at home, and the second unaccounted for. The girl's parents have filed a missing person report. Flyers will be posted everywhere today, the media has received press releases, and well, the community, influenced by her parents' distress, will be up in arms, I'm quite sure. In small towns such as this one, it will be all hands on deck come noon today."

"And who is missing girl?"

"Courtney Taylor. Do you know her?"

⌘ ⌘ ⌘

Flo's heart fluttered, a confusing mixture of shock, sadness, and satisfaction overwhelming her. Courtney Taylor. She had put the girl out of her mind, and successfully so, after the incident at Hollow Vista High School in mid-fall. The mention of her name however brought the ugliness back as if it had just happened.

Flo had been working in the science wing. Since the beginning of the school year, she had been enduring the taunts of Courtney Taylor, though she had no idea at that time what the girl's name was. That came later. What Flo did assume, and quite rightfully so, is that from the first time the pretty, willowy blond had lain eyes on Flo, she had detested her. And why? Flo had no idea.

It had been the very first day of school. Flo had pushed her cleaning cart through the double door entryway at the end of the science wing to begin her shift only minutes before the students were let go. She had noticed Courtney . . . Courtney and a few other students, crowding the exit of one of the classrooms. Although smaller in stature than many of the others, Courtney stood out. Dressed provocatively in a hot-pink, low-cut tank top and skin-tight jeans, she flashed a smile at a tall boy whose hand was positioned on her butt. Flo's glance in the direction of the students had been perfunctory but it was enough apparently to set Courtney off. The girl twisted her head toward Flo and glared at her menacingly.

"What are you looking at, old lady?" She spit the words venomously, before her mouth set in an ugly snarl. Her eyes narrowed to slits and one hand knotted on her hip.

The girl's hostility took Flo aback, but she said nothing. Instead, she tucked her head downward, bent her legs deeply at the knees, and put her weight against her heavy cart full of cleaning supplies forcing it farther down the hallway. She heard shrill snickering behind her followed by one masculine, vulgar slur. The boy's words, on the heels of the prior, unsolicited affront struck instantly at Flo's sensitivity. Although as an adult woman she might have ignored the offensive slight from a few, immature adolescents, the fact was that it cut to the quick, planting Flo back in time. In a nanosecond she was a teenager herself again, enduring yet again the taunts of a fellow student. *Get ahold of yourself, Flo. She's a kid and for God's sake; you're an adult. Ignore her. Ignore them all.*

The brief interaction with Courtney and her small band of friends should have been the end of it, but unfortunately for Flo, it was only the beginning. Day after day, when Flo passed through the hallway entrance with her cart, she was met with stares, hoots, snickering, garbled mumblings, and unintelligible words spoken between clinched teeth, and Courtney was the ringleader. While nothing was spoken directly to Flo after the first day, she was painfully cognizant of the fact that she was being targeted. She managed effectively to disregard the taunts until one, unforgettable moment.

It was Halloween. Flo and the other custodians detested the holiday because of the mess left in its wake. By the end of the day, without exception, the halls on Halloween were left riddled with candy wrappers, half-eaten chocolates, smashed popcorn, and wads of chewed gum, leaving a grand mess to be cleaned. Dreading the day, Flo uncharacteristically arrived minutes late to work and hurried to the science wing's custodial closet to retrieve her supplies. She tugged the door open and looked into a vacant space. Her cart was missing. She turned abruptly and trotted down the hall. She had not moved forward more than twenty feet when she slid on an oily patch of tile and fell head first onto the floor. Hard. Her legs crumpled beneath her and her forehead smacked into the rigid, floor surface stunning her. For a moment she was so dazed she saw and heard nothing. It was as though the whole world had ceased moving. And then it began . . . laughter . . . only tittering at first until Flo crawled to a sitting position in the puddle of oil. Then the chortling began in earnest. She tried to focus on who was laughing but she was dizzy and her vision blurry. Finally, she sighted the wheels of her cart inches from where she had fallen. Looking up, she was horrified to see a young girl with her hair sprayed grey and knotted in a bun. She wore dirty, baggy pants, a faded, blue work shirt, and tennis shoes. Charcoal lines had been drawn beneath her eyes and alongside her nose and mouth. Two front teeth had been blackened to appear missing. Most horrifying of all, however, was that a protuberant, Paper Mache blob, the size of a walnut, had somehow been attached high on the girl's cheek. She leaned on the custodial cart and smirked.

"See anybody you know?" the girl giggled.

Flo wanted to cry. She had been tormented many times in her life, but this blatant maltreatment was the height of abuse. She struggled to stand, sliding once again in the oily mess. Her knee whacked into the tile, but she was able to grab the edge of the cart with one hand. She pulled herself up, holding shakily to the handle. Her lips began to quiver. She glanced about the hallway at her audience, some of whom had gone silent. It did not take a genius to see that she was hurt and humiliated. *Maybe there is a conscience somewhere here.*

At that moment, she felt a hand on her shoulder. It was Chuck Lindsey, a science teacher, who obviously had heard, and perhaps even seen, the commotion.

"Flo. Come with me. And you, Courtney Taylor, do not move one step," he demanded.

Chuck guided Flo into his classroom and helped her to a chair. "Don't get up. I'm getting the school nurse to check on you."

When he left the classroom, Flo heard Chuck sternly reprimanding the remaining students. "Show's over," he said finally, "Now get out of here. Get to class."

What Flo did not see was Chuck motion for Courtney to follow him. He took her by the arm and led her to the principal's office.

⌘ ⌘ ⌘

"Mrs. Gray?" George Murphy asked. "Did you know her? Did you know Courtney Taylor?"

The detective had not taken his eyes off of the little woman who had gone silent and was glaring at the wall in front of her as if in a trance. "Mrs. Gray?"

"I did. I do. I know who she is," she mumbled.

In the minutes that followed Flo clarified her response. Though vague in detail, she described the harassment and the ugly incident that had injured and humiliated her. The confrontation, she explained, had resulted ultimately in Courtney being reprimanded and suspended from school for ten days. Flo had suspected instinctively that revenge for the punishment would follow when the girl returned to school, but that did not occur, at least not overtly. Flo was sure, however, that she had felt the girl's eyes bore into her when she had passed by and her back had been turned. She had been certain. Now she was convinced. *I was right. Spoiled brat. She was bound to get payback sooner or later. And it's come to this.*

"It's come to this," Flo said out loud. "I had no idea when or how, but I thought she would retaliate. Initially I thought it would be right away and I worried, but in time, I put the girl out of my mind. I forgot about her. But now this."

Flo fell quiet again, her eyes scanning the floor.

The detective and the officer exchanged glances but were silent for a full minute before George finally spoke. "Well, I think this will do it for now. Thank you, Mrs. Gray. You've definitely shed some light on this case and given us a possible motive to consider. You've been very helpful. We'll be in touch."

Flo stood, nodded without speaking, and numbly walked out of the police station to her car where she sat motionless for several minutes, her thoughts tormenting her. She had loathed the likes of adolescents like Courtney Taylor her whole life. They were misguided and mean. Yet Courtney was only a young girl at the cusp of adulthood. *How can I resent her now? She's disappeared and possibly is hurt or in harm's way. I don't know why I should even care, but I want to help set this straight. I need to help, but how am I going to do that?*

Flo shivered with the reality of the unknown bearing down on her. *I shouldn't even care.* She was unable to formulate a feasible reason why she did, but her inner sense of right and wrong had hold. *Let them find her. Let them find her.* The words played over and over, a relentless, alarming refrain that would not let go.

CHAPTER TWENTY-FIVE

GEORGE

Within minutes of Flo Gray's leaving, George was in his office phoning Susan Wallis. His grip on the phone tightened with each ring. Finally she answered.

"Hello?" he heard. Susan's voice was soft, hesitant, questioning.

"George Murphy," he said. "Hope it's not too early."

"No. No, of course not. I was up at sunrise," she admitted. "Sleep hasn't come easy."

"I understand. I called early because some new information has surfaced and I have a question or two for Jenny. Was wondering if she's awake."

"I can check, and, uh, Detective Murphy, I know a bit more about what happened to the girls too. I should have called you last night, but Jenny got sick, and I, well, I wasn't doing well myself. I was just planning to call you, when my cell rang."

"What's up?" he asked simply.

"Well, Jenny remembered who accosted her. She doesn't have a name, of course, because it was a stranger, but she does have a description of sorts. Last night after you left, she yelled for me to come upstairs. She sounded so frightened. When I rushed into her room she was pressing her fingers into the gash on her neck. She had been crying again. 'I know a man did this,' she told me. 'It was a man dressed all in black, his face covered with a mask. He wore a black sweatshirt, a hoodie.'"

"And, there's more," Susan continued. "Jenny said he smelled horrible. When she was telling me, describing the smell, like booze and filthy perspiration, it was as if she was sensing the odor all over again, right in the room because she became very agitated and started to retch. She managed to tell me 'I'm going to be sick,' and then she began hyperventilating and gagging more. She made it to the bathroom but vomited all over the floor. By the time I got her settled down again, I was feeling ill myself and I had a mess to clean up, so, I decided to put off phoning you. I'm sorry."

"It's okay. It's okay," he assured her. George, in no way, wanted Susan Wallis to feel as though she had done anything wrong. He had the new information now. That's what counted.

"I know now," he continued. "And, thank you. Look, Susan, I have the Taylors coming in this morning, so I can't get over to your place just yet, but I do have a burning question for Jenny."

"Let me see if she's awake," Susan responded, the words *just yet* lingering.

"I'm heading upstairs now," she added as she tramped up the stairway.

She grabbed the bannister firmly with one hand while gripping her cell phone in the other. When she reached the landing at the top, she took in one, deep breath and then hurried to Jenny's room. The door was open partially and she peered in. A small lamp had been turned on and it cast a soft, yellow glow on Jenny's face that was otherwise colorless. With the absence of makeup and with her tangled, long, auburn hair strewn about the pillow, she looked fourteen. Upon hearing Susan enter, Jenny's eyes fluttered a bit and then closed tightly before she opened them wide. Dark circles beneath them confirmed the depth of her distress. Susan ached for her.

"Jenny?"

"I'm awake. Didn't sleep very well."

"Me either," Susan admitted before continuing. "Look, I have Detective Murphy on the phone. He wanted to speak with you if you were awake."

"Aw, not more fucking questions already. Shit." She pulled the thick quilt up to her chin and sneered before her mouth set in a childish pout.

"Jenny Wallis!" Susan snapped, certain that George had overheard her daughter's vulgar retort. "He has a job to do. Don't make it harder for him." Her voice had taken on a defensive tone.

"Okay. Okay. Shit. I'll talk to him."

"She's up," Susan said to George, "but tired." She wanted to add the word *irritable* too, but refrained. She understood the potential for a minor, domestic skirmish. *Keep the peace, Susan.*

"I'll only take a moment," he replied having overheard the girl's profanity as well as detecting her crossness.

Susan handed her cell phone to her daughter and stood by, listening. *For God's sake, Jenny, be polite.*

"No. I didn't sleep very well," Susan heard Jenny acknowledge. Her voice was solemn, flat, her eyes closing for a moment. "Yeah, I remembered more after you left last night. I told my mom. Yeah. Well, I can remember a man. He grabbed me by my hair and my neck, yanked me out of Courtney's car after she crashed it. I remember a big hand taking hold of a bunch of my hair. It hurt like hell. No. Asshole came out of nowhere behind us, driving a truck. No. He didn't really say anything. Any noise he made was muffled. No. I did not see his face. He had something over it – a black mask or cloth, or something. And he was wearing a hoodie, I think, black too. His whole head was covered. I don't have a clue what he looked like, but I do remember he reeked. He smelled like sweat . . . nasty, dirty, disgusting sweat . . . and beer, and cigarettes, and maybe even shit. It was gross."

Jenny stopped talking for a moment. Susan watched her free hand touch the wound on her neck before gripping the edge of the quilt until her knuckles were taut. She was listening.

"A guitar? No. She didn't have a guitar. I didn't see her come out of the house, and she startled me when she opened the car door. 'Let's get the hell out of here,' she yelled and we took off. She didn't have anything with her. A guitar wouldn't have fit very well in her car anyway. Why are you asking about a guitar?"

Susan had not heard George Murphy's response, but within seconds, Jenny had shoved the cell phone toward her and muttered, "Holy shit." Then she snuggled back under the blankets and covered her entire head.

Susan could hear another muffled curse word – *shit* – from within the cocoon of covers as she left the bedroom and closed the door firmly behind her.

"Detective?" she asked, wondering what to do next. *Where do I stand in all of this?*

"George," he replied. "Look, I have to go. I see the Taylors at the receptionist's window. Jenny was helpful. Thank you. And thank her. I'll call later."

And he was gone.

"Bye," Susan said into dead silence. She wanted to cry.

⌘   ⌘   ⌘

"About time you showed up." Bennett Taylor's manner had not altered one iota from the day before and George found himself recoiling internally. *What a jerk. Is he this way all the time?*

"Busy morning. Investigation's picking up steam," he responded, his voice hoarse from lack of sleep.

"Well, let's get on with it," Bennett demanded as though he were in charge. His thick arms crossed his chest as he broadened his stance. "Brought some reinforcements."

Behind Bennett Taylor stood his wife, Jill, who appeared corpselike and frail. Her face was ashen aside from two rosy smears on each cheek and her oily hair had been pulled back in a tight French twist and skewered with a leather fastener. Opaque sunglasses partially obscured her eyes, but George determined quickly that sleep had evaded her as well for they were dark wells. Flanking Jill were two young men, boys really, both wearing baggy, knee-length shorts and loose t-shirts, one bearing an image of a scantily clothed female sipping from a Corona beer bottle and the other emblazoned with a faded, green, marijuana plant laden with buds, its fronds thick and full. Both teens were muscular and tanned, both solemn, and each one sneering brashly as though they assumed they were quite capable of taking over the investigation at any moment.

George was quick to size up the two as smug, privileged, and certainly a bit foolish to arrive at the police station in attire that was more fitting for a party. His judgment aside, however, they were there, and he suspected Bennett Taylor had reason to believe the teens would be of help, eager to join in on a search for his missing daughter.

With his suppositions squelched, at least for the moment, George asked bluntly, "And you are?"

Before either could answer, Bennett interrupted. "Jimmy Nelson," he said pointing to the taller of the two, "friend of the family, of Courtney's, for years. They grew up together. And Cole, Cole Jackson . . . goes to the high school. Wrestler."

For George, Jimmy Nelson's name registered immediately. He was the one Jenny Wallis had said was *crazy in love* with Courtney. Jenny's insistence on that fact had imbued George with a passing interest in Jimmy as a possible suspect, although that implication, George believed now, was dead wrong. Two many fingers were pointing in other directions. As for Cole Jackson, George knew only that he evidently had impressed Bennett Taylor as a wrestler, and that he simply was along for the ride, for whatever reason that might be.

"Boys." George nodded, acknowledging the adolescents in a manner that in no way usurped his authority. They were kids.

George then addressed the Taylors, "Mrs. Taylor, Bennett, let's all go into the conference room where we can assess next steps."

With not one further word, the foursome followed the detective into the small room that had been vacated only minutes before by Florence Gray . . . Flo Gray, the high school custodian whose home, according to Jenny Wallis had been ransacked, without question, by her friend, the Taylor's very own daughter.

⌘   ⌘   ⌘

Next steps did not come easily. George Murphy had to be careful. While he had information relevant to the case of missing Courtney Taylor, to this point nothing had been confirmed as hard fact. His sources were sketchy at best: Chester Flack, a broken, winery worker who still lived at home with his elderly mother and Jenny Wallis, a willful teen whose memory had been compromised by the ingestion of God only knew how much alcohol on the night Courtney disappeared. Jenny Wallis clearly had endured an attack by an unknown assailant - that was true, but unfortunately for George Murphy, hazy details of the ordeal had been emerging from her memory at a snail's pace.

How reliable is any of this shit anyway? George was aware he had a long way to go in solving this one . . . a long way, and time was crucial. Every minute that passed threatened Courtney's survival. *There's not enough fucking time.* The accuracy of that reality loomed in George's thoughts unbridled.

⌘   ⌘   ⌘

By the time Bennett and Jill Taylor departed the police station with Jimmy Nelson and Cole Jackson they knew more. And so did George Murphy. George informed the Taylors that two individuals had seen a large and loud, black truck, possibly a diesel, at the scene of the accident; in addition, the same truck had been sighted by one of those persons the next day.

"Someone, a person of interest in the case of Courtney's disappearance," George elaborated, "was seen driving in the vicinity yesterday. We have a vague description." George only revealed to the listeners that a man, seemingly a tall man with long hair, had been spotted driving a black truck out on Bending Vine Road. "The truck was a match of the one seen at the accident site. We have a credible witness."

George chose to add nothing more. The details in regard to the man's evil looking eyes or his rank odor were, to this point, periphery in nature. Sharing that information, George determined, would only muddle the minds of any would-be searchers. Yet, he did have one more bit of news he was obligated to share.

"There is something else you need to know though, Mr. and Mrs. Taylor," he added.

"Spit it out," Bennett snapped. He sighed forcefully and slammed a flat palm on the table in a gesture that indicated he was quite done with this ordeal.

"You need to be aware that your daughter, Courtney, has been implicated in a case of vandalism that occurred inside a local residence on the night of the accident," he stated.

"Oh, that's bull! And why are you bringing up something like that now?" Bennett retorted. "The only matter of importance right now is that my daughter is gone. Missing. Why are you accusing her of a stupid case of vandalism at a time like this? What the hell? Besides, kids vandalize all the time. It's part of growing up."

George was a bit taken aback, but he continued, leaning assertively forward so quickly that Jill was visibly startled, a tiny squeal escaping her mouth.

"This was not a simple case of vandalism," he stated. "The incident, that includes the defacement of personal property, has created a great deal of stress for the victim. A great deal. We need to get to the bottom of this issue as well."

"Oh for God's sake. This is ridiculous," Bennett growled. His face had grown crimson and his hands had clenched into tight fists.

A tense moment of silence ensued before Jimmy squirmed awkwardly in his chair, clearing his throat as he did so. With a voice husky and low he began to speak directly to Detective Murphy for the first time ever.

"Look, Detective, I know you have a ton of things to deal with right now, but for us, for me . . . well, we just need to find Courtney." He suddenly was a lost child. He covered his face with his big hands and began to cry, his wide shoulders shuddering uncontrollably. An anguished moan finally issued from his throat. The room otherwise had grown silent around him, not one person wanting even to breathe, until he looked up once more. "We have to find her, Detective Murphy. She's my best friend. I love her. I've loved her all my life."

"We'll find her, Jimmy. We will." Jill's voice, so often silenced it seemed, was soft, clear, and determined. Instantly she was at Jimmy's side, one arm encircling his broad back and her hand clutching one of his.

George stared at the two, incredulous at what he was observing. *Have I been dead wrong about her? She's stronger than I thought. Maybe beneath the façade, Jill Taylor is rock solid. She'd have to be to handle that jackass she's married to. And thank you God, at least she's found her voice.*

And so had Cole. "Yeah, dude, we will find her, you and me. We'll start now, this minute, and we won't stop," Cole managed.

The bravado Cole had displayed earlier was absent at last. George observed the transformation with awe. These were not the two, surly, young men who had stood behind the Taylors only an hour before. These were friends, united in purpose. George wanted desperately to believe that these kids, amid all the professionals and family participating in the search would be the ones to locate Courtney Taylor, and soon,

"Okay, everyone. Here's the plan. One step at a time."

CHAPTER TWENTY-SIX

SUSAN

A persistent pounding on the front door jarred Susan from her musings. With Jenny resting upstairs, having insisted quite rudely on having her privacy, Susan had slipped into her favorite, faded jeans, an old Hollow Vista High School sweatshirt that Jenny had discarded years before, and padded barefoot into the kitchen. She had eaten a buttered English muffin, savored a cup of milky tea, and had settled in on the living room couch to correct a final set of her students' math notebooks. *One more week to go until blessed summer. Kids are ready. I'm more than ready. God, Jenny is difficult. So much like her father. I've spent two nights and a day waiting on her . . . worried, frightened, caring, all of the above, and she had the audacity to snap at me with a rude, "Leave me alone, Mother, for once. I need some fucking sleep."*

Where had Susan heard those words before? Zach. Of course the demand had been slightly different – *"Leave me alone, Susan, for once. I need some fucking space."* – but the intonation had been identical. In both instances, and in countless others like it, when Zach still had been around, Susan instinctively had cringed and then retreated. And each time, as if on cue, moments afterwards, she had admonished herself for doing so, but by then it was too late. The damage had been done. Zach already had zeroed in on her reaction, noted it, and filed it away, storing it in a dark place until the next time. Zach had learned very quickly on in their relationship that Susan's reaction to insult was withdrawal and that knowledge gave him power. Without fail, in the face of his ranting she lost her voice and sulked away to be alone or to busy herself with a mindless task. And here she was again, huddled alone on the living room couch, having escaped the verbal abuse of her daughter. *Shit. What's wrong with you, Susan?*

Sliding the stack of notebooks to one side, she jumped up, having been startled by the knocking at the front door. She peered through the wide window first, drawing the drape to one side only enough to see who was there. Two young men were slouched against the wooden railing adjacent to the door. Susan did not know their names, but their faces were familiar. *Classmates of Jenny's, I bet.* She opened the door just as the shorter of the two reached forward to knock again.

"Yes?" she questioned.

"Mrs. Wallis? I'm Cole Jackson and this is Jimmy Nelson. We're friends of Jenny."

"And Courtney," the second teen added.

An awkward moment followed before Jimmy spoke again. "Uh, we heard about the accident, and about Courtney, about her missing. My folks and hers have known each other forever. Their ranch is next to our place, outside of town. We were at the police station this morning, meeting with Detective Murphy - you probably know who he is - and Courtney's parents, figuring out how to help. The Taylors are pretty upset."

"I can imagine." Susan face grew warm with a silent shame. No. She had not put herself in the Taylors' place, not for one second. She had been too overwhelmed with Jenny's condition, but at this instant, she was overcome with deep, if latent, compassion. She cleared her throat. "They must be frantic."

"Well, we're going to be searching the area, along with some other people, looking for Courtney, and we need to get going pretty quick, but Cole here, thought maybe we could speak to Jenny first. Is she here?"

"She is, but she is asleep right now. Exhausted. Obviously, as you mentioned, you're aware of the accident, and, well, Jenny was injured by . . . was injured and is pretty emotional about what happened. Courtney's her best friend, you know."

"And mine." Jimmy's voice quavered.

Oh, God. Is he going to cry? "Come in, come in," Susan offered. "Just for a minute. I don't think Jenny is awake and certainly not up for company, but I can mention to her that you are here, just in case. Wait here."

As she began to ascend the stairs, Susan remembered that Jenny had mentioned both Jimmy Nelson and Cole Jackson's names to Detective Murphy, neither with fond regard, if she recalled correctly. Jimmy had been a constant in Courtney's life, the yin and yang of an ill-fated relationship, it had appeared, and Cole, what had Jenny said? *Ah, yes. "He creeps me out," she told George and me. I remember. Even telling Jenny they are here is probably a mistake.*

It was.

Susan pushed open the door to Jenny's room to find her sitting up on the bed, eyes wide open, and her arms crossed protectively across her chest.

"Who the fuck's here?" she asked. "The idiot's pounding woke me up."

"Two guys, Jimmy and Cole. I told them you were asleep, not up for company."

"And that would be right. Jesus, Mom, are they in the house?"

"They are in the living room."

"What the hell? Get them out of here, Mom. I can't bear to see anyone right now. It brings it up. It brings everything back up." Jenny began crying again, this time a silent stream of tears. No noise. No sound.

"I'll get rid of them." Susan responded with abject obedience.

With the door closed firmly behind her, Susan made her way down the stairs to face the unwelcome visitors. She was blunt. "Jenny's not ready to talk to anyone. She needs rest now. You'll need to go."

There was no argument. Jimmy and Cole simply turned and walked toward the door though Susan was sure she heard Cole exhale as if in frustration. *You don't always get what you want, Cole.* The thought came to her with unexpected venom, her innate protectiveness for Jenny having taken hold yet again. *She doesn't like you.*

"Good bye, Mrs. Wallis," Jimmy managed.

"Good bye." And *good luck with the search* she had wanted to say, but the words were strangled in a grip of despair and uncertainty. Saying anything more would have been meaningless.

⌘ ⌘ ⌘

Susan did not return to Jenny's room right away. She didn't have the energy for one more bout with the girl. Instead, she wandered through the kitchen, slid on a pair of well-worn, leather sandals, and walked outside to her garden. The sky had been grey all morning, a combination of low fog and a layer of altostratus clouds that had suggested rain, and although perhaps a drop or two had fallen, the sky was beginning to lighten. *Somewhere up there is the sun. I sure would welcome it.*

Susan tilted her head backward searching the sky for any hint of sunlight, but was disappointed to see only a broad, translucent, silver circle far in the distance. She shivered slightly, just as a sudden, brief gust of wind blustered through the oaks, the prickly leaves grating against one another, fingers on a chalkboard. It was an annoying, screeching noise that flamed her current and escalating state of agitation. She looked around the backyard sensing a presence. *Mother?* It was a foolish thought. Her mother was gone, dead long ago, but if the truth were known, Susan relied on her mother still. She always had trusted her words of wisdom, her uncanny insights, her ability, somehow, to see beyond the now, and her deep belief in nature's subtle messaging. *Your spirit is here, Mama. I know it.* A second gust of wind whistled a mournful sound, low and deep; it whipped Susan's hair into her face at the exact moment she heard the owl. *An owl in the daytime - someone is dying, someone is reaching out from somewhere beyond. Which is it? Are you here to protect me, Mama, to protect Jenny? Is someone dead?* The raptor's hoot was more of a trill, deep and harsh, like a foghorn on a distant shore. It called for minutes, its meaning obscure, ambiguous, but Susan could not take herself from this place, not until, at last, the owl was silent. *It's Courtney, isn't it?*

Susan turned blindly toward the house, her eyes stinging with tears, and in her haste, she stumbled badly, catching herself before she fell. She stopped still to steady herself, her breath coming in gasps, and at that moment she definitely knew she was not alone. From the side of the house a figure advanced. She started at first, until she saw him. In only a moment she found herself looking directly into the dark, worried eyes of George Murphy.

CHAPTER TWENTY-SEVEN

COURTNEY

I'm not going to make it. He was here again, I think. Was he? Wait. Was I dreaming? Yes. No. I'm so confused. Courtney sat perfectly still, her head tilted against the outer wall of the barn. And she remembered. Yes, he had been back, threatening her with menacing aggression from beyond the chained gate. That had been when? *Early morning?* Time was lost. She had begun to perspire and shiver at the same time. Her cheeks burned from the inside out and she slapped at them with icy, cold fingers. *I'm sick. Dizzy. Am I going to die here?*

Panicking, she shifted from a sitting position to her knees. *Stay with it, Courtney. Stay with it.* But her resolve was eradicated by a frightening visage that formed in the air in front of her. Her captor's face, that hideous fiend, suddenly loomed there, a ghostly translucent image that wavered ominously and cackled, "I can do anything I want. Think about that all day, missy."

I'm in a nightmare, a fucking horror show. She was. She knew it. And so far, only Satan had been there to see.

Satan, where are you? It was her final thought before she fell backwards, unconscious, into the hay.

CHAPTER TWENTY-EIGHT

CHESTER

By the time Chester had pulled himself together and was driving down the rural highway once more toward the Nelson ranch, he was behind schedule. *Damn, I'm late and I'll hear about it too. Oh, fuck it. I don't give a shit. I'm doing Conti a favor.*

When Chester finally arrived, James Nelson's initial acknowledgment of him was brusque and rude. "About goddamn time somebody got here," he hissed.

Filled with instant distaste for the ill-mannered man, Chester's instinct was to bite back immediately, but he restrained himself. Instead, he narrowed his eyes, cleared his throat, and heartily spat into a boxwood hedge that bordered the driveway. He then turned to face James Nelson, eyeing him critically. The man was tall with broad shoulders, a cleanly-shaven, chiseled face, and neatly trimmed, snow-white hair. He wore tight blue jeans, a plaid, flannel shirt, and a black, fleecy vest stretched over a distended belly. He oozed affluence.

Immediately upon pulling onto the concrete driveway Chester had noticed Nelson sauntering down a series of wide, stone steps from a spacious veranda at the north end of his massive estate. By the time he addressed Chester though, he had reached the center of the driveway, where he had squared off and stood, legs spread, his face glowering.

"Took you long enough," he added, scowling. "Sure as hell don't have all day."

"Engine stalled," Chester lied. "Took time to tinker with the damn thing."

Nelson harrumphed, clearly not believing. "Look," he snarled, "we have a situation here, so I want this stuff moved off my property immediately. My workers can give you a hand with the heaviest pieces, but the rest is up to you. Need this out of here pronto."

Chester nodded. "I'll get at it," he said flatly although several obscenities, begging to be freed, circled his thoughts. *Jackass.*

As he was moving toward the sizeable pile of barrel staves and myriad, assorted, vineyard equipment, a red Mustang screeched to a stop swerving into a narrow space beside the truck. Two teenagers threw open the doors of the car, slamming them hard behind them. One, a younger version of James Nelson, glanced harshly at Chester as if he was unwelcome, but he said nothing. Instead, he sprinted up the stairs and into the house. The second teen followed more slowly, his shoulders slumped forward as though burdened in thought.

Within moments, the young men, along with James Nelson, exited the house and walked rapidly toward an enormous barn, passing as they did a large corral in which several horses trotted and ambled in random patterns. Though the creatures were majestic, Chester observed them with nervous apprehension. Horses frightened him but he did not know why. Perhaps it was their size, their unpredictability. He was fixated on the animals though, and was stone still, unmoving, when a short, muscular, mustached man advanced toward him.

"Boss says you need help loading this stuff," he said, gesturing toward the pile.

"Yeah, could use it," Chester mumbled, not allowing eye contact with the man.

"Well, let's get at it. Boss wants it out of here pretty quick. Got a bigger situation around here to deal with." The man seemed eager for conversation.

"Yeah, and what's that?" Chester asked.

"Boss's friend's daughter has disappeared. Runaway. Kidnapped. Who the hell knows? Guess folks are gathering here to start up a search party."

Chester's gut tightened. *It's the girl that was in the accident out in front of my place. These folks know her. Well, I'll be damned. Small, fucking world.* An irrational surge of guilt gripped him as it had earlier in the day but he attempted to quash it. *The onus for this shit isn't on me.* He knew he was correct, but the niggling reality was that he had not arrived to the scene of the crash soon enough to stop what surely must have happened next, and therein lay his culpability. He couldn't shake it. *I hid. I hid until it was too damned late.* His thinking exasperated him even more for it was alien. He truly never had cared deeply about another person in his life.

Steeped in discomfort, Chester's eyes began to dart, first from the worker's face and then to the ground, to the sky, to the truck, and finally to the pile of supplies. At last he spoke.

"Yeah, heard something in town this morning about a girl missing," he admitted.

"Yeah, she's the Taylor kid. Taylor's property butts up against the Nelson's. The families have been friends forever. Loaded. They're always partying and traveling together here, there, and God knows where else," he added, his voice edged with smug authority.

"Well, hope someone finds her," Chester replied tersely before turning to the task of loading the truck. "Better get humping on this job."

He said not another word, working in a needless fury, until the job was nearly complete . . . only one final pallet left. He had grabbed a few staves from the pile and was turning to throw them into the truck when he noticed something odd. Propped behind the remaining stack of equipment, and tucked beneath a plastic tarpaulin, he discovered an old, scratched guitar.

"What the devil's this guitar doing here?" he asked.

"Ah, one of the workers found it in one of the old, dilapidated outbuildings at the other end of Nelson's property where all this stuff was stored. Hell, the barn where this equipment was piled up hasn't been used for years. Guitar was leaning up against all this other shit like it belonged there. Guy who found it says he grabbed it thinking it might be of value, but it's not worth anything. Out of tune, a string missing, spine cracked. The thing is just junk as far as I can see. You can toss it. I'm sure the boss doesn't want it," the ranch hand said.

"I don't want the damn thing either," Chester answered, "I'll throw it away in the dumpster back at the winery. Least it'll be out of your hair."

"Yeah, that works," the man agreed. "Well, looks like you can handle the rest of this. I'm off to work with the horses. Have a good one."

"Yeah," Chester said to the man's back. The one-word response was barely audible.

With the truck fully loaded, Chester climbed into the driver's seat, planted the damaged guitar on the floorboard, and backed out of the driveway. In the distance he saw that several more people had gathered by the entrance of the barn beyond the corral. Three all terrain vehicles were lined up in front.

Guess they'll be fanning out all over the countryside to see what they can discover. If anyone were to ask me I'd say it'd be a dead one.

⌘ ⌘ ⌘

Chester drove home before heading back to work. He had left his lunch box at the winery, but home was closer, and he was starving. *Mother will have some sort of shit stewing up on the stove. At least old Bertha still cooks for me. Hell, that's about all she's good for any more. I have to wonder sometimes when she'll finally give it up and say, "Done with you" to her despicable life. Ah, shit. Focus Chester.*

Maneuvering the stake side truck down the lane to his house was more difficult for Chester than driving his old pick-up there. The winery vehicle was wider, heavier, and seemed drawn to every pothole, many of which had deepened during the rainy, winter months. Chester's entire body shifted from side to side as the vehicle's tires slammed into countless ruts and holes; he gripped the steering wheel with both hands to keep the truck from shifting sideways, instead forcing it forward toward his house. *Shit! Damned truck!* Of course, in his mind, the truck was to blame for his difficulty. He did not consider for one second the fact that he was driving much too fast and that speed on the crumbling country lane had a definite bearing on the rough ride. *Don't know how the hell I'll get this damned thing turned around once I get to the house. There's not enough blasted space. Damn, I shouldn't have come down this way. Stupid. Should have gone straight to the winery.* He was so distracted by his thoughts that he nearly rammed into a little Honda parked adjacent to the front gate. *Shit! Who the hell is here?* He threw the truck into park, unthinkingly grabbed the guitar that had been knocking from side to side on the floorboard, and jumped from the truck. He opened the front gate, strode rapidly up the walkway to the wooden porch and came to a dead stop. He was face to face with Florence Gray who stood just inside the door.

"What the devil are you doing here and where in the hell is my fucking mother?" he asked crudely.

"I'm right here. Don't be so damned cantankerous, Chester Flack," his mother, Bertha, barked, her voice cracking like splintering glass.

She stepped from behind Flo and glared through the screen at her son. "What are you doing home this time of day, what kind of monstrosity did you drive up here, and what the devil do you have there?" Bertha's questions spewed out one on top of the other in quick succession.

"I'm hungry," he replied, ignoring Bertha's other queries. "You got something cooking in there?"

He looked at his mother's weepy eyes, so deeply sunken into her wrinkled face, and wondered how she could see at all. Then he turned to Flo. "And what are you doing here?" he snapped for a second time.

"I came to tell your mother, and you for that matter, though I doubt you'd care a hoot, about my house being ..." She stopped in mid-sentence, her gaze falling to the guitar in Chester's hand.

"What are you doing with that?" Flo asked, her voice a squeak. "That's mine. That's mine. That's my father's guitar. How did you get it?"

"I found it. It's a piece of shit," Chester told her.

Flo ignored his vulgar elaboration. "Found it? Where? It's mine. It was stolen from my house. Give it to me."

She reached for the instrument but Chester maintained his grip, obstinately pulling it away from her. He was unconscious of why he made the move, but Bertha, always observant of her son, knew instinctively. The hateful and insensitive action on Chester's part, as subtle as it may have appeared, was borne from an innate meanness. Both she and he had been burdened with his callous disposition since his birth.

"Chester Flack, what are you doing? That guitar's not yours and you know it," Bertha admonished.

"So. And how do I know she's telling the truth?"

Flo bristled at his insult. "It is mine. It belonged to my father before he died. It's all I have that was his, Chester. Now, give it to me."

Reluctantly he shoved the guitar toward Flo who grabbed it by the neck with both hands. One of the strings vibrated with her touch, a sound emanating deep and lifeless. She glanced down at the instrument as if to make sure she was miraculously holding it once more and then she looked up at Chester who towered over her.

"And you'd better tell me now, right now, where you found this, because it was stolen, Chester, right out of my house. Did you take it?" Flo believed, without a doubt, that

Chester Flack was not above stealing from her or anyone else.

"I didn't steal your stupid guitar. Who would want the damned thing anyway? It's a piece of crap," Chester replied.

"It may not be in perfect shape, but it's important to me. It belonged to my father," she said again.

"Where'd you get it?" she added.

"I told you, I found it."

"Chester!" Flo was frustrated by his evasiveness. "Where? Where did you find it?"

"Hell, Flo. What difference does it make? You have the damn thing back."

"It makes a difference to Flo, Chester. Isn't that enough?" Bertha declared, inserting her opinion, as best she could, into the baffling conversation that, to her way of thinking, was going nowhere.

"Look." Flo began speaking again. "I came by here today, Chester, trying to be a decent neighbor, to tell you and your mother that my house was vandalized and my father's guitar, this guitar, was stolen." Flo clutched the guitar possessively before continuing. "Besides that, a number of my husband's paintings were damaged, some destroyed completely, and well, I've been quite upset. Had the police over, went to the police department to file a formal report, and well, I wanted to give you folks a heads up that somebody is up to no good around here."

"So that's why I saw you there," Chester said.

"Where?"

"At the police department."

"I didn't know you noticed me, but I'm pretty sure I saw you brush by and rush in there like you were on a mission of some kind. Why were you at the police department Chester?" Flo was bewildered.

"Oh, I was there for a reason all of my own," Chester disclosed, suddenly growing irrationally irritated to be caught up in this conversation. He clinched his teeth together hard, the muscles of his jaws visibly working in response. His eyes narrowed, he shoved clinched fists into his pockets, and he took a giant step backward. *Retreat. Retreat.* The current situation – being confronted by a woman he hardly knew – had thrown him off balance. It took him back in time, to many times, when he had felt as he was feeling now, trapped in a snare, being rebuked by someone – a teacher, an authority figure, the parent of a classmate, a bullied student who had finally found a voice, a parent, yes, a now very dead parent. In every instance when Chester had felt cornered, anger had overwhelmed him, crushing any ability to reason. Burdened by his fury, his instinct always had been to run, to put distance between himself and the perceived antagonist who sought to set him straight. He began to fidget like a captured criminal. *Need to get the fuck out of here. Shit. I should have gone straight back to work. But, hell, how could I have known Florence Gray was going to be here gabbing with Mother?*

As if purposely fueling his anxiety, Flo would not let up. "Where'd you find the guitar, Chester?"

He gave in to her. "I found it at the Nelson ranch outside of town this morning. Old man, Conti, my supervisor, sent me there to pick up a stash of vineyard equipment Mr. Nelson wanted to get rid of. It's the stuff piled in the stake side there. Anyway, while I was loading up I noticed a guitar propped up on a pallet of barrel staves. One of the ranch workers had found it in a barn where this equipment was being stored. Guess he figured it didn't belong to anybody so he grabbed it. Think he would have kept it if it had been in better shape. Told me to get rid of it."

Chester fell silent then. He was finished. Done. Or so he thought.

"Wait," Flo said, cocking her head to one side. "Something's wrong."

"There's a lot seems to be wrong," Bertha blurted.

"Wait," Flo repeated, speaking to Chester. "The Nelson ranch you said? They have a kid, Jimmy Nelson. He goes to Hollow Vista High." She paused and turned to Bertha. "Don't know if you know this, Mrs. Flack, but I work at Hollow Vista. Custodian. I know a bunch of the kids there, some by name, some by face, and right now I'm thinking something's odd here. Seems another student, Courtney Taylor, who hangs out in the same group that Jimmy Nelson does, has disappeared. Was told about it this morning at the police station. Have you heard about that?"

"Why, no," Bertha said, her hand covering her mouth, at the exact second Chester spoke once more.

"Yeah. I know about it. I know more than I want to know about it."

"Chester?" Bertha turned on him, accusing with a word.

"Mother." Chester's body stiffened, the troubling feeling of responsibility and guilt cloying with his conscience again. "Remember the accident Saturday night down at the end of the lane? I told you about hearing a crash, checking it out."

"Oh, dear, Chester. I don't remember anything like that. What happened?"

Chester sighed. His poor mother could name every doll and pet she ever had owned and she bored him with countless memories of adventures in her childhood, but she couldn't tell him what happened yesterday, or earlier the same day for that matter. *Not a good sign.* With as little elaboration as possible Chester related his knowledge of the incident involving a young woman's car accident and her subsequent disappearance. At Chester's mention of seeing a truck at the scene, Flo blanched.

"I'm sure I heard a truck too, near my place right after it was ransacked. I was a little groggy because I had been in a deep sleep, but once I was fully awake, every sense was alert. I remember distinctly hearing a truck screech onto the highway that night. I told Officer Sanchez as much. Could it have been the same one?"

The trio stood silent for a few seconds. Finally, Flo spoke once more. "There's a connection, Chester, between the accident and the vandalism at my place. There has to be, because I also found out this morning that the Taylor girl has been linked to my case. Someone, I'm not sure who, has implicated her as the vandal. But the truck . . . I'm confused about how the truck fits in."

"I don't know about that, but I'm about to add more shit to the stew," Chester revealed. "See, the reason I was at the police station this morning is because I saw the truck that left the accident site another time, the day after, and I caught a glimpse of the driver, too. A man. Long hair. I didn't want a thing more to do with this damned mess, but had to tell the cops 'cause, well, because, I couldn't get any fucking sleep and shit, a girl's missing. Police know."

Flo's mouth had opened, her jaw slack. She shifted her feet slightly and her hand shot up to finger the black mole on her cheek before she spoke. "So the accident was Saturday night, same night someone sneaked into my house. Sunday you saw the truck again, and today my father's guitar turns up out on the Nelson ranch. There has to be some kind of connection. And besides, I know for a fact that Jimmy Nelson and the Taylor girl hang out at school. I've seen them together many times."

"Yeah? Makes sense they'd be together. Ranch worker told me this morning that the Nelsons and the Taylors are friends. Do shit together all the time. That's probably why a search party was formed this morning, out at the Nelson place. Folks are looking for the missing Taylor girl now," Chester responded.

"Sure wish I could help somehow," Flo murmured wistfully. *I shouldn't care. Courtney's a spoiled, little bitch. She was cruel to me.*

"Why would you want to help find her when she's maybe the one who messed up your place?" Chester asked.

"Don't know really. Guess it's my weak point. She has parents. Parents love their kids, don't they, Mrs. Flack? The Taylors must be frantic. I know my parents would have gone crazy with worry if they'd lost sight of me, except that didn't happen. I lost them instead, but that's another story." Flo's shoulder's slumped forward and her gaze fell to her shoes.

Bertha ventured a step closer to Flo, took her hand, and patted it repeatedly. "It'll turn out," she croaked. "You just wait and see." Though Bertha was losing her mental faculties at a rapid pace now that she had topped ninety, remarkably she retained an innate empathy for the feelings of others. Flo was sad. Bertha had no idea why; nor was she clear what it was that would *turn out*, but a pat on the hand had seemed apropos.

Frowning, Chester watched the interaction between the two women. *What the hell?* He shook his head from side to side before abruptly brushing past them into the kitchen. "Need some chow," he muttered curtly.

As he sat alone at the kitchen table, Chester mulled over the conversation with Florence Gray. His thoughts became a battleground. *Fucking women. Instead of dealing with shit they get all sentimental. Hell. So she lost her parents. So? Lost. She can't even say the word. It's die, Flo! Everybody's parents die. What's the big deal? And who knows what the Taylors think about their kid. Maybe they can't stand her. Been known to happen. I know that one for a fact.*

A ghastly visage of his father's corpse instantly emerged in front of him and he gawked at it stupefied. Herbert Flack's body, bloody and stiff, hovered in a wavering haze. His face was chalk white and his eyes and mouth were open wide in surprise or fright. Perhaps it was both.

Served him right, the son of a bitch. Parents love their kids? Bullshit. It's only right that people get what they deserve, isn't it? Maybe that Taylor girl is getting just what she deserves too. Looks like she was a spoiled brat to me, driving her own BMW at seventeen, living in a fucking mansion, out boozing it up, fucking up other people's lives, fucking up my life. Why should I feel guilty? Damned little bitch. And why is Flo all jacked up about this girl? Who gives a shit? Thought all Flo cared about was getting her stupid guitar back. You'd think it was a prize. Christ. What a piece of shit. Like mother.

Instantaneously, as though shoving her husband, Herbert, into oblivion to gain the upper hand, Bertha Flack's image appeared. Chester fixed on the mirage of his mother - a tiny, shriveled body, hollow eyes, sallow, wrinkled skin. She gestured at her son reprovingly and she sneered, her open mouth revealing a coated tongue and missing teeth. Her boney fingers rose to her lips and she blew him a kiss, filling the space between them with the foul and reeking breath of a dying soul. He gagged.

Is old Bertha dying? How long is she going to hold on? Christ, forever. She's a pain in my ass half the time. Parents love their kids, Flo? They have funny ways of showing it. They sure have funny ways of showing it, don't they, Bertha Flack? You, sure as hell, should know something about that.

Chester started from his musings. He surveyed the empty kitchen as though fearing a witness to his thinking was lurking in some corner. *Damn, enough of this, Chester. Get your head on straight. You've got work to do.*

Awash in perspiration, Chester left the kitchen and walked into the hallway. He noticed that Flo Gray's car was gone, and that his mother was propped up in her rocking chair in the living room, sound asleep, her mouth open in a wide oval. Her hands lay in her lap like dead birds. He looked around the room, somewhat dazed, the familiarity of the place smothering him. He was drained, for he had been drawn into too much exhausting conversation this day and it had not set well. Recovering his wits would take time. He knew it. It was far from irrational then that when Chester left his property in the early afternoon to return to work he took with him two items: a butcher knife with an eight-inch blade and his hunting rifle. And why? He could not have justified *why* to anyone.

CHAPTER TWENTY-NINE

FLO

Instead of going back to work after departing from Chester Flack's house, Flo drove straight to the heart of tiny Hollow Vista where the police station, a small, community, medical facility, the morgue, and the post office were lined up in a row. She parked in front of the police station and ambled up the steps into the lobby. Behind the glass partition she saw Janice Cochran sipping from a can of soda while talking animatedly to young Officer Sanchez. Flo had no idea what the two were discussing, of course, but it must have been an intense topic because neither of them looked in her direction for a full minute. She watched Janice's free hand gesturing, her index finger shaking in a furious motion as if she were scolding a naughty youngster. Officer Sanchez looked down on Janice, his face serious, before it transformed completely; he grinned broadly and broke into a hardy chuckle. It wasn't until then that he saw Flo, looking, she imagined, like a forlorn child wondering in which direction to turn, for if the truth were told, that is exactly how she felt.

"Mrs. Gray." Partially muted by the partition, her name was a whisper.

She nodded at the officer and summoned him to the window. Before he could take a step, however, Janice took command. "How may I help you?" she asked.

"Oh, yes, Mrs. Gray. You were here earlier," she added, scowling.

"Yes, I was." Flo's reply was terse. She had met Janice initially that same morning and while the woman had been professional, she had imparted a condescending edge that had made Flo's neck flush with prickly heat; now, for a second time, Janice looked at Flo as if she were an annoying nuisance that she would have to handle yet again. Her lips pursed and one knotted fist dug into her hip. She tucked her chin downward and raised an eyebrow as if to say, "So, get on with it," though she uttered not one more word.

"I'd like to speak with Officer Sanchez, if I might. I have some new information about my case. He'll want to know," Flo stated.

"I'll have to see if he has time, right now," Janice said, glancing toward Officer Sanchez who had retreated to the back corner of the front office. "Wait," she demanded, turning her back toward Flo.

Why do some people make life so difficult? Flo wanted an answer in the worst way. *First was the alarming, home invasion, next the discovery of a robbery, then that ludicrous conversation with Chester Flack and his poor mother, and now this – a haughty bitch with the bearing of a badger.* Flo bit her lip. *Christ. Officer Sanchez is right there, Janice. Just get him.*

Fortunately for Flo, Officer Sanchez did make time for her. As he ushered her into the same conference room where they had spoken earlier that day, Flo glanced back at Janice who was shuffling through a stack of papers, while her eyes focused directly on the conference room door. The young officer noticed Janice as well and was astute enough to sense Flo's discomfort in the face of the woman's brusqueness and watchful eye.

"Don't worry about Janice Cochran, Mrs. Gray," he assured Flo in a hushed voice. "She apparently has been running the show around here for years. I've barely gotten use to her myself. She comes off a little impolite sometimes, I know, but don't take her disposition too seriously. She won't bite. Now, what can I do for you?"

"I only need you to listen for a minute, Officer," Flo said once she was seated. "First, you need to know that I have my father's guitar back."

Office Sanchez's eyes widened and he cocked his head in surprise, but he said nothing; instead, he listened quietly as Flo explained why she had stopped by the Flack house on her way home for lunch – for the simple reason to let Chester and his mother know about the home invasion. "I was only trying to be neighborly and warn them to beware," she said before expounding on details of her conversation with Chester Flack.

"So that's it," she said as though she were finished; yet she continued talking. "I'm no detective, officer, but there are some strange connections, seems to me. I was sure you needed to know that Chester found my father's guitar out at the Nelson ranch this morning. That's one problem solved, but the fact that Chester says he found it where he did seems odd to me, because Jimmy Nelson and the Taylor girl, the missing girl, are friends. They run in the same crowd. I've seen them with the same bunch at the high school many times. And Chester Flack told me he'd learned from a ranch hand today that the Nelsons and Taylors are as thick as thieves. And they've formed a search party. Did you know that?"

Officer Sanchez nodded. "I was aware. In fact I'm heading out to the Nelson property as soon as we're finished here."

"Well, I sure hope someone finds the Taylor girl. It's such a shame. Everything that has happened this weekend is so confusing, and I'm concerned because somebody out there, and God only knows who, has been playing a big hand in the whole mess. My head's swimming trying to put two and two together."

Flo looked at the officer as if he surely had a logical answer for her, but he only sought to console her. "Look, Mrs. Gray, try not to worry. We have a team of professionals and other folks working as hard as they can to find the Taylors' daughter. The information you've provided is very helpful, and thank you for coming in, but now, go on home. Get some rest. A member of our support staff will be coming by later. Did you remember that?"

She had not, but she indicated with a nod that she had. "I should be there," she said. "Thank you."

The officer escorted Flo to the door to the lobby. "Take care, Mrs. Gray. It'll all turn out," he said.

Turn out. There were those words again, sliding so easily from the mouths of Bertha Flack and Officer Sanchez, two people as different as black and white. Flo cringed. *Empty words. Turn out? Turn out, how? Am I to assume that "turn out" means something good will happen or will it turn out to be another tragedy? God knows I've suffered through enough of those.* Like a sad song, the mindless phrase – *It'll turn out* - played in Flo's mind until she was home. Alone there, she imagined the possibilities. It was not pretty.

⌘ ⌘ ⌘

Absorbed with her disconcerting imaginings, Flo wandered to the back bedroom where her husband's paintings were stored. Countless oils and acrylics were propped against each other in random disarray, a few pastels and pen and ink drawings were tacked to the walls, and hundreds of other sketches were piled in stacks on a drawing table, having been untouched since Randall's death. The soggy mess of slashed and shredded pieces that had been thrown in a heap on the floor, however, captured Flo's attention once more. Looking at the damage, an absolute desecration to her way of thinking, made her heart ache. She swayed sideways, suddenly dizzy, but regained her balance by grabbing the doorjamb at the same second she heard a pounding at her door. She flinched. *Oh damn, someone from the police department.* She was wrong.

Through the window she spotted a dirty, red pick-up truck, its front bumper jammed against her fence. *Chester Flack?* It had to be.

When she opened the door, Chester stood before her looking a sight wearing his camouflaged pants and jacket, a filthy, hunting cap, and holding a rifle, pointed fortunately toward the ground. He said nothing, but glared at her as though she were the enemy, his deeply set, black eyes boring in on her.

She addressed him sternly. "What are you doing here, Chester?"

"Thought about what you said," he managed, his lip bulging with a wad of tobacco. "Went back to work this afternoon and, goddamn it, couldn't get a lick done, so I fibbed to old Conti, my boss. Told him I was sick and high-tailed it out of there. First time in my life I've done that." He shuffled his feet nervously before he continued. "Goddamn it, Flo, I don't want any part of this shit, but every direction I turn, someone is dragging me back into it."

"What are you talking about, Chester?" she asked.

Chester Flack never could have revealed the turmoil in his gut, the feeling of responsibility, however irrational, that had continued to pester him since the night of the accident. *I ought to have moved in faster. Done something.* The thoughts had been relentless, but they were his alone. Never would he disclose a revelation of remorse, of plain, ordinary shame, to a woman he hardly knew. It would be a sign of weakness. It would be crazy. Even his mother had been denied. So he lied. "You said there was a connection somehow between me finding your old man's guitar out on the Nelson ranch and the disappearance of that girl. Why do you think that, Flo? It doesn't make sense."

She looked at him blankly, suddenly confused herself as to why she had made the connection. "I'm not sure," she said. "It's a gut feeling, that's all. Courtney's been implicated in the vandalism, the guitar was stolen, and then it was found at the home of her friend. How did it get there, Chester? Who put it there?"

"I don't know, but I'm ready to look into it," he said. *The fact is I have to look into it.*

"What in the world are you talking about?" Flo frowned and crossed her arms across her chest in a gesture of self-protection.

"I'm talking about driving around, doing a search of my own. Can't hurt. Guess I'm thinking the more folks out there combing the area, the better." Chester shuffled his feet once more and looked down at the porch. His stomach was knotting uncomfortably, and he clinched his hand tighter on the rifle as though loosening his grip would release his secret. Finally he looked up.

"Look, at my house today I heard you say you wished you could do something to help the girl's family because they had to be desperate, or some shit like that. Hell, I don't give a good goddamn about those people, but you got me to thinking. So, hell, I thought about it and decided, damn, I'll have a look myself. I stopped by cause I wondered if you might want to come with me . . . to look for her . . . seeing as how you wanted to help." There. He had done it. In Chester's own, bumbling manner, he had asked.

Flo was baffled by the invitation but somewhat intrigued as well. But Chester Flack was crazy. Everyone in town thought so. How smart would she be to pile into Chester's truck with him and drive off to God only knew where? The question lingered momentarily, but in a twist of unbridled fate, rationality eluded her.

"Let me get my jacket and lock up," she blurted.

Within minutes Flo had strapped herself into the front seat of Chester's pick-up, in the place that had been his mother, Bertha's alone for years. Chester revved the engine, took a sideways glance at Flo Gray, and spat out the window. She grabbed the door handle with one hand, the seat belt with the other, and braced her feet on the floorboard. She knew what was coming.

"What the hell, Flo," he shouted above the noise of the motor. "Let's see where the fucking road takes us."

And with that, he stomped on the gas pedal and sped away, a cloud of gravel and dirt left in the wake of his truck.

Flo gritted her teeth, scrunched up her shoulders, and stared straight at the roadway. *Good grief, Flo Gray. What mess have you gotten yourself into now?*

CHAPTER THIRTY

GEORGE

He was unsure why he did it. He did not have time. He imagined the Taylors waiting. Jill would be upset, sniffling into a handkerchief, her face forlorn, while ruddy-cheeked Bennett Taylor would be irate, pacing and cursing under his breath. They were expecting him at the Nelson ranch any minute to confer about the search for their daughter. But he was close. And it was easy to rationalize. *It's a check-in visit . . . on Jenny. What is wrong with that?*

George steered his car onto the long driveway that would take him to Susan Wallis's house. The trek had gained new familiarity to him and as he neared the two-story structure he experienced an odd contentment. Once parked by the gate, he stepped from his car, walked quickly to the front door, and knocked softly so as not to awaken Jenny, who surely still would be resting after her ordeal. He fully expected the door to be opened immediately, but when it was not, after several more taps, he stepped back surveying the front porch and yard. It was eerily quiet. He ventured from the covered entryway and peered around the side of the house. Far in the distance he saw her. Susan was standing alone in her garden, her eyes cast upward to the sky that swirled with threatening, grey clouds. He watched her there, wondering what she was observing for she was a statue, still, dark, and silhouetted by muted light from the sky. An owl called, its hoot an extended, mournful cry. George shuddered at the exact instant Susan moved. She ducked her head, twirled around in his direction, and began running. The wind caught her hair and whipped it across her face. He watched her stumble, stop, and then lope forward, her head still facing downward until at last she looked up only feet away from him. Her cheek was smudged with dirt, her lips trembling, and her brown eyes glassy with tears. The moment she recognized it was George in the shadows, she began to cry, real tears that told him more than he was prepared to understand. *She is so sad, vulnerable, and, oh God, so beautiful.* His heart quivered, an alien, perhaps forgotten sensation that unnerved him. And he knew. *I'm falling in love with this woman.*

They faced each other, only inches apart, he looking down at her face and she, in reciprocating fashion gazing at him, her weeping silent. And in that moment, he instantly was afraid, fearful of touching her, yet too anxious not to reach out. As though any semblance of control had escaped him, he extended his hand and stroked her gently on the arm. She did not move away. Instead, she leaned forward, resting the side of her face and one flat palm on his chest. His arm was around her instantly and he pulled her entire body to him.

"Oh Susan," he whispered, resisting an instinct to kiss her on the top of her head.

"George," she murmured, her voice muffled against his chest. "I heard a daylight owl, and I'm so scared. I'm not sure we'll ever see Courtney again."

He could feel her shiver. "We're going to find her. We are," he assured her. "Come on, let's go inside."

She turned her body but did not pull away from him. With his arm still around her, he slowly guided her toward the back, screened porch, and as they walked, her hand moved up to the hollow of his broad back. In the brief silence that followed both must have come to terms with what was happening to them, for once inside, he drew her to him once again and held her, unspeaking. She had stopped crying by then, her fear and silence curbed and replaced by an inexplicable, floating sensation.

"I'm not sure what to say," she whispered.

"Say nothing," he told her. "Nothing."

He parted from her only enough to touch her chin with his fingers, and then he kissed her, once on the forehead, and then again, full and lingering, on her lips. When he pulled away, her eyes remained closed for a moment and then she opened them and stepped back, her cheeks tingeing pink.

George's face was serious. "Well, Susan Wallis, I guess we may be entering new territory," he said. "I hope I haven't been too impetuous."

"No. No, it's perfect," she replied. "I've been thinking that it – our meeting each other, I mean – might evolve in time. I had hopes it could."

He perused her face. "You are a beautiful woman, Susan, but you have to know that when I turned into your driveway today, this is not what I remotely imagined would happen. That's not to say I'm not glad it did though." A touch of a smile crossed his lips before he continued. "We can't put the reason we met aside, especially not now, but I have to say that for me, being with you today, though unanticipated, is an amazing positive in the recent change of events around here."

Susan smiled.

"And it is so nice to see you smile instead of cry," he added.

"Yeah, sorry about that," she said. "I've been teary all day." She paused. "George, why did you stop by? You usually phone first."

"I'm not sure. I thought I could check on Jenny and I wanted to see you. Simple."

"I like that."

"And now, I have to leave. I'm late already. A search party has been organized at the Nelson ranch. Another officer is overseeing the operation, but I need to check in. The Taylors will expect it. They've demanded it, in fact." George's face had become serious. He continued, "And Jenny's okay?"

"She is getting back to her old self," Susan told him. "She becoming more challenging by the hour and, to be honest, has been a bit rude to me. When she needs me, she has no problem having me cater to her, but now that she's feeling a little better, she's regained that inherited edginess and a mind of her own. I spent some time outside to get away after the boys left."

"Boys?"

"Two young men showed up asking to see Jenny. Jimmy Nelson and Cole Jackson. Friends. Jenny wanted no part of them though. Told me to send them away. That was this morning."

"I actually met those two early this morning at the station. The Taylors had them in tow," George revealed. "Teenagers - hard to figure out sometimes."

"Amen to that," Susan agreed.

"Look, I'd love to stay here, but I really have to get going. May I call you later?"

"Of course."

"I have no idea when it will be, when I can call, but I will. You're okay, right?" he asked.

She nodded.

"Stay inside. Lock up," he said before reaching for her once more and kissing her quickly.

He was out the door before she could reply. She stood at the window, watching.

"Bye," she whispered as he drove away. "Bye, for now, George Murphy."

⌘   ⌘   ⌘

George was correct. When he arrived at James Nelson's ranch, Bennett Taylor was loaded for bear. George saw him first, pacing the Nelsons' veranda and wearing what looked to be garb fit for a safari – a wide, floppy-brimmed hat complete with chin strap, a poplin, multi-pocketed, bush jacket, and bloused pants tucked into tall, black, leather boots. The bland, khaki color of his apparel was a stark contract to Bennett's face that was only a shade lighter than deep, current red.

Holy shit. What a get-up. George could not refrain from judging and wondering what the reasoning was behind Bennett's attire. *Is this a game to him? Surely it's not.*

"Where in the hell have you been?" Bennett snarled. "You should have rolled in here half an hour ago."

George tensed. Though he fleetingly considered the notion that his visit to Susan, had anyone else known, might be deemed an impropriety on his part, he was not sorry for it; nor did he have any intention of offering an excuse for his tardiness to this blowhard. "I spoke to Officer Sanchez. It looks as though the search is underway as planned, and I'm assuming you will be joining a group."

"No, no. I have no intention of traipsing around the countryside. That's a job for younger people and, of course, for law enforcement, which points to the obvious fact that you're not already out there doing your job scouring the county in search for my missing daughter." Bennett fanned his arm in the direction of a distant, brush-covered hillside as he continued. "Hell, a shitload of other folks, unlike you, have been gone for an hour or two, hell bent on locating Courtney. The fact that you're still standing around here . . . now, that's a shocker to me. I don't mind telling you. Time to do your job, Murphy," Bennett declared.

"Watch yourself, Bennett. You'd better just stand back for a second. And be careful of accusing me of not doing my job," George retorted. He detested the fact that Bennett Taylor's bearing provoked him, but it did. He was aware that with every minute in the presence of the man, he was growing more and more incensed. Apropos to Bennett's character, however, the man ignored George's comment as if he had not even heard it and continued on, focusing again on himself.

"Besides I have Jill to contend with right now. Woman's a basket case. She kept me awake half the night with her blubbering. 'Goddamn it, Jill,' I told her, 'Shut that shit up or else.' Brought her over here so Nelson's old lady can take a shift in dealing with Jill's ridiculous behavior for a while. Christ." Bennett looked at George then as if he were an old friend and actually chuckled. "Goddamn, old man, I could use a couple of stiff drinks and some sleep."

For a rare moment in his life, George Murphy had to search for a response, so appalled was he by the man before him. Finally he decided simply to agree with Bennett, although he could not abstain from edging his words with sarcasm. "Yeah Bennett, sounds like a drink is exactly what you need. A good old-fashioned shot in a moment of crisis is sure to do the trick. Got to take care of first things first, right? And as for me, I'm talking off. No need for me to waste any more of your time by hanging around. Besides, I need to get going so I can do my job."

George turned his back to Bennett, took the steps down to the driveway two at a time and slid into the front seat of his squad car. Through his rear view mirror he could see that Bennett had turned away as well and was sauntering back toward the Nelsons' residence. His shoulders were thrown back and his arms swung at his sides in wide arcs as if he didn't have a care in the world.

Amazing, simply amazing. George watched in abhorrence, chewing his lip and nodding his head from side to side until Bennett had disappeared completely from view. It was not until then that he started and revved the engine. He maneuvered slowly back onto the highway at the exact moment he was certain he heard the distant roar of another vehicle. He looked in the direction of the sound and noticed instantly a black truck rounding a wide bend not half a mile down the road.

CHAPTER THIRTY-ONE

SUSAN

Though it was not yet dusk, the cloud shrouded skies made it appear so. The living room was dark, cold, uninviting. Susan turned toward the staircase and ascended slowly, dreading another bout with Jenny. At the girl's bedroom door, she stopped. She could hear nothing, not even the of soft resonance of music that routinely filled the room. Susan pushed open the door, peered inside, and immediately was met with a muffled outburst.

"Leave me alone, Mother. Shit. I told you I need some fucking space. Go away!" Jenny's entire body was buried beneath the blankets, her head barely visible and turned to the side on a thick pillow that deadened the sound of her voice.

"Will you be wanting something to eat soon?" Susan asked, regretting immediately that she had posed the question.

"Hell no. I'm already nauseous, Mom. You know that. The thought of food really makes me want to puke. And I hurt all over. Shit, Mom. I just want sleep. I just want to forget. Go away. Leave me alone for once."

Susan did not reply. She simply shut the door, this time with a sharp snap that left a not so subtle message of her own. *Oh, Jenny. You make me weary.* How many times had she muttered the same phrase under her breath, except to Zach? *Ah, she's a carbon copy of him in so many ways. She has no concern whatsoever about how I'm feeling. It's as though I'm a non-entity to her as I was to him. That's unless she wants something.*

⌘ ⌘ ⌘

After the interaction with Jenny, Susan had lost her own appetite, but she forced herself to nibble a few crackers with Brie cheese, before returning to the stack of ungraded student notebooks still piled on the couch. She was disgusted with herself for having not finished her work earlier. *I'll give the rest a quick perusal and slap a grade on them, the higher the better.* Such an approach toward correcting her students' work was unusual for Susan, but she wanted the task over and done. She was exhausted from her worries about Jenny and Courtney but, moreover, satiated with the memory of George Murphy's kiss. Concentration eluded her. She had leafed through only two notebooks when her mind began to wander and she was back in George's arms. *Delicious.* She closed her eyes hoping for George's image to linger there, but fatefully that did not happen. Instead the face of Zach Wallis, the husband who had left her stranded and vulnerable so many years before, surged into focus. And she knew why. Jenny. Her daughter's behavior had ramped up her tension. It was the identical feeling of anxiety with which she had existed for years before Zach's departure. From the beginning, Zach's mercurial nature had strained their marriage. Seldom was he positive or upbeat. On the contrary, he was usually either silent and reclusive or angry, hurling insults and unjustified verbal abuse at Susan who often was blindsided by his unpredictable and unfounded hostility. After Jenny was born, Zach's sustained silences, juxtaposed with his acute pugnaciousness, became an everyday norm, and Jenny was present to see . . . to see, to learn, and to mimic. While Jenny had moments of normalcy, she was prone to tantrums, often hurling herself onto the floor, throwing her toys, and shrieking as loudly as she could. She also pouted. It was not unusual to watch her transform into a silent, brooding brat - her lower lip jutting out, her arms tight across her belly, her hands in fists, and her eyes menacingly fixed on the object of her ire. Following Zach's departure, when Jenny was eleven, her bouts of anger subsided. The negative standard by which she had modeled her conduct had disappeared from sight and she was forced to look to her mother for guidance. Susan, being the exact opposite of her husband in personality, exemplified restraint, respect, kindness, and spirituality. In time, Jenny's manners followed suit, although she remained headstrong and edgy at times . . . like now.

Why doesn't she just get the hell out of here? Susan flinched and swallowed hard, appalled by her own thinking. Yet she understood. Jenny's belligerent attitude had contributed to Susan's conjuring of the phrase, lifted as it were, from a file in her memory, for those were the words she had muttered over and over when Zach was at his worst. *Why doesn't he get the hell out of here?* Though she had loved Zach on some level, she had detested him as well and often had wondered, with the two emotions prominently existing at the same time, which would win out? *Well, Zach took care of that.* She never had to choose because eventually he was gone. In the aftermath, she let go of both - love first, and then the hate. In his case, neither was worth hanging onto. With Jenny, however, Susan's sentiments were much different. Her love for her daughter was deep, unwavering, and though, on occasion, Jenny irritated her to the core, she had never wanted to lose her. Never.

That stark realization, at a time when her sensibilities were being tested to the limit, catapulted Susan back in time. And her heart raced with the memory of the time she almost did lose her little girl.

Susan and Zach, with Jenny in tow, had taken a rare drive to the ocean on a fall afternoon when the normally stubborn, shoreline fog had pulled back, far off shore. The cloudless, cobalt sky had allowed the intense, Indian summer sun to warm them, lulling them into a lazy stupor while the ocean heaved and surged, its potential anger hidden beneath a wash of awesome beauty. Zach and Susan lay on a blanket in the sand on an empty beach, back to back facing in different directions and surely thinking thoughts as unalike as they were.

How two, such disparate individuals had found each other had mystified, Susan's mother, Rachel, from the beginning, but she had said nothing. An old woman need not interfere with the workings of the universe, she had reasoned, but her heart ached with the knowledge that this union would fail. She was sure of it. Some day, her daughter would cry and she would not be there to pick up the pieces of a broken heart.

Jenny was snoozing on a beach towel next to her parents, her sandaled feet buried in the sand. Her cheeks had grown rosy from the intensity of the sun. Only three then, she was a veritable bundle of energy. Down time was rare. It was not unremarkable then that Zach's snoring awoke her. She crawled on her hands and knees and stared at him, skewing her nose in revulsion of the raspy sound. At last she stood and waddled to her mother who was curled into a fetal position, one arm shading her eyes. Jenny stroked her leg, finally jostling it with her tiny hand, but Susan was dead asleep as well, oblivious to her daughter's touch. Thwarted by her attempt to attain the attention she so desired, Jenny turned toward the sea.

"Swimmy, Swimmy," she cried, her voice barely audible, no match to the crashing waves.

She began to toddle forward, but fell, her hands, cheeks, and knees instantly scalded by the burning sand. Though she screamed in pain, "Hot, Mommy, hot," she ran, confused, in the opposite direction, away from her mother and toward the incoming, ocean waves that had become brutally fierce in the short time they had been there. Fortuitously awakened by Jenny's small cries, or perhaps by an inexplicable, maternal instinct that something was awry, Susan sprang from the blanket and chased after her little girl who by this time was only inches from the water.

"Jenny. Stop. Jenny," Susan shrieked, but it was too late.

A large wave swept Jenny off her feet and pummeled her like a rag doll before thrashing her into the sand. The child's arms flailed, attempting to grab hold of something, anything, but to no avail. She was dragged backwards, head underwater, into the ocean.

"Get the kid. Get the kid," Zach, suddenly aware, yelled from his place on the blanket. "She's going to fucking drown."

By that time Susan had rushed into the water and was turning in circles trying to locate Jenny. Finally she fell to her knees at the exact second Jenny's little body was hurled toward her. She grabbed at the child just as Zach reached them both. He wrenched Susan by the arm, pulling her away with one hand while he snatched Jenny by the hair with his other hand. He dragged them both for several feet before he let them go dropping them in the wet sand like dead fish.

"You fucking idiots," was Zach's pronouncement on finding that his wife and daughter both had survived. "Get your shit together so we can get the hell out of here and go home."

Susan had never forgotten that moment. *Jenny was wailing both with fright and pain, for the Pacific Ocean was cold and she was bruised. Jenny's sandals were missing, her t-shirt torn. Susan's own heart was beating furiously and her breathing was ragged and labored. She was shivering uncontrollably but managed to pull Jenny into her arms, hugging her tightly.*

"Don't cry, baby. You're safe," she cooed, nestling Jenny's head into her neck. It was then that she looked up, expecting Zach to be hovering over them, but that was not the case. He was gone, already fifty yards down the beach.

While Susan, exhausted from her exertion, clutched Jenny's small body, she watched Zach turn and scream, "Come on, you two. Move your feet, Susan. Let's go."

"I should have known then," Susan said out loud, ruminating on the unsettling memory, still vivid after so many years. "He didn't love me, or Jenny either." *But what I did know for sure, right then and there, was that he would walk away for good some day, out of our lives, hopefully forever.*

CHAPTER THIRTY- TWO

COURTNEY

Something's wrong, I know it is, Jimmy. You can fix things. Can't you? I think we're going in the wrong direction. The road to the tunnel is that way. Let's run. If we run we can get there in time. Jimmy? Why aren't you fucking listening to me? Oh shit, Jimmy, I think we're lost for good this time.

Courtney awoke once more, delirious and rambling gibberish in the throes of nonsensical dreams that mocked her helplessness. Her face was awash in perspiration but she was freezing cold. She must have flung the scratchy, horse blanket to the side as she slept for now she was exposed and shivering uncontrollably. Though her sight was blurry and she burned with fever, she frantically twisted her aching head from side to side trying to locate the blanket. At last she found it, partially wedged into the hole in the outer wall of the stall. With icy fingers she numbly picked at the fabric in order to free it and with the effort of her feeble tugging, eventually it mercifully released. She struggled to sit so that she could wrap the blanket around her once more, but her wooziness made any movement excruciating. Though exhausted by her effort, finally, she managed to cocoon her body in the folds of the nasty, wool blanket. Leaning against the splintery, wooden planks of the outer wall of the barn, her head lolled to one side only inches from the opening that she had enlarged only the day before when she had harbored the tiniest hope.

CHAPTER THIRTY-THREE

CHESTER

Without saying another word to Flo Gray, Chester drove straight down the rural highway that ran through town toward the Nelson ranch while Flo held on. Under Chester's demonic control, the old truck rumbled along at one speed - sixty miles an hour. It didn't seem to matter to Chester if he was on a straightaway, rounding a wide curve, or turning ninety degrees. He kept his foot planted on the gas pedal, his hands gripping the steering wheel, and his eyes, fortunately, on the road. As a motorist, he was something of a savant, gaging angles, sensing the pitch of a road, judging distances, and evaluating how weather conditions, hot or cold, influenced a driving surface. As long as he could peg the speed of his trusty truck at sixty, he was good to go. Even hills didn't slow down Chester Flack, although, in recent years, the truck had begun to labor a bit, the engine's roar deepening with even the slightest ascent. Chester would ease his body forward closer to the steering wheel as though that subconscious movement was all the assistance the truck needed to move forward, and at the apex, he would lean back again, satisfied and reassured.

After speeding along for several miles, Chester maneuvered his truck into the circular driveway of James Nelson's ranch in the exact spot he had parked earlier in the day to load the winery's stake side. With a piercing shriek, metal scraped metal when Chester slammed on the brakes and when the tires screeched to a stop a faint smell of rubber filled the air. The entire truck seemed to groan as if in pain when the ignition was turned off. Flo sat motionless, her heart pounding. Though she still held a death grip on the seatbelt and door handle, with the ceasing of motion, she began to calm down. She could feel the springs beneath the worn seat covering settle and creak as though they too could relax again. When her breathing normalized, she looked directly at Chester who had not yet bothered to check on the wellbeing of his passenger. No. Not Chester. He was in another world, adjusting the rear view mirror in every which direction in order to see what lay behind.

"Whew, Chester, that was some ride," Flo finally squeaked, her voice exposing her anxiety.

"Got you here," he snapped before offhandedly declaring, "God damn, the ride's half the adventure."

"I have to admit it was an adventure all right," she agreed, "though it's a little more excitement than I'm used to."

"Where are we, anyway?" she added.

"Nelson ranch. Where I picked up all that shit this morning. Why, right over there's where I found your old man's guitar." Chester pointed to the edge of the driveway that was bordered with low, neatly trimmed boxwoods.

"Oh, there?" Flo asked rather inanely, gazing at the spot as though she were looking upon a patch of holy ground. Her eyes grew glassy. "Well, I'll be damned."

Her musing was harshly interrupted by a gruff voice hollering outside, a short distance from the house. "What do you want? And who the hell are you? You're on private property, you know."

Chester turned his head to see who was bellowing at them before he climbed out of his truck. "Who the fuck's that?" he asked and though not speaking directly to Flo, he continued. "It's not the same dude who was here this morning. Sure as hell isn't old man Nelson. Saw that jerk up close and personal this morning."

Flo watched Chester slam the truck door hard as if to make a statement that he could be any damned place he wanted to be. He began striding toward the man who was tall, broad-shouldered, red-faced, and swaggering, step-by-step, down the staircase as though he owned it. Chester was certain he knew better. *Who in the hell is this jackass?*

Not to Chester's surprise, the man's bellicose behavior continued. "You'd better listen up, buddy. You need to get that rattrap off this driveway before it drips oil and grease all over. Probably already has." The man took a few steps forward and tilted his head downward as if trying to spot a slick of some kind beneath the truck bed. The red of his cheeks deepened as he bent forward, and when he straightened again, he staggered slightly sideways. He huffed in one big breath before continuing his rant. "I don't know who in the hell you are, but this is private property, and you don't belong here. You need to leave immediately. That means now. Get that piece of shit truck and whoever it is you're hauling around in it, the fuck out of here. We don't need worthless lowlifes around here."

The verbal assault was all Chester needed. *This son of a bitch better watch his mouth. He's liable to get his ass shot.* Chester's entire body had tensed. He had been here before, in the face of unfounded belligerence. With recurring inevitability, Herbert Flack's disturbing, ashen visage flashed before him. *You think I won't take you out too, ass wipe?*

Even though his words masked his sinister thoughts, an angry scowl stole across Chester's face. "Looking for the guy who owns this spread," he said. "Believe his name's Nelson."

"Nelson's not here. Besides I'm damned sure he wouldn't have any reason to deal with the likes of you," he replied. A noticeable odor of whiskey pervaded the air as he spoke.

The more the man talked, the more Chester bristled inside. A concurrent control took over, however, enabling him to remain outwardly composed so that he could bargain a bit. He needed information. "Look, I work in Conti's warehouse over at Bending Vine Winery. Believe one of the winery vineyards butts up to this place."

"So?" The man, who was perspiring profusely in layers of perfectly pressed safari gear, had moved to within five feet of Chester. He stood with his legs spread, his shoulders pulled back, and his fists digging into his waist. His eyes had narrowed to slits, his lips were drawn tight, and Chester could actually hear the man grind his teeth. His stance was a practiced posture of intimidation . . . but Chester was unfazed. *This guy's a drunken piece of shit. I could knock him over with a flick of my finger.* Chester continued.

"So, I was here this morning loading up equipment that Mr. Nelson wanted hauled away – a bunch of shit Conti could use at the winery," Chester offered candidly before fabricating a lie. "One of the ranch hands seemed to think there might be more stuff up for grabs at a barn somewhere on another part of the ranch. Thought I'd drive over, see what was there, and take it off Nelson's hands. Just need directions. Doing the dude a favor."

"Nelson doesn't need a favor, not from you, and not now. He's up to his ears in a more important matter. So you just pack your ass on out of here. Now, before I call the cops." The man paused for a moment. "Matter of fact, you'd better watch yourself because the police are scouring the vicinity as we speak."

Chester understood immediately that the search for the missing Taylor girl was in full swing. Why else would cops be all over the area?

"Cops?" he asked, in an attempt to feign his knowledge of the affair. *This creep doesn't have a clue what I know.*

"Indeed they are."

"What's the problem?" Chester attempted to ask the question as innocuously as he could.

"Missing person. My kid in fact," he said, his face impassive; not one shred of angst or sadness was evident.

Chester took a step back. *Hell. This jerk is Courtney Taylor's father.* The man in front of him had taken a folded, white handkerchief from his pants pocket and was wiping his forehead just as a woman walked onto the veranda.

"Bennett," she called. "What is it? Who is that?"

Bennett Taylor frowned. "Crazy bitch," he murmured before yelling, "Get inside, Jill. Now. It's nothing."

He then turned to Chester. "Looks to me like you're more trouble than you're worth. My wife is a hopeless mess already and your showing up here, probably up to no good, is enough to put her over the edge. She's not used to riff-raff. Now get the fuck out of here."

"On my way," Chester replied. Then he spoke again, seemingly to himself although loud enough for Bennett

Taylor to hear. "Guess I'll find that barn on my own. It can't be that hard."

Bennett Taylor jumped on the comment. "Nelson's got over a couple thousand acres. Outbuildings and corrals all over the place. I suggest you get going, stay on public roads, and keep the hell off Nelson's private property. I'll be warning him, and the cops too, about the likes of you. So, watch out."

The warning did not set well with Chester, but he turned his back to Bennett Taylor, strode to the driver's side of his truck, and hopped inside. He looked directly at Flo and said with absolute certainty. "That arrogant asshole is Courtney Taylor's dad, but he's not as smart as he thinks he is. He told me enough. Says folks are doing a search right now for his kid, but told me to stay off Nelson's private property. The dude, Nelson that is, owns over two thousand acres. Shit. That could be two or three miles down the road. And you know what we're about to do? Drive around until we spot a barn or two and when we do, we're going to do a little investigation of our own."

"Chester, I'm not sure we should. I don't want more trouble. Besides, I just remembered that someone from the police department was supposed to stop by my house to take photos of the damage and dust for fingerprints this afternoon. I should be there."

"Goddamn, woman. I dragged your ass out here cause you said you wished you could help find that girl. You said that plain as day, and guess what, like it or not, right now, that's what you're going to do. Your ass is along for the ride."

Chester started the engine, glanced in the rear view mirror at Bennett Taylor who had retreated to the stairs, and peeled out, leaving a cloud of white exhaust behind.

For the first time in two days, the shadow of responsibility that had burdened Chester eased, for he had a semblance of purpose. He was not about to mention that to anyone though, especially not to Flo Gray. She would think he'd lost his marbles.

CHAPTER THIRTY-FOUR

FLO

She could do nothing about it. Flo was stuck. Chester was on the road again and she was holding on for dear life. She actually never had contemplated how she would die, even in the aftermath of her parents' and husband's heinous deaths years before. But she considered it now and one thing was certain. Perishing in a fiery, vehicle accident was not her first choice.

"Chester," she yelled. "Slow this thing down." But her plea was to no avail. Either Chester couldn't hear her over the groan of the engine and the whoosh of rushing wind that battered his hunting cap and tore her hair from the trademark bun, or he was ignoring her outright. She was quite sure the latter was more apt to be true.

Consequently she was confined in the cramped cab alongside Chester Flack for three more, harrowing miles, clinching her jaw until it hurt. She had twisted her nerve-racked body slightly in her seat so as to keep her unlikely companion in her sights, but because of the awkwardness of her posture, the edge of the seatbelt had begun digging into her neck. Though she was terribly uncomfortable, she was afraid to move lest she'd strangle to death right there in the front seat of Chester's age-old, rusted, pickup truck.

In a sudden flash her imagination took hold. *Flo felt the seat belt become taut against her neck, and she heard herself gasp, clearly having drawn her last breath. Her head drooped to her chest, her body was stone still, and the spirit inside her was hurled into a bright, white silence. And all the while, Chester forged ahead down the highway at a flat sixty-five, oblivious to the corpse of the little, old custodian growing cold beside him.*

Flo was pulled from her imaginings by the motion of Chester's truck spinning in a one hundred and eighty degree arc through a swath of deep gravel that lay to the side of the highway near the bottom of a long grade.

"Hot damn," Chester hollered as the rear tires of the truck sank slowly into the loose gravel like a lifeless body in quick sand.

"Always wanted to do that! Hot damn," he shouted again. He began stomping his feet on the floorboard and wildly pounding the steering wheel with both hands in a display of frenzied exhilaration.

"What in the hell did you just do?" Flo shrieked.

A cloud of dust had risen from the shifting gravel, engulfing the truck, inside and out. It swirled angrily throughout the interior of the cab, refusing to settle and shrouding both Flo and Chester in an opaque, gritty film. Flo began coughing uncontrollably while Chester slapped at his paunchy belly and laughed until muddy tears ran down his cheeks into the scruffy stubble that Flo assumed was the beginning of a would-be beard. Flo glared at the man quite taken aback by his bizarre reaction to almost killing them and in silent torment rebuked her own lack of judgment that had put her there. *I should never have gotten into this ridiculous truck in the first place . . . especially not with Chester. His crazy shenanigans are going to be the death of me. I hate to think what's next.*

What actually did occur next was not anything Flo ever could have imagined, and in the end, she found herself hard put to articulate the details, not because she couldn't remember, but more to the point that she wanted to forget.

⌘ ⌘ ⌘

Once the veil of dust had begun to settle, Flo was able to control her coughing, but she felt as though she had swallowed a handful of abrasive cleanser. Never had her tongue and mouth been so parched and she yearned for water as never before. The simple thought of one tiny sip of any liquid induced an involuntary response to her thirst. She began smacking her lips, the tacky sound reverberating annoyingly in her head. And though she knew she looked a fool, she could have cared less. At that moment misery consumed her thinking. *Dying from dehydration sure as hell isn't my choice of a way to pass on either.*

At least Chester's guffawing had lessened into a drawn-out succession of chuckles that varied in intensity and volume. The confounding laughter continued for some time until at long last, he was silent. He glanced in the direction of Flo, frowned at her, let go with one more, loud chortle, and bellowed, "What the hell's wrong with you, Flo? You look like a dying carp."

"What the hell do you mean?" A sudden acute disdain welled inside her. "Well, obviously this crazy stunt of yours, and all the gravel dust it's raised up, hasn't fazed you one bit," she croaked. "I darn near choked to death and now I'm so thirsty I can hardly swallow."

"Well, hell. I can take care of that problem."

"You have water?"

"Hell no. Don't drink the stuff." He reached across the cab, gave the glove compartment a quick thump, and it fell open revealing wads of paper, a leaking pen, a half-empty pack of Camel cigarettes, a faded package of chewing gum, a sparsely bristled hair brush, and a pint of Jack Daniels. He seized the bottle of whiskey, unscrewed the cap, and shoved it toward Flo. "Here, have a swig."

"I don't want that nasty stuff," Flo retorted. She raised a flat palm toward him and wrinkled her nose in disgust before falling into another bout of coughing.

"Have it your way," he said, taking a hefty mouthful of the whisky and then swallowing hard. "Whew! Good shit. Sure you don't want some? It'll cure what ails you."

Though Flo scowled and nodded in the negative, Chester continued to hold the open bottle of Jack Daniels within inches of her face. She could smell it – an ester-y aroma, combining the essences of malt and oak. As she took in the odor, a distinct tingling tormented her nasal passages. She snorted and hacked once more before giving in. "Okay. Give it to me."

The bottle was warm. Flo placed her mouth at the rim of the opening and took a tiny sip. The result was twofold. It burned her throat dreadfully but, at the same time, soothed her agonizing thirst.

"Go ahead," Chester encouraged. "Drink more than that. You don't have to guzzle the stuff, but I promise it'll kill that cough."

Flo raised one eyebrow, disbelieving, but did as Chester told her. She took in a mouthful of the amber liquid, swilled it around in her mouth, and gulped it down. Her reaction was instantaneous. "Oh, phew, that crap burns like hell." And it did. She could feel the heat from the alcohol slide down her esophagus and inflame her gut. "Shit, Chester. I'll stick to wine, thank you very much."

"Got to admit it cured your cough. Plus you don't look like a fucking, dying fish anymore," Chester said, chuckling. He then took another hefty swig from the bottle before tightening the cap and shoving it back into the glove compartment. The door of the compartment screeched annoyingly as Chester slammed it shut. For a few awkward moments all was silent, until Chester sighed and said to himself, "Guess I'd better check out what kind of pickle we're in."

He threw open the door, nearly falling as he exited into a deep trench that had been etched out by the force of spinning tires. The entire expanse of gravel had shifted with the intensity of the truck's movement and a mound of it was wedged beneath the truck, tightly lodged against the bottom of the transmission housing and left, rear axle and tire.

"Shit," Chester muttered. "This doesn't look good."

He then began to curse in earnest, directing a foul and lengthy tirade directly at the truck as though the weary vehicle had a mind of its own and was solely responsible for Chester's predicament.

Flo's entire body tensed as she listened to Chester's haranguing, but was unsure whether to stay seated or to join Chester outside. Chester made the decision for her.

"Get on out here, Flo. This goddamn truck is so crammed in here I'll never get it out," he yelled.

She opened the passenger door and stepped out. Although Flo was a short, slight woman, the gravel crunched and shifted beneath her weight. The unstable surface made her unsteady and she tottered around the front of the truck like a feeble invalid. When she reached the spot where Chester stood brooding, he scowled at her as if she shared the blame for the jam they were in, but directed his ire at the truck.

"Piece of shit, truck. Son of a bitch can just rot here," he snarled. "What a goddamn mess."

"Well, Chester, this is hardly the truck's doing," she countered.

He glared at her as if she were crazy, his dark eyes scowling menacingly, and for the first time since she had been in Chester's company, Flo was a bit fearful of him. She knew his reputation, had heard the speculation about whether the death of his father years before really had been accidental, but surely it had been. He and his mother, Bertha, had sworn to it from what she'd heard, and clearly he had not been charged. That aside, however, Flo never had felt more uncomfortable with anyone in her life, and she was stuck . . . stranded, in fact. She was daunted by the unforeseen, stark reality of her predicament. *Christ, Flo. How and why did you get yourself into this situation? Chester Flack is a nut case.*

Her self-admonishment was interrupted by Chester who with one, firm strike with his thick boot kicked a dent the width of a head-sized boulder into the quarter panel of the now-ensnared truck. Startled by the rash and unexpected action, Flo flinched, stepped backwards, and lost her balance on the uneven gravel. She fell onto her butt hard, her hands jamming into the sharp rocks as she attempted to catch herself. The impact jarred her whole body and she winced in pain and shock.

Chester wheeled around when he heard the sound of her fall, but only stared, unmoving, as though he had no clue what to do. Flo did not move, but she watched Chester warily while she blindly picked at the tiny shards of gravel that had pierced the palms of her hands. Chester's evident lack of concern astounded her. *Surely any other person would have helped me to my feet. What's wrong with him? Seems like Chester doesn't take responsibility for anything.*

In that regard Flo was wrong. A good chunk of Chester's anger, misdirected toward his truck, an inanimate object that could not retaliate, was the result of his quick assessment that his ability to find the missing Taylor girl, however remote the chance was anyway, now would be hampered. Although it was out of character for him, a man who found self-satisfaction in his conscious detachment from others, Chester was suffering deep inside with the realization that his hesitation on the night of the accident had contributed to the girl's apparent abduction. And though he understood at some level, that such thinking on his part was a paradox in keeping with his natural bent, he could not stop the torment. Now, confounding that issue, Flo was in tow, and with no mode of transportation, they had no choice but to resort to walking.

Leaving Flo still sitting on the ground behind him, Chester stomped to the cab of the truck once more and climbed in. In his gut he knew it was a futile effort, but he turned the key in the ignition. The engine fired as it had for years but even though he pumped the gas pedal and silently willed the vehicle to move even an inch, it did not budge. In fact, the exertion on the vehicle caused the front tires to sink further into the gravel as though they were absurdly mocking Chester's efforts.

"We're doomed," he whispered, and followed with a shout out to Flo. "This fucking thing isn't going to move at all. You have a phone with you?"

"No. It's at home. Didn't bring a phone, purse, anything. Just have my jacket and keys. We left in such a rush. Do you have one?"

"Hell no. Never in a million years would I have use for one of those damn things." He paused. "Well, hell, we're going to have to hoof it then, cross-country. Want to keep off the side of the highway."

"Hoof it? Walk? All the way home?" Flo asked, dumbfounded by the suggestion. "We're miles away."

"Yeah, well, six miles or so. Probably less if we hike cross-country." He looked at her as though his proposal was perfectly rational.

"Look, if we have to walk, shouldn't we stay on the side of the highway? Maybe we can hitch a ride into town," she said although the idea of catching a ride with a perfect stranger was far from appealing. Being there with Chester, a mere acquaintance, was bad enough. She shuffled her feet and gazed nervously about as anxiety began to mount.

"Not when I'm lugging this on my shoulder," Chester argued, pulling his rifle from a gun rack mounted inside the back window. Clutching the rifle in one hand, he began rummaging with the other under the seat of the truck, eventually producing a large, butcher knife and a wad of greasy rags. He leaned the rifle against the side of the truck and began spreading out the rags, one on top of the other. When there was a stack of six, he placed the knife in the middle, wrapping it carefully as though the blade were a fragile treasure. After he had tied a short length of bailing wire around the rags, he shoved the bundled knife in Flo's direction and said, "Here, you're going to have to hold this while we walk."

Flo took a step backwards as if repulsed by the idea of carrying what she considered a concealed weapon.

"I don't think so," she stated, tilting her chin upward in a gesture of defiance. "It's your knife. You take it."

"Damn it to hell, Flo," Chester hissed. "You're fucking useless."

One word. *Useless.* Flo's reaction was visceral, a punch to the gut that made her stomach lurch. She made a move toward Chester and hissed. "I'm a lot of things, Chester Flack. Useless is not one of them. Keep your condescending comments to yourself." Burning with a surge of adrenaline, she turned around in a full circle as though looking for a way to escape, but it was a pointless impulse. "Pathetic," she added.

Her contempt for Chester was growing with each passing moment. *What an inept human being. He put us in this quandary. He'd better get us out.*

She watched Chester heft the rifle to his shoulder, gather the bundled knife to his chest, and reach once more into the cab of the truck. He hit the glove compartment with the butt of his fist and when it fell open, he grabbed the half-empty bottle of whiskey and shoved it into his trouser pocket.

"Let's go," he demanded. "Going to be dark in a few hours."

Flo watched Chester's boots crunch across a stretch of gravel in a direction opposite from the road. He stopped momentarily before squeezing through an open space inexplicably notched in a row of Manzanita shrubs not twenty feet from the now entrapped vehicle that he was abandoning it appeared, without an ounce of regret. Flo looked back one final time at the old truck, that, only hours before, she had envisioned as a potential death trap. She then turned on it just as Chester had, mustered her resolve, and followed him beyond the opening in the shrubbery. The somewhat odd, and, to Flo's way of thinking, ominous-seeming access led to a brick-wide path edged on both sides by an entangled mass of poison oak, huckleberry, coyote brush, sage, and wild buckwheat. Close by she spotted knots of California poppies, the bright, orange blossoms vivid amid a breadth of browns, umbers, and myriad shades of green. In the distance, valley oaks and live oaks dotted the landscape. They stood like sentinels, their ancient, gnarly branches giving only slightly to a chilly breeze. Flo looked farther down the trail and caught a glimpse of Chester disappearing behind a spindly stand of Ponderosa pines. She quickened her pace so as not to lose sight of him altogether. Under no circumstances did she want to be stranded in the middle of nowhere, alone, and though Chester had proven to be an unsavory and quite disagreeable companion thus far, he was all she had, her only hope of getting home. *At least he's a hunter and acquainted, I assume, with the countryside. Surely he knows where we're going.*

As Chester hiked farther down the trail, without ever looking back to see if she was behind him, Flo realized that her predicament could potentially become life threatening. She was at Chester's mercy, plain and simple. The stark veracity of the fact that her safety depended on a man who was not wrapped too tightly was like a knife to the belly. *Chester is such an eccentric, and oh, so unpredictable. I'm not sure I can endure much more of his impulsive behavior. But I can't let him out of my sight either. As much as I hate it, I need him. I need that crazy asshole.* She began hyperventilating, the short, rapid gasps leaving her light-headed and shaky, but she stumbled forward, calling in a croaky voice, "Wait, Chester. Wait for me."

CHAPTER THIRTY-FIVE

GEORGE

By the time George's white, unmarked police cruiser reached the distant curve on the rural highway where he had spotted a black truck speeding, he found nothing. He was positive he had seen, and heard it, at the exact moment he had pulled out from the Nelson's driveway on his way to connect with the team of folks searching for Courtney Taylor. *What the hell?*

The sound of the motor had been piercing, a whining roar, that had captured his attention instantly. And why? It was all because of Chester Flack. Surely it was, for Chester had planted the seed. At the police station, Chester, in his own awkward manner, had reported that the black truck he had seen at the accident site, and later on, cruising down Bending Vine Road, had had a deafeningly loud engine. Retention of that fact was indubitably the reason why George had honed in on the strident sound immediately.

Even though George had accelerated quickly, pushing his tough and powerful V8 engine to its limit in order to apprehend the motorist, the truck, and its driver, had vanished. When he reached the spot where he was certain he had seen the vehicle charging around the curve, there was nothing. No roar. No screech of tires. No tread marks. No exhaust fumes. Nothing. *Damn. Where the hell did it go? Am I imagining shit?* As George pulled off the road and parked at the far end of the curve, he tentatively considered the possibility. *It's the pressure I'm under, I guess. And I'm exhausted.* George could think of no other reason for his confusion, and that consideration exacerbated his worry.

This current, missing person case was the only one for which he had had immediate, administrative oversight . . . ever, and it was a daunting position, even in a sleepy community such as Hollow Vista. The town was not a likely hot spot for criminal activity, the earlier murder of Sherry Mitchell, the local, real estate agent, followed by the shootings at Hollow Vista High School being the only exceptions; and even those tragic and shocking events had not been orchestrated by a hard core criminal, but by a misguided, unhinged old woman, a weary teacher who, in her own, deranged way, had sought relief from life's miseries.

George's thoughts had wandered back to those incidents provoked by the fact that the latter had taken place at the high school where the missing girl, Courtney Taylor, was a senior . . . as was his daughter, Angie . . . and Jenny Wallis, who, if fate had played a different hand, possibly could have been abducted as well. She had been let go though. *And why was that?* Clearly Jenny had been manhandled. The poor girl had injuries to show for it, but she was alive, and safe at home with her mother . . . *with Susan.* Was Jenny lucky? Certainly in comparison to Courtney she was.

She had been traumatized though. *And whose fault was that?* George's thoughts would not settle. *Where does responsibility lie in such cases? Is it the fault of the girls themselves, foolish teenagers who were drinking, driving, and behaving recklessly? Does it lie in the hands of an evildoer, an unknown, faceless character with little or no conscience? Is the offender the man Chester described, the longhaired guy with menacing eyes? Why, maybe Chester himself is, in part, responsible.* He alluded to the fact that he had hesitated, *reaching the accident scene too late to affect the outcome. No. It's not fair to fault Chester. What about the girls' parents? Are they to blame for not watching closely enough? Did Susan falter somewhere along the way? No, surely not.* George's thoughts turned to Bennett Taylor, the brash, abrasive boor who was Courtney's father. When George had left him, standing on the veranda of the Nelson estate earlier, Bennett had been more intent on finding himself a shot of vodka or whisky than in dirtying his boots to search for his own daughter. *What kind of parent is he . . . really? And what is Jill's role in Courtney's life? The woman's upset, I know, but isn't she simply wallowing in self-pity right now, as though she's the primary victim? What is important to these people? Is it family? Friends? Is it affection for each other or their love for their daughter? They obviously have given Courtney every material item she could want. No. Emotions - love and affection - don't light the Taylors' fire. How could it? Bennett has been so miserably condescending and aloof even in the face of a potential tragedy. What's wrong with that guy?* George chewed on his lip and stared at the empty roadway until his eyes blurred. Fuming at the mere thought of Bennett Taylor, he slammed his hand on the steering wheel and cursed. His gut began to burn, and in that second he was perfectly clear. Courtney was not Bennett Taylor's prime concern. The man's major interest was firmly entrenched elsewhere. *Money. It's money*

*that drives Bennett Taylor, that son of a bitch . . . money first, above
anything, above anything else at all.*

⌘ ⌘ ⌘

Though only a few minutes had gone by, George had the
absurd feeling that he had been stopped on the side of the
road for hours. *Shit. Have to get moving.* Without further hesitation, he angled his cruiser onto the highway once more,
his eyes scanning the bordering fields for any members of
the search team. At the one-mile mark, he detected two,
all-terrain vehicles topping a hill, not fifty yards away. He
pulled to the side of the road once more and scrambled out
of his car, motioning frantically as he did in order to gain
the attention of the drivers. One of the men obviously saw
him and gestured in recognition. George watched the men
park the four-wheelers, and wait as he clambered through
tall grass up a steep grade to meet them.

Jimmy Nelson, alongside Cole Jackson, was seated on
one vehicle, while an older gentleman who was a virtual
doppelganger for Jimmy, operated the other.

"Hey, fellas," George panted, a bit winded as a result of
his hasty hike.

"Detective Murphy," Jimmy acknowledged. "This is my
dad."

"James Nelson," the man said, extending his hand to
George.

"George Murphy. Detective. Good to meet you," George
replied. He looked from Jimmy to his father before adding,
"Amazing resemblance."

"Hear that often," the older Nelson admitted. "Guess I
can't get away with not claiming him."

Jimmy rolled his eyes and smirked uncomfortably. George noticed.

"No luck yet, obviously," he said aiming to diffuse the awkward moment by changing the subject.

"No, nothing," James admitted, as he hopped from his vehicle to the ground. He went into an immediate stance that mimicked that of Bennett Taylor: fists at his waist, feet spread wide, and chin tilted up in a show of patent arrogance. James Nelson was tall, broad-shouldered, and muscular, although a rather large, distended paunch aged him. And though his face, neck, and arms were tanned, his cheeks, in contrast, were ruddy, perhaps reddened from too much wind and sun.

Or maybe it's an overindulgent lifestyle. After all, he and old Bennett are apparently best friends. George caught himself. *That's enough, George.* He was well aware that any further judgment could entrap him, thwarting his ability to stay focused on what was important - the investigation.

"So, how long have you been out here, and where have you been? I'm assuming Officer Sanchez offered instructions as which areas to search. He constructed a grid of the area, I know. Methodically covering one section at a time is the way to go. You are staying in touch. Right?"

"Yeah, we've been in constant contact. Thank goodness for these," James said, tossing his cell phone from one hand to the other before continuing. "We've covered about one square mile pretty thoroughly. Looked into ravines, creek beds, a few outbuildings here and there, but nothing."

"It's pretty frustrating," Jimmy added. His voice was husky and he wiped at his eyes with the back of his hand.

"I know a good many folks are hiking their assigned areas. Have you seen any other vehicles though? All-terrain, trucks, anything?" George pried.

"No," James replied, "though Bennett, that's Courtney's father . . ."

"Oh, I know Bennett," George inserted.

"Well, I talked to Bennett a while back. He said some lowlife in a beat-up, old, red truck was at the house nosing around earlier."

Chester. "Really?" George gave James no indication that he was quite sure who the *lowlife* might be.

James continued. "Yeah, guess the guy was the worker old man Conti, from the Bending Vine Winery sent over earlier to pick up equipment I wanted to unload. I had only a passing interaction with him then. Had him get right to work. Bennett thought the guy was full of shit though. Supposedly the guy said my ranch hand had told him there was more equipment up for grabs. Seems he was looking to find the barn where I had stored a shitload of winemaking paraphernalia for years. Guess he wanted to help himself to what was left of the stuff. Odd. Anyway, Bennett wanted to give me a heads up that the creep, who just showed up in my driveway out of nowhere, was pretty belligerent, and apparently ripe and ready to trespass onto my property. Bennett was pretty sure he was apt to cause trouble."

"Interesting. That information would be a bit disconcerting," George answered, his mind already racing. "Look, I need to be heading out now. Contact Sanchez if you find or need anything. Anything."

George couldn't get away fast enough. He turned on the men abruptly and scrambled down the hill, sliding onto his butt twice before he reached his cruiser. In seconds he was speeding down the highway with one person in mind. *Holy Shit. What is Chester Flack up to now?*

CHAPTER THIRTY-SIX

SUSAN

In the aftermath of her spontaneous re-envisioning of the haunting and unforgettable day of Jenny's near drowning, Susan began shivering, not from cold, but with fright. How was it that a horrific event that had occurred so many years before had been conjured so vividly? Surely it was because of the possibilities, the potentialities, and, yes, the realization that in an instant, because of one, wrong turn, one misstep, her life could have been altered forever. *And Jenny? But Jenny did not drown. She is safe. Asleep. Upstairs.*

She closed her eyes once more, and Jenny, the toddler, was in her arms again, her wet hair matted with sand, her small body trembling, and one, tiny fist clutching the skin on Susan's neck so tightly it might have hurt had the context of their embrace been different. Susan could remember still, feeling her daughter's heartbeat, a rapid, palpable pounding that had mirrored her own. They had clung to one another - mother and daughter, female to female, in a bond that Susan knew never could be breached . . . never . . . not even in death, for at that instant, Susan sensed Rachel's presence once more, not remotely, but deep inside, where her mother's essence resided as though the two had never parted. Susan's heart ached.

"Oh, mother, how did I, did we, arrive at this place?"

Susan understood at a profound level that her mother could not answer; nor would she have responded definitively were she still alive. It had not been Rachel's way to dwell on the past, to predict the future, or to exert effort for control over what was not in her power. Instead, she had relied on her gift of intuitiveness, of allowing nature and instinct to guide her path. She had valued questions rather than answers.

"Isn't it true that we must make our own way?" Rachel might have offered. "Haven't you gotten yourself along this far? You will know, Susan, in which direction to turn. Trust yourself."

The fanciful counseling only confused Susan more. *Trust myself. That notion is daunting as it is, but I'm not on this road alone. What about trusting others, Mother? In just whom, on this Earth, can I put my trust? Who should anyone trust? It's a risk, isn't it? Of course it is. Life is a paradox, one inconsistency after another, but hell, I have no choice but to move forward, do I? It's one step at a time until I can see for myself, what's around the next bend. Keep moving along, Susan. Trust yourself.*

⌘ ⌘ ⌘

Susan brooded for some minutes more before her mind silenced itself. She took in the sounds of the house – the hum of the refrigerator, a ticking clock, the screech of a branch brushing the front window, a soft, whistling wind beyond the front door, her own breathing. In an odd way, the normal rhythms of her home gave immediate, and much sought after, comfort. It was fleeting, however.

Susan looked toward the staircase. *I should check on Jenny.* She shuffled barefoot to the base of the stairs, but stopped short, her hand resting on the bannister. *Ah, motherhood, with all its unpredictable complexities.* Her thoughts went to Jill Taylor. *I wonder how Courtney's mother is coping right now?* Susan had met Jill only twice. Once was when Susan had dropped Jenny off at the Taylors' estate for a barbeque and an overnight; the second was in passing at a high school fundraiser. Though Jill had offered a small smile and was amiable, saying a few words about needing to support the girls and their school activities, something about her created an uncomfortable distance. It was Jill's reserve, perhaps, or the eyes, deep blue and melancholy. Susan had never forgotten the woman's forlorn expression. *If she was sad then, how must she feel now? And what about Courtney? And George? What about the others, who are searching right now? How are they all faring?* Susan was struck again with the cruel reality that Jenny's best friend had been dragged away, surely into harm's way. *What are the possibilities, the probabilities, really, for finding that poor girl? And how, in the end, if it turns out badly, am I going to support Jenny?*

Susan sighed, mounting the stairs, one slow step at a time. Outside Jenny's room she paused once more, unsure. Would Jenny be calm by now? Or would she be rude, upset, enraged? Susan was not sure she could trust herself to reason in any cogent manner with the girl on the other side of the door if the latter was the case. *Trust yourself, Susan.* She opened the door slowly. The small lamp on the end table was still on, casting a yellow glow on an empty, unmade bed. Jenny was conspicuously absent and the room still, the quiet there as silent as a grave.

Susan flinched, the shock of what she was seeing, and conversely not, forcing a wave of adrenaline through her body. She trembled, clutching the doorknob for stability, for she was suddenly light-headed and weak. *Where is she?*

"Jenny," she called. "Jenny."

A quick search of the upstairs gave her no answers. Jenny was gone. Susan's emotions began to overwhelm her. Shock quickly gave way to anger. *How dare she? How dare she leave without a word? And where is she?*

Susan ran down the stairs, looking into every room and calling Jenny's name over and over until her voice became a whisper. *Where is she?* As though drawn to her own place of comfort Susan stumbled through the kitchen, crossed the screened-in, back porch, and wandered outside. The afternoon had turned chilly. Susan, still barefoot, stepped blindly onto short tufts of weeds that dotted the backyard. They dug painfully into the soles of her feet, but she did not stop. At the edge of the garden, she paused and turned back toward the house. In that instant, an eerie burst of wind spun like an invisible dervish across the lawn just as the resident owl's sorrowful *who-who* sounded from its hiding place nearby. Susan's heart fluttered with an overwhelming sense of dread. And then she saw her. Jenny.

Wrapped in the afghan she had cherished her entire life, Jenny was on the ground, sleeping like an abandoned urchin beneath a giant oak. Her long, copper hair was splayed out around her head, her eyes were closed tightly, and her cheeks, were rosy now, perhaps having been touched by the wind. Susan rushed to her daughter's side, and knelt down beside her. Jenny stirred slightly but did not awaken. As Susan gazed at her, she was overcome with a combination of anger, frustration, regret, relief, and love, the emotions so raw and real, it was as though she had stepped into a fairy tale . . . with an ending that was dubious at best.

Jenny's impulsiveness, her mood swings, and her insensitivity continue to throw me off. And here we are again. It was a fact. Her daughter's brash actions, her restlessness, her profanity, all, were reoccurring, unpredictable affronts to which Susan had uncomfortably had to adapt, but so be it. At this moment all that mattered to Susan Wallis was that once again, her daughter was safe.

CHAPTER THIRTY-SEVEN

COURTNEY

She had no idea he had come back, but he had. He tried to rouse her by slapping her cheek with the back of his hand, but his brutal effort proved useless. What ominously occurred instead was that his crushing grip on her body caused her to fall utterly limp like a stricken animal. He seized her naked shoulders then with sharp, dirty fingernails that dug into her flesh. Her arms flopped backwards onto the fetid hay and the fingers of each hand began to curl involuntarily inward. He shook her violently.

"Wake up, Missy," he hissed, spewing her neck with vile saliva.

Her eyelids fluttered, but closed once more. She was a rag doll, incapable of fording off her attacker. Even when he pummeled her into the bed of straw, she did not respond. She was too weak, too sick, and drained of any hope. So she lay there, her heartbeat rapid but her breathing barely audible. She was beyond vulnerable and barely conscious when he took her again, thrusting inside her over and over until finally he was done. A loud, horrific snort of sickening pleasure shattered the silence of the place. When he sat back at last and stared at the frail girl in front of him, he sneered and then he chuckled, "Got you good this time, Missy."

He finally stood and dribbled urine into a corner of the stall before cinching his trousers with a fraying, braided belt. The waning glow of the afternoon sun, that at last stubbornly had burned its way, in sparse and random patterns amidst the mantle of clouds, sent slivers of filtered light through cracks in the outer barn wall. The eerie, meager luminescence was enough to illuminate a mass of telling scars that lined the brittle skin of the man's long, skinny forearms. The shining, silver tracks surely bore an unspeakable and murky story of years of obvious, chronic, intravenous drug use that somehow had brought him, consumed with demented desperation, to this place in time.

Plainly oblivious to the dramatic situation in which he was embroiled, the man stared down at Courtney once again and chortled. "Don't worry Missy. I'll be back. You be ready now."

He turned abruptly, threw open the gate, and charged to his temporary, sleeping quarters at the far end of the barn. At this point he had only one thing on his mind. *Yes sir. It's time. Time for this old boy to get jacked up one more time.* In his haste for just another, luscious taste, however, he fortuitously had overlooked one simple detail – to padlock the gate. And, as chance would have it, when he had slammed the gate shut, the concussion of metal on oak, had forced it to swing slightly ajar. It wasn't open much, but perhaps enough if anyone ever was to become aware.

CHAPTER THIRTY-EIGHT

CHESTER

With Flo Gray yards behind him, Chester hiked down the narrow trail for a quarter mile, away from the highway and the abandoned truck that was trapped up to its axles in gravel. *Damned thing. The fucker will have to sit there until I'm good and ready to have it hauled out. What a fucking mess that damned truck has gotten me into.* His thoughts in placing blame on the poor truck were as irrational as his behavior had been that day, but he never could have acknowledged that fact, likely because he was unable to step outside of himself to comprehend. From the time he had been a small child, without an inkling why, he had generated rash and absurd dramas that had charged him with adrenaline, exhilarated his spirit, and perhaps, if the truth were known, given him a reason to live. Impulsivity had driven him . . . always, and thus, over the years, he had gained the reputation as being something of an imprudent character and a completely socially inept lout with no filter whatsoever. It was a saving grace that he never had cared for one second what other folks thought though. *Who the hell needs people anyway? They're not worth the powder to blow them to hell.* To his way of thinking, that notion had saved him. He had stayed to himself, alone as much as possible, where he was unscathed by the whims and wills of the general public. His mother, Bertha, had been the only person allowed into his world, and that had been only on the periphery where he held her annoying presence at bay. It was veritably so that people, not one single person, had been a priority for Chester Flack . . . ever, until, for some inexplicable reason, now.

⌘   ⌘   ⌘

Although the day had been dreary and gloomy early in the morning, the clouds had given way to a hazy sky, the elusive sun having warmed the air, if only slightly. As a result, though the walk had been a relatively easy one, Chester had begun to perspire quite heavily. Trickles of sweat burned his eyes and ran down the sides of his face, dripping onto the collar of his shirt. He slowed to wipe his brow with a dirty handkerchief that had been stuffed in his pocket for weeks. Then, for the first time since he had set out, he looked over his shoulder to see if Flo was still following him. She was plodding along fifty yards behind him. *Christ. Should have never dragged her along. And now she's slowing me down. At this fucking rate, we'll never get home.* Chester could not control his reasoning. He simply was incapable of considering the consequences of, or accepting onus for his own actions; instead he rationalized that something, or in this case, someone, was responsible for the untenable position in which he found himself. *Goddamn it, Flo. Hurry up.*

"Get a move on, Flo," he yelled. "Hustle, woman."

Though she resented his tone, Flo stepped up her pace and soon was at Chester's side, panting a bit from the effort. Chester was leaning against a gigantic boulder that was plopped confoundedly on the side of the trail. *How the hell did this big, old rock get here? Seems out of place.* She tilted her head, baffled. *Hell, and so am I.* Flo's analogy held weight in her mind for she was a bit bewildered as to how she had lost her good sense and had allowed herself to become stranded in the middle of nowhere with Chester Flack.

While she caught her breath, she watched Chester dig into his shirt pocket for a can of chewing tobacco. He pried off the lid, took a pinch of the stuff, and tucked it inside his lip. Flo frowned.

"What the hell, Flo. You'd better wipe that God-awful expression off that mug of yours. You look like the devil."

"Why do you do that, Chester? You're going to wreck your teeth chewing that nasty tobacco, not to mention get lip cancer."

"Chewed most of my life. Habit. And I like the taste. Yep. Wintergreen. Besides, it's my fucking business what I do, not yours. You can keep your own damned opinions to yourself," he slurred.

Flo opened her mouth to reply, but then closed it just as quickly. The last thing she wanted was an argument with Chester. Not now. She stared at her companion as if seeing him for the first time. *He sure is a scruffy looking mess. He has decent eyes though.* It was true. Chester's eyes were dark brown, almost black and deeply set, but Flo detected a flicker of vitality there, as though beneath his crotchety façade a more pleasant spirit was conceivably hidden away. His cheeks and chin were sprinkled with days old, greying whiskers and she could see that his face was furrowed beneath them, but he had a strong jaw. His lips were pleasant enough, too, although with a wad of tobacco lodged between his cheek and gum she was beyond wary of what lay beyond. Chester's voice drew her from her reverie.

"Holy crap, Flo. Would you stop gawking at me? What the hell's wrong with you?"

Flo looked hastily away. She had not intended to set Chester off again, although from what little she understood about the man, he was two shakes away from flying into a rage at any time. In a mundane action that lent the awkward situation a modicum of normality, she reached to her face and protectively patted the black mole on her cheek. The unsightly growth was an odd comfort.

"Didn't realize I was staring," she mumbled.

"Well, you were," Chester admonished. He glanced farther down the trail. "Let's get the hell out of here. Doubt we'll make it home before dark at the rate we're going."

"Great," Flo replied, dejected by that ominous possibility.

"Now, what the hell do you mean by that?"

"Nothing. Let's go." Flo determined instantly to bury her emotions, and from that moment on, to keep any comments to Chester to an absolute minimum. *Chester Flack is a loose canon.*

⌘ ⌘ ⌘

For an hour and a half, Chester continued to lead the way down the narrow trail that eventually widened for half a mile and then disappeared altogether. He and Flo stepped across a wide pasture through thick, tall, browning grass that slowed their progress. Finally Chester stopped, hopped over a dilapidated barbed wire fence, and stumbled forward to the middle of the adjacent field where, like a weary, bewildered mongrel, he perused the horizon, turning around in a complete circle three times.

"This way," he yelled. "There's an outbuilding yonder. Don't know about you, but I need water. Might be a spigot there. You thirsty?"

Flo nodded. Her throat was dry, her lips parched, and her cheeks chapped by the tepid sun and wind. The intermittent, pesky gusts had tugged her hair from its customary bun and strands flew up and about into her eyes and mouth. She swatted at her face, annoyed. She was tired too. Though her job as a custodian constantly kept her on her feet, and she often had wondered how many miles she covered in a day cleaning the hallways and classrooms of Hollow Vista High, this was different. She was certain a blister was blooming on her left heel. It stung with every step but somehow she mustered the drive to go on.

The two hundred yard trek to the building Chester had spotted was difficult. Grass gave way to barren dirt that was dotted with rocks, some only inches in diameter and others as large as head-sized boulders. Chester picked his way, eyes facing downward, across the swath of land, while Flo followed closely. Their footsteps churned up dust and sent myriad insects and alligator lizards scurrying over rocks and into tiny crevices. Chester made it a point to stomp savagely on countless gopher mounds along the way intent, it was clear, on seeing to the critters' demise, yet he was visibly startled when a long, thin, king snake slithered across the toe of his boot. He reacted by kicking frantically at the serpent and sending it arcing into the air.

"Get the fuck away from me," he hollered. He turned flustered to see that Flo had noticed it all. "I hate snakes," he admitted. "All of them. Any kind."

Flo nodded, understanding, but she said nothing.

Chester paused after booting the snake, glanced around the rocky terrain for any others, and then cautiously moved on. He reached a small berm just short of the outbuilding. On one side of it was a small, gnarly, oak sapling competing for its existence among a knot of scrubby Manzanita bushes; the rest of the small hill was dotted with sparse patches of blooming dandelions and foot high nettles, their purple flowers defying any creature to chance a stinging touch. Both Chester and Flo kept their distance.

When at last they reached the building, they faced a solid, twelve-foot wide wall of oak planks.

"Must be the back side," Chester said. "Has to be a door or window somewhere. Let's walk around."

With Flo his shadow, Chester moved tentatively around the structure for fifteen or twenty feet to the opposite side where he stopped dead. "Holy shit."

He had halted so quickly that Flo nearly slammed into his back. "What?" she asked, startled.

Chester was gawping into a dark, cavernous space where both he and Flo could see the reflection of light from a filtered sun wavering on the front bumper of a large vehicle. A wide, wooden door, that obviously had been used to secure the building had been raked backwards and was leaning precariously against a spindly pine. The door was badly warped, the top door hinge was rusted, and the entire, upper bracket had been twisted out of place. Shards of splintered wood lay on the ground.

"What?" Flo asked again. "What's the matter?"

"It's that fucker's truck."

"What are you talking about, Chester? Whose truck?"

"The truck that drove up on the accident. I'm sure of it. Saw it again the next day with this longhaired, evil-eyed son of a bitch driving it. Remember, I told you that that's why I was at the police station . . . to fill in old, Murphy, the detective. Holy shit."

Flo stepped back from the truck a few steps as though repelled by it. "What is it doing way out here?"

"Hell if I know. But if I were to be a betting man, I'd say it's being stashed so it, and the fucker who's been driving it, can't be found. I mean, who the hell knew this ramshackle, old shack was even here?"

Chester scratched his head and squinted, searching the bushes that lined the dirt lane that led to the dilapidated shed, before striding directly to a spot just inside the entrance. He reached out and touched the hood of the engine with a flat palm. "Warm. Engine's still warm, barely. It hasn't been parked here too long though, and I'm willing to bet the ass wipe who was driving it isn't too far away either."

Flo was instantly fearful. The rate of both her heart and breathing intensified. She wiped her palms, moist now, on the sides of her pants. Her instinct was to run somewhere, anywhere, but that notion, she knew was ludicrous. She had no choice but to stay.

"What are you going to do Chester?" she asked, her voice hoarse, mouth dry.

He whirled around so quickly she jumped. "Find him, but first, I'm going to take care of business."

Chester chucked the securely wrapped butcher knife he had been carrying onto the ground, furiously pulled the rags from around it, and marched back to the truck. Flo's eyes were riveted on him. *What the hell?* Chester glanced menacingly in Flo's direction with his fist clutching the handle of the knife. *Oh God, what is he doing?* Her heart, she was sure, skipped a beat.

He promptly turned from her though, walked to the side of the truck, and drove the knife into the sidewall of the left, front tire. Flo expected a deafening explosion, but instead heard only a loud pop followed by a long hissing sound. She watched, her mouth agape, as the truck slowly listed to the left. Chester worked in a quick fury, circling the vehicle with his weapon until every tire had been punctured. It took several minutes for the hissing sounds to stop, and then there was silence, save for a rustle of leaves as a critter or two surely scuttled for shelter in the dense undergrowth.

Like a man hell bent on seeing his mission through to the end, Chester carried the knife, swinging it slightly, back to the pile of rags where he rewrapped it carefully and tossed the bundle at Flo's feet. Then he reached for his rifle that he had left propped up against a vertical support near the entrance of the shack, backed up twenty paces, raised the weapon and fired twice, once into the front of the engine compartment and then at the front windshield. The bullet left a clean hole right above the steering wheel.

"Sure wish that jack ass had been in the driver's seat about now," Chester snarled.

"Sure glad he wasn't," Flo mumbled, terrified once more that Chester might overhear.

Though Flo's ears still were ringing from the concussion of the rifle blast, Chester's declaration had been ominously clear and her body trembled with the realization that it was quite possibly a portent of what lay ahead.

CHAPTER THIRTY-NINE

FLO

The unexpected shots fired from Chester Flack's rifle had been startling not only to Flo, but to a few other folks as well. George Murphy had heard the blasts from his position on the side of the highway where only minutes before, he had discovered Chester Flack's unmistakable, old, red truck pitched awkwardly in a ton of gravel on a runaway truck ramp. From a half mile away, in a different direction, James Nelson, his son, Jimmy, and Cole Jackson had heard too. And in a barn not one hundred yards away from the shed that Chester recklessly had fired into, Courtney Taylor roused once more. Though the shots may have initiated a part in her awakening, it was frantic pawing outside the wall of her stall that ultimately pulled her into a vapid and fragile consciousness.

Spooked by the blasts of the rifle, Satan had begun galloping wildly around the weedy track adjacent to the run-down barn until finally he sought shelter next to it, near the stall where Courtney had existed for more than two days. Frightened and impatient, he stomped the ground. His ears flickered back and forth and he began snorting; with his upper lip curled, he sucked air in and out noisily. Those frantic sounds had been what triggered Courtney's stirring. *Satan.*

Slowly she opened her eyes and rolled in the direction of the outer wall. Through the hole she had enlarged earlier, she could make out the horse's dark, lanky legs and she heard the gritty thump of its steel horseshoes grinding into the packed earth with each anxious movement. *Satan. Don't leave me.* Groaning, and with profound effort, she crawled on her hands and knees to the wall. When she reached it, she unsuccessfully struggled to sit upright. Though her mind had insisted she could do it, her body denied her. Too weak, she was able only to slouch in the straw and tilt her aching head against the lower edge of the opening where, whether real or imagined, Satan's muzzle abruptly and fleetingly nuzzled against her hair. The connection was not enough however. Caught up in the angry and unpredictable hands of fate, as Courtney tugged the horse blanket tighter around her with numb hands, her eyes closed once more and she fell into an almost comatose sleep, unaware if Satan's presence beside her would be her salvation or her final undoing.

⌘ ⌘ ⌘

Flo had reeled backwards when Chester shot his rifle, the reverberation from the discharge of the weapon staggering her. Instantly, normal sounds became muffled and she felt as though her ears were stuffed with cotton. She was irritated with Chester for being a reckless fool, as well as with herself for still being in his company.

"Why didn't you tell me you were going to shoot that thing, Chester? At least I could have covered my ears."

"Didn't know I was going to shoot it myself 'til I did it," he asserted, and then he chuckled. "Sure was fun though. Look at that fucking truck, all blasted up and sunk down to its bumpers. Creep who owns it won't be going anywhere."

Flo shook her head in disbelief. *I'm not sure Chester has control of all his faculties about now. God only knows what he'll do next.* She shuffled her feet, blindly rubbed her hands up and down on her pant legs, and glanced around anxiously, praying not to see a stranger or two escaping the entanglement of dense undergrowth to attack them for trespassing.

"Look, don't you think we ought to move on out of here, before someone comes? Surely someone heard those rifle shots," she said.

"I don't know, or care, who heard them," Chester answered, "but you're right. We're going to move on . . . on down this road. I want to see if it leads to where I think it might."

"What are you talking about, Chester?"

"I'm talking about following the trail. See hear? Boot prints, pointing in both directions. Whoever owns this truck has been coming and going and I bet the jackass is not too far from here right now."

Chester began walking down the dirt lane away from the damaged truck. "You can stay here or come with me, but it's going be dark sooner than later, so you'd better decide fast."

"I'm coming with you." *Don't have much of a choice, do I?* As Flo began to follow Chester, her mind became a jumble of questions. She settled on one. "One thing, Chester," she asked, "Why is it you're after this particular guy? Why him?"

"Because he's the one who took that girl," Chester said. He had turned toward Flo, squared his body, and was glaring at her with such intensity that she trembled.

"How do you know?" Her question squeaked out in a whisper.

"I just know. I feel it in my gut. I watched that truck barrel off into the night, as loud as a semi, away from that girl's wrecked car." In that moment, without one iota of personal comprehension as to why, he confessed. "I watched, Flo. Like a jackass, I just watched. Got there too late to stop the bastard."

Chester gulped and looked from side to side, his eyes darting as though he were a trapped animal. And for Chester, he was, for he had been caught. Deprived of the ability to filter his thoughts before speaking, he had blurted out a truth to Flo Gray, a woman he barely knew, and a person who would judge him for being a coward. He was sure of it.

The shackles of his contrived shame had been broken though, and in uncharacteristic fashion, he continued to blather. "I hid, Flo, like a scared kid, afraid to get involved, afraid it'd be more trouble than it was worth. And then I heard later what happened . . . that a girl had been driving that car . . . that she was missing. I swear to God I didn't see a girl that night. By the time I got to the accident site, the car was empty. But, I'll tell you one thing, Flo Gray, before I even reached the wreckage I saw and heard that fucking truck. I'll never forget it. The driver took that girl. I know it, in my gut. And, well, I have to try to make it right. I don't give a shit about people, Flo, never have, but this, this thing has me burning inside . . . and it's my own damn fault for being chicken shit."

Flo could not believe she was hearing Chester's words, an admission of remorse, and for once, she felt sorry for him. "You shouldn't feel guilty, Chester. What happened to Courtney Taylor is not your fault. And, besides, look at you. You're obviously not scared now."

Chester swallowed hard. Besides his mother, not one other person in the world had ever let him off the hook. For a second he was numbed by Flo's blunt and earnest comment, but the feeling was short-lived. He glanced back once more at the battered truck in the shack, tightened his hand on his rifle, spat into the dirt, and with a renewed resolve took command, disregarding, at least openly, Flo's attempt to placate him.

"Come on, Flo," he directed, in the mellowest tone he had used all day. "We need to get a move on."

Without hesitation, she fell into step behind him once again. The two walked down the narrow lane that was flanked on both sides by thick growths of Manzanita, scrub oaks, poison oak, and myriad grasses and low shrubs. The lowering sun bore down on the trees causing them to cast eerie shadows about the place. Flo hurried forward as Chester moved farther away from her. She was consumed with apprehension. Losing sight of Chester was not an option.

Abruptly, after nearly thirty yards, the dirt lane veered sharply to the left. Directly in front of Flo and Chester, barring their way forward, was a decaying, wooden fence that surrounded what appeared to be a deteriorated, horse racing, practice track. On the far side of the track was a barn that was so old and dilapidated that it appeared to list, in its entirety, to the right.

"Well, I'll be damned. Bet that's the place where all Nelson's winery supplies were stashed. Holy shit. A good wind would blow that fucker over," Chester said, while pushing at the fence until the top plank splintered to the ground. He stepped over and onto the track. "Come on, Flo. Climb over."

She managed to heave herself over the broken fence and continued alongside Chester walking the track until they were closer to the barn. Though yards away, they could see that the planks of wood on the outer wall were marked with rotting holes and gaps of various sizes. Damp moss coated the surface of the oak boards where their jagged ends met the earth and the slightly pitched roof appeared to be smothered in a thick layer of lichen, leaves, and other decaying vegetation.

"Looks like that roof could give way any second. No wonder Nelson wanted to clear out all the shit he had stored in there. Roof goes, everything beneath it will be smashed into rubble," Chester asserted as if he were an authority on such matters.

"How do you know it's the same barn? It might not be," Flo suggested.

Chester shot her a look of annoyance. "Bet you money it is," he said. "Ranch hand at Nelson's estate told me, straight up, that all that equipment I loaded up had been moved yesterday out of an old barn that sat right next to a practice track. This is it. I'll bet money. Come on. Let's go in . . . check it out."

"I'm not so sure that's . . ." Before Flo could finish her comment she heard a loud snort. A sudden, startling movement emanating from behind the barn drew her attention, but she stood, paralyzed in place, as an enormous, black horse began galloping directly toward Chester and her.

What the hell? This is it. We're finished. At the last second, however, before barreling over them, the horse swerved to one side, the animal's underbelly passing not more than a foot from Flo's head. Once past them, the horse slowed its pace to a slow canter. It did not take its eyes from them, however, even as it circled back in their direction. When it stopped at last, it lowered its head, pawed the earth, and began a series of low, aggravated snorts. Flo watched, frozen in fear, as the horse's ears flicked back and forth and its long tail swished wildly before settling flat behind its huge rump.

"Oh my heavens," Flo whispered, chancing a glance at Chester who, drained of all color, was on his knees beside her, still clutching his rifle.

"Holy shit," he murmured. "Where in the hell did that devil come from?"

Flo talked through her teeth, afraid to move even her lips. "From behind the barn. Charged out of there. That horse has been spooked."

"Might have to shoot it."

Flo's eyes widened. "You can't shoot it, Chester."

"Didn't say I was. Said I might have to." He did not move for a full minute, but then he stood slowly and began to take deliberate sidesteps in the direction of the barn. "Stick with me, Flo."

Flo was his shadow once more, but she did not take her eyes from the place where the horse, the intimidating, black giant, had stationed itself. In what seemed an eternity, Flo and Chester reached the barn door. While the horse had watched their every move, shaking its muzzle up and down menacingly, before positioning its head high in statuesque perfection, it miraculously had not moved toward them again. With her back pressed against the jamb of the barn door, Flo could see that the horse's glassy, brown eyes remained locked in on them. To Flo's way of thinking, the animal was communicating, clearly having implored their attention through its aggressive behavior and perhaps now, with its cautious reticence, entreating them to beware. In that odd moment of observation Flo shivered with an uneasy feeling that made her pause, forcing her mind to consider countless reasons why.

Beside her, Chester stepped backwards through the wide opening of the barn, reaching out to Flo as he did. He tugged on her jacket sleeve. "Get in here, Flo, before that crazy beast comes after us again."

Flo backed in behind him. Her heart was beating rapidly as a result of the frightening, close encounter with the horse, yet she continued to wonder. *Why did that horse charge at us like it did? Why did it do that and then veer away? Why did it hold back? Why? Was it trying to communicate something?*

"Chester," she said. "I'm not so sure that horse is crazy. I think it was trying to get our attention."

"Well, it sure as hell did that," he replied, turning to gaze into the dusky bowels of the near-empty barn. A smattering of barrel staves and empty wine bottles littered the ground near the entryway. A row of ten-penny nails supported an array of worn, horse tack: cracked, leather harnesses, reins, and a few bridles. A length of heavy chain dangled loosely from the lock of a distant stall door and dank straw lay in piles throughout the place. The air was chilly and the barn was creepily quiet, save for the occasional scuttle of scurrying vermin beneath the wooden floor and a low, distressed neighing from the agitated, black horse now somewhere outside, beyond a far wall.

"What now?" Flo asked with guarded curiosity. *God only knows what Chester will be up to next.*

He had turned in a full circle, twice, much as he had done earlier when in the open field deciding in which direction they should venture. *He must be thinking. Circling to get his thoughts straight. Odd. Oh dear, Flo, what a mess you're in.* "Don't know, Flo. Guess we should explore the place while we still have some daylight."

The thought of losing light while stranded in the crumbling outbuilding caused Flo's stomach to lurch. *What if Chester's right? What if the roof caves in? What if we're stuck in here all night?* She began to tremble and shift her feet from side to side. One hand raked against the mole on her cheek while the other grabbed at her hair, now completely loose from its bun.

Oblivious to Flo's nervous twitching, and clearly unaware of her musings, Chester continued. "Come on. Maybe there's a lantern somewhere."

Chester moved to the side of the barn where a number of cattle stalls were located. The first was wide open, the gate having been removed or rotted away; the second had a wooden gate that was raked open awkwardly. Inside was a trough of dirty water and a pile of carrots and decaying apples. A half-empty bucket of oats had been knocked over sideways, much of the contents in a pile on the floor beside it.

"Probably home to that crazy horse out there. Stinks like a goddamn pig sty in here," Chester said, shaking his head in disgust. "Even that beast out there deserves better than this."

The third stall was equipped with a heavy metal gate that was ajar a few inches. Coiled over the top rung was a thick, steel, welded chain unattached to anything, it appeared. An open, rusty padlock was looped into one link. Chester reached for it and then curiously snatched his hand away.

He swirled around to Flo, "Don't like the looks of this. Got a feeling."

"What?" she asked.

"Don't touch the lock or chain. I'm going to pull open the gate a little so I can see in."

Chester grabbed the end of the gate with a firm grip and pulled it toward him. The outer edge dug into the wooden floor for a moment but he was able to lift it upward, freeing the gate to swing outward a few feet. He moved through the opening and into a small stall filled with hay and reeking of feces and urine. The outer wall was riddled with openings, some slivers, others wider cracks, all letting in the remaining light of the day. At the lower corner of the wall, a wash of light fell through a larger hole on what appeared to be a bushel sack of some kind leaning against a supporting timber. Beyond the hole Chester could see the front legs of the black horse moving ever so slightly as it pawed the earth.

"There's nothing here but a sack of garbage," he said, "but the horse is out there. I can see its legs." Chester was speaking quite loudly thinking Flo was outside the gate, but he turned to find her less than a foot behind him.

"I don't want to be left alone," she told him.

He flinched when he heard her admission but said nothing. He began to step across the hay-covered, wooden floor back toward the slightly opened gate, knowing that Flo would be at his heels, but he stopped suddenly. Something was wrong.

As if Chester Flack did not exist at all, Flo had moved forward in the opposite direction, sinking to her knees beside the sack. She reached for it gingerly and pulled it toward her. Courtney's limp, naked body fell free from the horse blanket. It was ice cold. Flo felt for a pulse and called out, her voice cracking.

"It's the girl, Chester. It's Courtney. We found her. She's alive."

CHAPTER FORTY

GEORGE

Rifle shots. George was certain. He shook his head in disgust before pounding the front fender of Chester Flack's abandoned truck. "What is that crazy son of a bitch up to now?" he said out loud, his frustration building. He was uncertain, of course, that Chester had fired the shots, but with the old boy's truck having been deserted on the side of the road, buried up to its axles in loose gravel, and with Chester nowhere to be seen, it stood to reason.

He looked in the direction of the blasts, gaged the distance, and determined instantly in which way to go. George drove down the highway for several hundred yards, scoping the shoulder of the road for the entrance to Zinfandel Lane, a narrow, unpaved road that bordered the north end of James Nelson's property. *Not sure where this will take me, but at least it will get me closer to where those blasts came from. Somebody, probably Chester, was shooting at something.*

Zinfandel Lane, a road that was not more than twelve feet wide, twisted like the gnarly vine it was named after, one blind curve leading to he next with a few asymmetrical turnouts jutting out onto the shoulder into the rustic terrain. Though George assumed the lane was seldom traveled, it was deeply rutted, filled with potholes, and scattered with rocks that had inched upward, out of the packed earth. The cluttered, etched ground made for a rough ride. George was annoyed to hear his cruiser emit squeaky new noises as it rumbled over the rubble, but he could do nothing about it now. He had driven nearly half a mile . . . no turning back at this point. After one, last, sharp, right turn that banked blindly down a slight downhill curve, George came to a stop. In front of him, not fifty feet away he saw a ramshackle outbuilding, an old barn perhaps, that with age, had settled into the side of a slight knoll. The corner supports of the barn tilted precariously to the left, but George was drawn to it. He needed to take a look inside. He paused. Although it was not silent where he stood outside his cruiser, with chirps and flurries from birds and critters chattering in secret surroundings around him, the place was eerily still. He began to walk slowly forward, his concern growing. It looked as though the old structure could collapse with the slightest gust of wind. More importantly though, was the unknown. He had no idea what, if anything lurked inside. Experience had taught him to keep caution close at hand though. He reached into his jacket and touched the service weapon strapped to his chest. *I hope I don't need to use it.*

When, at last, he reached the building, he stopped and listened. He heard stirrings inside. Voices. A man and a woman were muttering, the tones serious and agitated. He drew out his pistol cautiously, pushed open a narrow, oak door, and peered inside. He was met first with the smell, the pungent odor of animal feces and moist hay, and then, in the muted shadows, the man. Chester Flack.

"Chester? What the hell are you doing here?" No sooner had George uttered the words than Flo Grey appeared. "And, Flo? What's going on?"

"We found the girl," Flo said, her words lined with wonder, with fear, with hope. "She's not dead."

"But damn near," Chester blurted.

"Let me see. Where?" George would ask questions later. He had many, already forming.

"In here." Flo motioned for George to follow her. She and Chester had managed to move Courtney to the center of the stall and had wrapped the blanket, stinking though it was, back around her again. It was all they had. "She's naked, Detective . . . and bruised. We covered her up the best we could."

George knelt beside Courtney, felt her neck for a pulse. "Stay with us, Courtney. Helps coming," he whispered to the girl, and then to Flo, he demanded, "Don't leave her. I'm stepping outside to radio for help."

Within seconds, George had reached his vehicle and had made the call for medical assistance, but his effort had not been fast enough, because inside the barn, in the minutes he had been gone, all hell had broken loose. He reentered the building to find a tall, rake thin, half naked man flailing a length of thick chain high in the air. Flo, George could see, was cowering in the stall beside Courtney and Chester was lying injured, his torso bloody and his arm broken, the ulna and radius clearly shattered. Not three feet from Chester, but out of reach, lay his rifle. The poor man was eying it desperately.

George leveled his weapon - a Glock 19 - at the lunatic who, clearly out of control of his senses, had no idea

George had entered the barn. His back was turned to the detective and he was so intent on swinging the chain that he was oblivious to George's encroaching figure. Over and over the raving madman thrashed the chain - against the metal gate of the stall, against the rotting floor of the barn, and precariously close to Chester once more. *I can't shoot a man point blank in the back. Have to stop this craziness though. What kind of psychopath is this guy?*

"Put down that weapon," George yelled his voice a re-sounding demand that put an instant end to the man's violent raving.

He turned toward George, leering at him with wild, bloodshot eyes before spitting onto the floor. A wad of spittle dribbled onto the man's scraggly beard. "What the fuck? Who the hell are you?"

George stood his ground. He pointed his gun menacingly at the man whose filthy hair hung in clumps nearly to his chest. "Get down on your knees and put your hands on your head. Now."

"Fuck you." And he ran. Like a demon possessed, the crazed man turned and sprinted the length of the barn, through the open door at the far end, and out onto what appeared to be a neglected horse track overrun with weeds. "Satan," he screamed. "Satan."

George fired a stern warning shot above the man's head. The force and velocity of the bullet caused the header at the opening of the barn to shatter, ragged spikes of oak spiraling down onto the hay. But the noise did not deter the runner. Instead, the blast propelled him into a full-out sprint. By the time George was outside the man was halfway around the track, spurred on by adrenaline and, George suspected correctly, methamphetamines. *Meth head. No doubt about it. Bet he woke from a stupor and took another hit. The jerk's all jacked up.*

George began to run himself in pursuit of the man but stopped instantly at the sight of a large, ebony horse rearing on its hind legs and pawing the air. The obviously spooked animal pounded its front hooves into the packed soil of the track four or five times in rapid succession before it stopped still. George cautiously backed against the side of the barn certain that contact with the horse could be deadly. The steed's ears were pinned back, its tail was swishing hard and fast, and it roared, a deafening squeal of fear and agitation. It looked straight at George before galloping off, around the track, directly toward the man who continued his sprint that oddly enough was leading him back in George's direction. *He's so wacked out he doesn't even understand he's on an oval track. The guy is crazed. No doubt about it . . . he and the horse too. What the hell?*

George could only watch. Another gunshot would make matters worse, so he held perfectly still and observed the drama play out. At the final turn, the horse, chuffing heavily, was upon the man as though vengeance drove him. Though the man shouted over and over, "Satan. Satan. Satan," the great animal paid no mind. Instead, it lowered its head and nudged the man's back, once . . . twice . . . and finally a third time – an intense shove that pushed the man forward onto his hands and knees. He staggered to his feet and growled Satan's name once more. "Satan, you fucking devil." It was the catalyst Satan needed, George supposed, because from his vantage point, he watched as the horse jammed into the man's back with such force it jolted him into the air. He landed several feet down the track, face down, stunned. The horse circled the man once, snorting loudly, before tossing its head into the air and trotting back toward the barn.

George did not hold back. He ran to where the man lay prone, slammed his knee into his lower back, and cuffed him. "On your feet, you piece of dog shit."

After a full minute, the man rose awkwardly and stood in the middle of the track reeling. His emaciated torso was drenched in perspiration and his trousers, slick with grime, hung from his skinny hips. George took a step backwards away from the man who reeked of cigarettes, sweat, and human feces. Another odor, akin to cat urine, emanated from his body. Even in the open air, the revolting smell permeated the space around him. George stifled the instinct to gag, grabbed the man's track-ridden arm, and forcefully guided him back inside the barn where he secured him to a post with the very chain he had used not minutes before to flog everything in sight.

After George had recited the perfunctory Miranda rights, the man opened his mouth as if ready to speak but he said nothing. Instead, his chin fell to his chest and bobbled there while his entire body began quivering irrepressibly, gripped as it was by the addict's latest ingestion of drugs. Looking down on what he considered a pile of living dung below him, George was filled with disgust, anger, and a small dose of sadness. *How is it that a person can get to this place?*

⌘ ⌘ ⌘

After checking on Courtney and Flo, who were virtually in the same spot where he had left them, George examined Chester. He was drawn up in excruciating pain. The broken arm was plainly visible, but George was concerned that he might have sustained internal injuries as well. Chester, whose face had drained of all color, could not tell George how many times he had been hit, so in battered misery, he could only wait, bearing the acute pain, until the medical team arrived. A sudden roar from outside the barn pulled George's attention away from Chester. *They're here.*

George rushed to the door of the barn hoping the sound was indeed from an ambulance or fire engine, but it was not. Instead, James and Jimmy Nelson, along with Cole Jackson, had powered up on their now grungy, all terrain vehicles. A curtain of displaced dirt and dust had ballooned up from the barren ground and enshrouded them.

"Heard rifle shots awhile ago," James announced through the haze, dismissing a more formal acknowledgement. "Thought they came from this direction. Caught sight of your cruiser from top of that hill," he added pointing to a moderate rise in the distance.

"There were rifle shots, all right. Heard them myself. Followed in the direction from where they came and ended up here." He paused, looking past James to his son, Jimmy. "Look, I have to tell you something else. Courtney was discovered here. Two folks, Chester Flack and Flo Gray, both from Hollow Vista, ran across this barn today and found her inside. Don't have all the details yet, but I'll get there." George spoke to James Nelson, but his eyes remained pinned on Jimmy who flew from the four-wheeler and began charging toward the barn.

"Hold on a sec," George warned, grabbing Jimmy's arm firmly. "She's here. She's alive, but Jimmy, it's not good. Courtney's been hurt. And you can't all barge in there. It's a crime scene."

"I have to see her," Jimmy said, his eyes pleading.

"I'll take you to her. James . . ."

George did not need to say another word. James understood. "Cole and I will wait out here," he said.

"And Jimmy, you need to know other people are inside there. Chester and Flo who found her and, well . . . the person I've arrested for her abduction."

Jimmy's jaw tightened and he tilted his head questioning, but he remained silent. Color bloomed to his neck and cheeks.

George continued. "It's a miracle that, by chance alone, Chester and Flo came upon this old barn today, and in wandering through, discovered Courtney. And it's equally astounding that I found them. So, there's good to be had, but at the same time, as I told you Courtney's hurt. I'm letting you go in Jimmy because, well, because I know how you're feeling. Exactly. She's like family."

Jimmy nodded. "Thanks," he muttered. It was the only sound he could manage.

⌘ ⌘ ⌘

Jimmy reeled in disgust when he took in the foul odor of the barn the moment he entered with George. "Damn."

George had released Jimmy's arm, but positioned himself close beside the young man. When his eyes had adjusted to the now darkening outbuilding, George touched Jimmy's back. "Come on," he said.

Just inside the first cattle stall, George stopped. "Flo," he said, "Courtney's friend, Jimmy, is here."

Flo stood immediately and backed away toward the gate and then outside to where Chester lay knotted against it in pain. She silently sat down beside him and did not move.

She watched Jimmy Nelson, just one click older than a boy, step through the hay to the side of his friend. And she listened to Chester's breathing, labored respirations that made her uncomfortably afraid.

When at last he looked down on Courtney, Jimmy did not hold back. He uttered a hoarse croak of sadness and began to cry, the tears, with uninhibited honesty, finally offering a modicum of relief. He knelt beside her, touched her cheek, and began petting her long, matted hair. "Courtney? Can you hear me? It's me, Jimmy. Can you hear?"

Courtney lay absolutely still, her breathing slow and shallow. "Courtney," Jimmy began again, "Help is coming. Can you hear me?"

He looked away from Courtney briefly to address George. "Can she hear me? Do you think?"

"I don't know," George admitted, "but if I were you, I'd keep talking. It can't hurt."

For five minutes longer, Jimmy whispered to Courtney as if her life depended on it, and perhaps it did, for she was breathing and stirring slightly when paramedics finally arrived.

In the long minutes before she was whisked to the ambulance by the medics, Jimmy stood, numb, a mixture of sadness, fear, and relief giving way to bubbling anger, for he had spotted the slumped form of person chained to a post.

"That's him, isn't it?" He directed his question to George.

"It's the man we found here," George said, not committing.

"He's fucking scum," Jimmy seethed, his imagination tormenting him with visions of what this monster had done to his girl. In a nanosecond his feeling of adoration for his best friend, for the love of his life, transformed into fury, into a hate so intense that he felt void of any control of his senses. It was physical. His teeth ground together involuntarily, his muscles tightened, and his hands became fists. "I want to pummel that fucker," he hissed too low for anyone else to hear. His heart began to beat faster, he could feel heat burning his cheeks, and he glared at the half-naked man as though wishing the proverbial *look* could, indeed, kill. Oh, how he wanted the fiend who had abused Courtney to suffer. And then he spotted it. Only feet from where Chester waited his turn for medical aid, lay a rifle.

This could be so simple. The thought played in Jimmy's mind for only seconds before he dashed to the rifle, grabbed it, and rotated the bolt. Instantaneously, before he could shoulder the weapon properly in order to shoot, he was slammed sideways onto the floor of the barn. The rifle was ratcheted from his grip by one strong hand. Though from the doorway, George had observed Jimmy's impulsive action, reacting immediately by yelling, "No, Jimmy," it was not he who had interfered.

"What the hell?" Jimmy muttered, as he crawled awkwardly back to his knees.

"You shouldn't want to do something like that, son," Chester's gravelly voice declared. "It's something that would stay with you the rest of your life."

Having collapsed beside Jimmy, Chester grimaced in pain from his effort in stopping yet another calamity. He had managed however, and in the aftermath of his exertion, his breaths came in pants. He examined Jimmy's face guardedly, all the while, gripping his rifle, with unyielding tenacity, in the only good arm he had. An uneasy silence consumed the space before Jimmy spoke.

"Why'd you slam into me like that? Why'd you stop me?" Jimmy asked, his voice anguished. "I wanted to off that scumbag."

Chester sighed in pain, in relief, and with profound empathy. "I know you did, son. I know how much you wanted to shoot the fucker dead. I know all too well."

He glanced fleetingly in Flo's direction before focusing on the face of George Murphy whose features, with the lowering sun's light behind him in the doorway, were hidden in shadow. Whether George had inferred anything from Chester's words to Jimmy, Chester had no idea. And it didn't matter now anyway. They had come for him. Paramedics were helping him to his feet for the short walk to the ambulance.

⌘ ⌘ ⌘

When the day was done, George went home. Home. *Have I been home in the past hundred days?* He had to wonder, for he was dog-tired.

"You found Courtney?" Angie asked.

"She was found, not directly by me, by some other folks – that crazy, old Chester Flack . . . you know . . . the guy who drives like a bat out of hell around town in that old, red pick-up."

"Yeah. He almost backed into me when I stopped by the station to see you. Didn't even look."

"Doesn't surprise me. The guy seems to live in a world of his own. Sure glad he didn't plow into you."

"Me too. Who else found her?"

"Yeah, you know her. Flo Gray, that nice, little custodian from your high school."

"Flo? Flo found her?"

"She and Chester did, by chance. I don't have all the answers yet, but I'll get the story soon enough . . . probably tomorrow. Just seeing those two together was surprising to me. They should be at the clinic now getting checked out. Courtney too. Paramedics did a great job." He put his hand to his head as though thinking hurt. "Right now, I need a bite to eat and a shower."

"Sit, Dad. I'll fix you something."

Angie warmed minestrone soup and made her father a ham and cheese sandwich. Then she sat with him, nibbling on crackers, anxious to hear what he could tell her. "Is Courtney going to be all right?" she asked finally.

"Yes. And no. Physically she'll recover, I think, but the trauma of what I believe she went through over the past couple of days will last. She'll need counseling for sure," he said, "as will a few other people."

George's thinking took him back to the barn.

⌘ ⌘ ⌘

By the time the ambulance had been loaded with Courtney, Chester, and Flo as well, Office Sanchez had arrived on scene in his squad car.

"Got here as fast as I could," he said. I was out in the middle of nowhere when I heard you needed backup. Hiked a mile and a half to get to my car. "Sorry."

"Everything is under control . . . for now," George told him. The Nelson and Cole kids took the quads back home by way of the highway, and James Nelson was able to calm the horse down."

"There's a horse out here?"

"Yeah. Gelding named Satan of all things. Poor horse looked malnourished and was spooked as hell, but Nelson knows horses. Guess that's why he's in the biz. Said he'd be able to rehabilitate the animal. He called his ranch foreman who's bringing a trailer out. They'll transport the horse back to his ranch, as soon as the help gets here. As for that shit bag in the barn there, we'll confine him in the back of your squad car for a ride to county jail . . . temporary custody, you can bet. Need to find out the guy's name though, and right now," he said, gesturing toward the semi-conscious man, "he's not in a condition to talk to anyone." George perused the side of the building opposite the stalls. "He has to have been holed up somewhere in this shack of a barn. Let's start looking. Christ. What a stinking shit hole."

With spotlights illuminating the area, the men were able to explore their surroundings more closely. At the far corner of the barn, barricaded with hay bales stacked three-high, they found the man's sleeping quarters. The floor was strewn with several, filthy t-shirts, tattered jeans, knotted socks, a well-worn pair of hiking boots, a black, hooded sweatshirt, an old, muddy, army-issue jacket, and oddly, coiled in one corner like a snake, was a lone, nylon, guitar string. A sleeping bag and dirty pillow were smashed up against the outer wall. On a wooden box in the corner lay drug paraphernalia: six syringes, two metal spoons, a container of aluminum foil, and four disposable, cigarette lighters. A half empty package of Camels and three empty beer cans were there as well.

"This guy seemed to have all the equipment he needed to get himself well adjusted," Officer Sanchez noted with sarcasm. "But where are the drugs? Must be some meth, heroine, cocaine, something around here."

"From the way the guy was behaving, I'd say he's on meth," George said, scanning the floor of the makeshift room once more for evidence. In one corner beneath a torn shirt, he found two old volumes. "There. Has to be."

He edged one book toward him, touched the cover with one finger, and flipped it open. The book had been hollowed out, lined with foil, and was one-third full of crystalline meth.

"Here you go. Jackpot!" George said.

Armed with plastic bags and gloves, the detective and officer gathered the items they found, later placing them in George's trunk. "I'd say we'd leave this stuff here until tomorrow," George said, "but I'd hate to see it go missing somehow. The way things have been going around here, anything could happen."

"You're right about that," Officer Sanchez agreed. "Hey," he said, shining his flashlight into one, dark corner. Check that out. Is that a wallet?" He had spotted a square of leather wedged under the corner of a hay bale.

"Looks that way," George said, grabbing the edge of the leather and pulling. The wallet flopped open. Inside was an expired credit card with the name so scratched and dulled it was unreadable, a ten-dollar bill, and a faded, driver's license. The photo was of a clean-cut, dark-haired man with brown eyes and an average-looking face. Nothing particularly notable caused George to dwell, but the almost indecipherable name on the license did. His heart actually skipped a beat.

"Oh, no," he said. "Shit."

CHAPTER FORTY-ONE

SUSAN

"Hello?" Susan answered her cell phone as she always did, with a question in her voice. Even today, when earlier in the afternoon life seemed to have offered her something solid to stand on in the person of Detective George Murphy, a simply stated *hello* for her, at any time, was implausible, if not impossible. Why? Though she may not have been able to articulate the reason, it was factually because of what life had wrought for her. Filled with countless, fickle twists and turns, a lifetime of experiences had set Susan back on her heels more than once, often enough, in fact, that certainty, in her view, was a dead bird.

When she was met with silence, Susan spoke louder. "Hello?"

"Oh, hello, Susan. George Murphy here."

"George." She was suddenly a schoolgirl. She felt the warmth of a blush.

"I have news, Susan. Good news." With dinner and a shower behind him, George had settled back on his bed hoping for a short nap, but sleep had evaded him. Every time he closed his eyes, he envisioned Susan. He knew he had to speak to her, and soon. *Jenny is going to want to know. And Susan needs to.* He had reasoned with himself.

"What?" she asked. "Did someone find Courtney?"

"Yes. And she's safe."

"Oh, thank heavens. Where? Who? When did this happen? Jenny will be so happy. I'm so relieved. Oh, George, this is good news." Susan's responses were tumbling one on top of the next.

"It is. I was hoping to stop by in the morning, Susan, because it's getting late, but I'm having a bit of trouble sleeping. Was wondering if I might drive over to your place now."

"Of course. Do." She paused before adding. "Is it all right if I tell Jenny?"

"Yes. Just let her know that Courtney is safe. I'll fill in some details when I see you." *And the details are not pleasant.* George was burdened by a capricious charge, for the suppressed information he held and soon would deliver, had the potential, he was positive, to open a wound. He was not certain he was prepared.

"Great. See you in . . .?" she asked.

"Half an hour or so," he calculated as both anticipation and dread began to well inside him.

⌘ ⌘ ⌘

Twenty-five minutes later, George stepped up to Susan's doorway anxious to see her beautiful face, but the door swung open wide to reveal her daughter, Jenny, barefoot, wearing sweat pants and a t-shirt, and draped in a pink blanket. She had been crying.

"Jenny, are you okay?" he asked.

"Yes. No. My mom told me about Courtney but I didn't know I'd feel this way."

George stared at the girl somewhat confused.

"I'm happy, Detective Murphy. And relieved, but I'm miserable too.

This girl is not making sense.

"I'm happy, but not just for Courtney . . . for me too. I'm relieved for myself because I'm off the hook. I don't have to worry about her any more. I have been so sick, so afraid, and I just knew that that awful man, the one who almost threw me out of his truck, the one who did this," she uttered a tiny shriek and grabbed her swollen neck, "was going to hurt Courtney bad. Maybe he'd do worse. Why are there people like him? Why? The world is so messed up. I've been sleeping and sleeping because when I'm awake, I'm so scared. What if that horrible person comes back? What if I had found out Courtney was dead. If she was dead and I wasn't . . . I couldn't bear that. It wouldn't be fair . . . her, not me." Jenny's voice was plaintive.

To George, the girl's thinking was muddled, her comments disconcerting, and yet ironically her words resonated with him. What if Courtney had not survived? What if? George understood the pain of loss at the deepest level and remembering caused his stomach to lurch. Yet, he could not find words at this moment to comfort the girl before him. *Focus. Think. Say something. I can give her a bunch of trite responses like life's not fair, this is a lesson, Jenny, feel the hurt and then let it go. Right. Like that's easy. Or how about, this is another turn in the road, Jenny. Life goes on. Yep. Life does go on, but saying goodbye hurts the worst when the story hasn't ended. Now there's a truth.* George's thoughts had silenced him. *Oh shit, the last thing I need to do is offer lame, crappy advice, as though I know what's coming around the bend.*

His reasoning was troubling. It left him not knowing whether to step back from the distraught girl or to move forward and comfort her. Behind Jenny, at the foot of the staircase he saw Susan, her face ashen, and her hands extended, palms upward as if to say, "I don't know what to do. I'm as confused as you must be."

Though Jenny was a young woman, at this moment she seemed only a child, clearly struggling to comprehend her world. She had stopped talking and had begun to sob. Her arms were straight at her sides as though she didn't know where to put them and her head tilted downward, her long hair falling forward, as her entire body heaved. George was unsure, but he moved toward her and gently placed his hands on her upper arms. She looked up at him a bit quizzically and then leaned forward. Without hesitation she put her cheek against his chest as if he were the father she didn't have.

"Thank you," she whispered.

George held Jenny there for several seconds and when she was ready, she pulled back. "Will I be able to see her?"

"I'm sure you will very soon."

"Okay," Jenny said, as though *very soon* was enough. She turned, walked to her mother, kissed her cheek, and simply said, "'Night, Mom," before trudging up the stairs.

When her bedroom door had closed firmly, George moved to Susan. He hugged her to him. "Whew. That was something," he murmured.

"I had no idea," Susan admitted.

Her comment arrested him. "Susan," he said. "There's more."

⌘ ⌘ ⌘

In her wildest imaginings, Susan could not have prepared for what she learned next.

"Let's sit," George said.

"Kitchen?" she asked. "I'll get you coffee or a beer?"

"A beer sounds really good." He managed a small smile.

"Jenny should be okay," Susan commented, as she flitted around the kitchen, opening a beer and placing a chilled mug in front of George. "The worst is behind her. This has been so traumatic though."

George's throat tightened. He could not respond. *Jenny may not be okay . . . not when she learns the truth.*

"What?" Susan asked, looking at the handsome face that suddenly had grown sober. Her thoughts were jumbled. *What's wrong? Why is he so serious? Is he angry? Does he not want to be here? But he asked to come over. He was so good with Jenny. And he hugged me. Surely . . .*

"What?" she asked again. She forced herself to abandon the emotions that were clouding her thinking.

"I have to tell you something, Susan, that I'm afraid will be a bit shocking."

She cocked her head, and gazed at him somberly. "What?" she asked for the third time. "Just tell me."

"We located Courtney in a barn at the far end of the Nelson family's property. Do you know where that is?"

"I know where the Nelson estate is. Yes."

"Well, Courtney's safe now, thanks to chance. But there's more. Someone else was in the barn with her. He's been arrested as the suspected assailant . . . and Susan, he's someone you know."

"What are you talking about?"

"In searching the area we found his belongings, among them a wallet, and a driver's license. The photo on the license, and his fingerprints as well, check out. Susan, the man in the barn was Zach. Zach Wallis. He's a troubled man, Susan. Violent, truly sick, and wracked by drug use." George hesitated. "I'm sorry. I'm sorry I had to be the one to tell you."

Susan's head began to swim. She was not sure she would not faint. Grabbing the edge of the table, she looked as far away as her small kitchen would allow. *Find a focal point. Swallow.* She began to perspire as nausea overtook her. *Don't be sick. Don't be sick.* Self-talk was all she had now. Her face had blanched white, tiny beads of sweat were visible on her forehead, her breathing had grown rapid, and her heartbeat felt alien. She placed a loose fist to her chest and closing her eyes, breathed in deeply. *Don't be sick. Calm down.* And suddenly Rachel, Susan's long ago deceased mother, the spirit thriving still, appeared once more.

"You'll know what to do," the old woman counseled. *"You will. Trust yourself."*

At that exact second, from far outside, Susan's daylight owl began to call, the recurrent, lonely hoot muffled and drawn out. It was the salve Susan needed. *"Oh Susan, how did you get to this place?"* The question she had begged of her mother – *"Oh, Mother. How did I arrive at this place?"* – finally had transitioned to its rightful home, to Susan alone. She understood completely, intuition aside and fate be damned, that she had arrived, by her own doing, to this place . . . to this place . . . to this exact spot in time.

She put both hands on the table before her and then reached out for George who took one of her hands into both of his. He gazed at her curiously.

"I feel as though I'm suddenly trapped in some kind of illusion," she explained. "And I don't like it. It seems someone, or something intangible, is trying to play a trick on me, to coerce me into heeding an errant call but I won't be deceived this time. The past is gone. Over. I've been down that road and I'm not turning back. Reality is right in front of me. It's here. Now. Everything will be okay, George, all of it for life is going to play out. It will. For the first time in ages I know I can leave past deceptions, even this hideous revelation about Zach, behind me. I will not buy into the drama. I cannot be weighted down by it. I can't . . . because I know where I'm going, and it isn't backwards. I'm more interested in what lies ahead, and I'm ready to walk that path."

Both Susan and George sat quietly for a moment before she finally spoke in a voice so soft he had to lean closer to hear. "You know I have to ask you one question, George. I hope it's not too rash of me to ask it, but I have to tell you, I'm set to move on. I just need to know one thing. Will you be beside me as I go?"

"I can't imagine an adventure I'd rather take," he grinned.

He stood slowly, not taking his eyes from her face. When he had pulled her to her tiptoes, he touched the top of her head with his lips and then he kissed her, long and sweet, for the second time that day.

EPILOGUE

The tiny town of Hollow Vista, as a whole, did not change much in the months, and even years, to come. It remained a sleepy community of individuals, who though different in myriad ways, were much the same, for they were human, fraught with emotions: love, hate, anger, sadness, joy, disgust, surprise, trust, anticipation, and too many sentiments to count. Both burdened and blessed with the power of choice, they made their ways, personified as they journeyed, by a road called life.

No one understood better than George Murphy who learned before it was too late that he could, without remorse, without betrayal, give himself permission to love a woman again. He was not certain if fate, luck, or simply chance, had played a role in bringing Susan Wallis into his life. That didn't matter. She was there and he was not about to let her go. And under the most implausible, and quite bizarre circumstances imaginable, much the same could be said of Chester Flack and Flo Gray.

Late at night when Chester Flack was released from the community medical facility after having met with the wrath of Zach Wallis earlier in the day, his left arm was in a dark, black cast and his battered torso had been taped tightly. He was bruised, and he ached, but he was alive. He went by taxicab home to his mother Bertha, whom he assumed would be consumed with worry and irritation at his tardiness. She was neither. Chester found her reclining as usual in the rocking chair she adored, but this time, she did not rouse. Sometime during the afternoon, he assumed, she finally had let go. When he found the nerve to touch her crepe-like skin, she was cold, rigor mortis already having taken hold. Bertha's passing broke Chester's heart but it also set him free. Flo Gray, remarkably, stepped in to fill the void.

Jimmy Nelson, unlike George and Chester, did not change the focus of his life. When Courtney Taylor was released from the hospital two days after she had been found, barely alive, in that stinking barn, she was told she could go home. She did not. As she always had done when she was faced with a dilemma, or was trapped in a predicament she could not see her way out of, she went to Jimmy. He had been her childhood pal, a forever friend, and, finally, she accepted, the love of her life. Not so were her parents. Bennett Taylor stubbornly was unwilling to relinquish his conviction that his daughter deserved what had happened. "She asked for it," he ranted. "She dresses like a slut and obviously makes stupid choices." And though Jill hated Bennett deep in her soul for his angry outbursts and undeniable loathing of her child, she did not dispute him. How could she? He was her husband. While they slipped away for a month to Europe, Courtney convalesced on James Nelson's estate. Though she recovered in slow increments physically, Courtney fought off depression, unknowingly cried in her sleep, and spent hours grooming the black gelding, Satan, in a corral adjacent to the Nelsons' lavish barn. Only time would erase the image of the heinous man who had raped her and held her hostage. And when she learned his name, she was undone, sobbing hysterically, before transferring her pain to the only person she could. The indelible cadence of Jenny's speech pattern, a mimicked version of Courtney's attacker's, had been the catalyst for her decision. She refused to see Jenny Wallis ever again.

After being convicted of a laundry list of crimes that included home invasion, petty theft, drug possession, kidnapping, and rape, Zach Wallis was ordered to state prison. Not more than six months into a lengthy sentence, he was found dead in his cell. Whether accidental or not, no one ever knew. The pruno he had concocted of rotten fruit, candy, and moldy bread had been laced, it was discovered, with tainted methamphetamine. He was found on the floor, next to his bunk, face down in a pool of vomit. His daughter, Jenny, was given his belongings – a tattered, leather wallet, a skinny, silver, wedding band, and ten dollars cash, all of which she tossed into a dumpster outside the courthouse where her father had been arraigned. She did not mourn; she did not cry. For Jenny Wallis her father's passing did not count, for one miserable second, as a loss.

And Jenny? Jenny moved away at the end of summer as she had planned. Her mother had found George, Courtney was with Jimmy and the Nelson family, and she believed herself to be independent at last. Being without a partner of her own did not faze her. Instead, she embraced her autonomy. After a few months of physical and emotional recovery, combined with finally accepting Courtney's rebuke of her, she knew she would move away, not bound to any other soul. Though she felt invigorated, strong, confident, and free, a niggling sense of apprehension played at her emotions, for she would be venturing, she was aware, into a world she did not trust. She snuffed her uneasiness deep inside, however, so that she could move on. As she drove away from home three months after graduation, she avoided looking in the rear view mirror for miles down the road. She had her eyes set on the future. Like her mother, Susan, for Jenny Wallis, there was no turning back.

"If you don't know where you are going, any road will get you there."

Lewis Carroll

ABOUT THE AUTHOR

Judith DeChesere-Boyle was born in Elizabethtown, KY, and with the exception of living for three years both in England and TX, was raised there. She first attended the University of Kentucky, and then moved to CA graduating from College of Marin with an AA degree in English with a Creative Writing emphasis and San Francisco State University with a BA degree in English. She attended Sonoma State University, earning two teaching credentials and a MA in Education with an English Curriculum emphasis. She taught English at the secondary level for many years, retiring early enough to pursue her love of writing more seriously. She raised two wonderful sons, Alex and Justin, and now lives in Sonoma County, CA, with her husband, Rick. Besides writing, she reads avidly, gardens, tends the family's pond full of koi, and walks her two German Shepherds three miles a day. She is the author of three novels, *Big House Dreams, Nine Bucks and Change,* and *Go With The Flo.* She also has written a memoir, *Tumor Me, The Story Of My Firefighter,* a tribute to the memory of her son, Alex.

Learn more at Judith's website: www.jdechesere-boyle.com

www.ingramcontent.com/pod-product-compliance
Lightning Source LLC
Chambersburg PA
CBHW071042250626
47159CB00002B/334